Praise for the National Bestselling Bookmobile Cat Mysteries

"With humor and panache, Cass delivers an intriguing mystery and interesting characters."
—*Bristol Herald Courier* (VA)

"Almost impossible to put down . . . the story is filled with humor and warmth." —MyShelf.com

"[With] Eddie's adorableness [and] penchant to try to get more snacks, and Minnie's determination to solve the crime, this duo will win over even those that don't like cats." —Cozy Mystery Book Reviews

"A pleasant read. . . . [Minnie is] a spunky investigator." —Gumshoe

"Laurie Cass spins a yarn full of red herrings and fascinating characters. Ms. Cass also populates Chilson with engaging folks to visit, and spending time with them is both relaxing and entertaining."
—Fresh Fiction

"Reading Cass's cozies feels like sharing a bottle of wine with an adventurous friend as she regales you with the story of her latest escapade."
—The Cuddlywumps Cat Chronicles

"Books, family, romance, and of course, a library cat make this a winning series for mystery readers and fans of these cozy adventures."
—Kings River Life Magazine

Titles by Laurie Cass

The Crime
That Binds

A BOOKMOBILE CAT MYSTERY

Laurie Cass

BERKLEY PRIME CRIME
New York

BERKLEY PRIME CRIME
Published by Berkley
An imprint of Penguin Random House LLC
penguinrandomhouse.com

Copyright © 2022 by Janet Koch
Penguin Random House supports copyright. Copyright fuels creativity, encourages
diverse voices, promotes free speech, and creates a vibrant culture. Thank you for buying
an authorized edition of this book and for complying with copyright laws by not
reproducing, scanning, or distributing any part of it in any form without permission.
You are supporting writers and allowing Penguin Random House to continue to
publish books for every reader.

BERKLEY and the BERKLEY & B colophon are registered trademarks and
BERKLEY PRIME CRIME is a trademark of Penguin Random House LLC.

ISBN: 9780593197738

First Edition: October 2022

Printed in the United States of America
1 3 5 7 9 10 8 6 4 2

For my mom.
Margery Joyce Milks Schnell
1934–2021

Chapter 1

It was a dark and dreary morning. And there was every indication that the darkness and dreariness were going to continue into noon, then into early afternoon, late afternoon, dusk, evening, and possibly into eternity. It was one of those days that made you wonder why you lived in northwest lower Michigan. A day that made you question every life choice you'd ever made, since the net result was a dull, sodden late March with no visible evidence that spring was ever, ever, ever going to show up.

"Mrr."

I grinned. Then again, all the paths I'd taken had brought me to this. I was assistant director of the Chilson District Library, head of the library's outreach efforts, and driver of the bookmobile. Plus, I had a wonderful fiancé I was going to marry on some indeterminate date, and I had a great boss, outstanding coworkers, supportive friends, and—

"Mrr!"

—and a black-and-white tabby cat who commented

on everything from quantum mechanics to the color of the inside of his eyelids.

My part-time bookmobile clerk, just as every previous clerk had done, tapped his toes on the cat carrier strapped to the floor in front of the passenger's seat. "What was that, Mr. Eddie?" Hunter Morales asked. "Did you say you were hoping for sunny and seventy degrees today and since the day isn't turning out as you expected, that Miss Minnie is to blame?"

I nodded in a sage-like manner. "And that I should be punished."

Hunter laughed, and I once again congratulated myself on hiring him. A few months ago, my boss had expressed an interest in expanding the hours the bookmobile was on the road. It was an excellent idea. The only problem was that we couldn't manage it with the existing staff. Sure, I was young (if you considered mid-thirties young, which I did) and eager for a challenge, but there are only so many hours in a day, and I'd quickly found that an overloaded schedule was too much for me and my other part-time clerk, Julia Beaton. Though Julia was a very young mid-sixties powerhouse, she'd already retired from one career and didn't want to work more than half time.

Thus the search had begun. The requirements sounded simple: have a commercial driver's license, drive the thirty-one-foot bookmobile through the many hills and lakes of Tonedagana County rain or shine, haul books from vehicle to library and back, help people find books, be patient and kind to all.

I'd desperately wanted to put one more item in the job posting, but my boss dissuaded me. "That's what the job interview is for," Graydon had said. "To see if it's a good fit."

He was right—I knew he was. And, anyway, how could I put "talk to cats," in the newspaper advertisement, let alone post that on the state library association's website and expect anyone to take me seriously ever again? Though Eddie was accepted by everyone from the library's board to the newest bookmobile patron as a permanent part of the bookmobile, it was quite a step from acceptance to conversation.

So it was with a hope and a prayer that I hired twentysomething Hunter Morales just after the holidays. Hunter and his wife, Abigail, were living with his parents while saving to buy a house. He was also taking as many college classes as he could to finish up a bachelor's degree in business while developing a clientele for his welding company. My aunt Frances was feeling the teensiest bit smug because she'd met Hunter in one of the woodworking classes she taught at the local community college and had recommended that he apply.

"It's possible I know just the person," she'd said, and she, too, had been right. He'd looked good on paper, and though neither Julia nor I had the courage to specifically ask him the "Do you talk to cats?" question during the interview, his sense of humor had sealed the deal.

I looked over at him now. Hunter was thin, almost a foot taller than my five feet, and had hair cut short to keep the welding sparks from burning holes in his head. Or so he said. I was fairly sure it was an excuse to run his electric shaver over his head once a week and save the hassle of getting an official haircut, but it was a good story, so I didn't call him on it. "In some climates," I said, "March is like a calendar photo. Hyacinths. Apple blossoms. Daffodils."

"Shh!" Hunter whispered. "Do you want Eddie to hear? He'll make you move somewhere warm and sunny. Arizona. Maybe New Mexico."

I scoffed. "He wouldn't like it there, either. Too hot in the summer. Fur coat, remember?"

"Mrr," Eddie muttered.

Hunter leaned down and peered through the cat carrier's wire door. "Sorry, bud. Looks like you're stuck with Michigan."

"Oh, I wouldn't say stuck." I flicked the blinker and turned off the road and into the parking lot of a white clapboard township hall. "Sure, it's dark and dreary, and the snow is still glopping down"—I nodded at the wafting snowflakes—"but a month from now the world will be transformed."

Hunter nodded. "Yeah, that's pretty cool, isn't it?"

I parked on the far side of the gravel lot and we quickly ran through the opening routine. Unlatch Eddie, rotate the driver's chair 180 degrees to serve as a computer chair, detach the bungee cord that held the castered chair, fire up both computers, and unlock the door for all who wished to enter.

Which was, at that point, a total of no one, so we continued our mutual admiration of springtime in Michigan.

With Eddie observing from the passenger seat headrest, we'd agreed that the worst part of this season was the eager wanderings of the skunk population, debated merits of purple versus yellow crocus (tied, one each), marveled over the fact that lakes could still be iced over while daffodils were blooming, mutually admitted to toe-curling delight when seeing the first hint of green leaves on maple trees, and had moved on to the topic of setting up a guessing contest of when the snow pile behind the library would completely melt when we jumped at a loud voice.

"You two actually enjoy this kind of weather?"

Hunter and I turned as one unit to face our first bookmobile patron of the day. I smiled at the elderly man. "Good morning, Mr. Valera. I didn't expect to see you for another few weeks."

Mr. Valera, who regularly threatened me with "Call me Herb or I'll call you Ms. Hamilton," finished climbing the stairs, shut the door, took off his knit hat, and banged an inch of snow onto the entry rug. His patrician silver hair did not, as my curly-haired mop would have, bounce in all directions at once. No, his hair did as he commanded and stayed where he wanted it to. That demanded respect by itself, let alone his innate kindness, empathy, and intelligence.

"If I'd been smart," he said, stuffing the hat into his coat pocket, "I would have continued my retirement habit and stayed in Florida until late April. But, no, I was lulled into complacency by the weather of the last week and thought, like a fool, that spring was here."

Last week had been sunny and mild, with temperatures warm enough to make you think about hauling the patio furniture out of the garage. I'd seen some people do that, but most of us knew better. Personally, I didn't move the snow scraper from my back seat into the trunk until Memorial Day.

My beloved fiancé had recently said that was because I simply forgot, but I said it was caution. Which made him ask why this was the one thing I was cautious about. Which made me start citing a list of Things That Made Minnie Hamilton Cautious, something that didn't go well because once I'd listed (1) pending asteroid collision and (2) the library's postage machine, I'd spent so much time defending those two items that I'd refused to make the list any longer.

Hunter interrupted my list reminiscing by introducing himself. Due to his varied schedule and because we were still revising bookmobile routes, this was the first time he'd been at this stop.

"Good morning, young man," Mr. Valera said, shaking hands. "And call me Herb."

Hunter nodded. "No problem, Mr. Herb."

Mr. Valera gave him a pained look and I laughed. "You should be grateful," I said. "We could be calling you 'Your Honor.'"

"You're a judge?" Hunter asked.

"Retired," Mr. Valera said. "Kicked out to pasture by the state of Michigan when I was seventy, whether I wanted to or not."

The Honorable Judge Herbert D. Valera had served as a downstate circuit court judge for decades. I had no doubt that he could tell story after story about courtroom drama, but he didn't seem inclined, and I wasn't sure I wanted to know. Circuit court judges had the power of sentencing life in prison, and making casual entertainment out of those circumstances didn't seem appropriate.

"So." Mr. Valera clapped his hands and rubbed them together. "Did you get those books I ordered?"

"Mrr!"

"Apologies, Edward." He moved forward and scratched Eddie behind the ears. The purrs were instantaneous and loud enough to be heard in the next county. "What's that?" Mr. Valera asked. "No one else has ever rubbed your head to your satisfaction? I'm the first one who has done so? Such a shame. What do you plan to do about it?"

I could answer that. Easily. "Complain about me at the top of his little kitty lungs at four in the morning and then bat something off my dresser and onto the floor and then push it under the dresser so I can't reach it."

Mr. Valera gave Eddie's head one last pat. "Maybe that's what happened to our sculpture." He was smiling, but it didn't quite cover his entire face.

"Sculpture?" I pulled the stack of books he'd ordered from the Reserved shelf and handed them to Hunter to check out. "I didn't know you were an art collector."

"Art? Me?" He laughed. "Not in this or any lifetime I can imagine. It was my parents who were the artsy types. My sisters and I grew up . . . Well, it doesn't matter. In the end my sisters, my cousins, and I were left with the family cottage just down the road and an odd collection of artwork, almost all of which has zero monetary value."

For a moment I longed to know about the childhood of young Herb Valera. Had his parents been artists? Had the family lived in Paris? New York? Had they met people like Georgia O'Keeffe? Jackson Pollock? But Mr. Valera was a private man, and if he wanted us to know, he'd tell us.

"Just almost?" Hunter was done beeping the books

with the scanner: biographies of Shirley Jackson and George Washington, a history of the seventeenth-century tulip mania, the latest Michael Connelly novel, and a copy of *Sonnets from the Portuguese*. He smiled and pushed the pile over to Mr. Valera. "So there's a painting worth more than its frame?"

"Oh, if only that were true." Mr. Valera took his books and tucked them under his arm. "The cottage is full of worthless paintings. The rest of the family has a conniption fit at the merest suggestion of getting rid of any of them." He shook his head. "Worst thing about a family cottage is every decision is made by committee. And I do mean every decision. That's the odd thing about this sculpture."

"What's odd about it?" I asked. "Is it weird-looking?"

"No, that's not it at all." He paused, then smiled. "Well, yes, it is weird—all angles and holes—but that's not the issue. The problem is it's missing."

"You mean someone stole it?" Hunter asked. "Did you tell the police?"

"If I was certain it was stolen, then yes, I would certainly inform local law enforcement." Mr. Valera put the books down on the desk and pulled his knit hat from his coat pocket. "But there's a complication with that determination."

The tone of his voice had shifted. In one sentence he'd been the kindly, humorous Mr. Valera who liked nothing better than to scratch Eddie's head; in the next he'd spoken in a way that summoned images of him in a black robe, sitting behind a massive oak desk, hands folded, as he somberly addressed the criminal he was about to sentence.

I shivered, happy that I wasn't a criminal and

even happier that I'd never had cause to appear in front of Judge Valera.

"You mean you're not sure it's missing?" Hunter asked the question mildly, but his disbelief wasn't hidden well.

Mr. Valera smiled. "As I said, there's a complication. Two, if you want to be accurate."

"We do," I said promptly. This earned me a nod of approval from the former judge, which made me more proud of myself than it should have.

He held up the index finger that wasn't holding a stack of books. "The first complication is this is a family cottage and items wander off from time to time. Though they eventually make their way back home, the simple system I developed of writing down what you take in a notebook dedicated to the purpose isn't always followed."

"So annoying." I rolled my eyes in sympathy but didn't mention that, if it had been my family cottage, I might not have always remembered to write things down myself.

"Yes, but the more serious complication is . . ." Mr. Valera paused, which wasn't something I'd ever heard him do. Normally, he spoke in clear and declarative sentences. No hesitations, no word stumbles, no self-corrections. It was something I admired tremendously, and I hoped to be more like him in that regard when I grew up. To have him search for words meant, to me, that the complication that faced him was a big one.

"It's okay," I said, and gave him our unofficial motto. "What happens on the bookmobile stays on the bookmobile. Confidentiality is a thing with us."

"Thank you," Mr. Valera said to me and Hunter,

who'd been nodding agreement. "This is more a personal difficulty than a truly private one." He suddenly looked sad. "Last fall my sister talked about sending the Conti somewhere to get cleaned."

I frowned. People did that? What was wrong with a dustcloth? Or a feather duster? Then again, I'd never owned a valuable anything. What I knew about the caretaking of pricey art objects could fit into two words: don't touch. That anyone would go to the trouble and expense of shipping a sculpture off for cleaning made me wonder how valuable it actually was.

"The full family agreed it was past time and my sister said she'd take on the project. Perhaps she did and the Conti is safe."

I was beginning to get a bad feeling about the story. "Did something . . . happen to your sister?"

Mr. Valera looked off into the distance. "She had a stroke in late October. She survived, but her recovery has been slow. Communication is still very difficult." He smiled wryly. "If she'd sent the Conti away, and if she had the record-keeping skills an earthworm might conceivably have, we'd have a paper trail. However, she inherited our father's capacity for paperwork and there are no records anywhere."

Ah, siblings. Nothing like them for heaping abuse. "So the sculpture might be sitting safe somewhere, waiting for pickup," I said. "Or it might have been . . . stolen?"

"We're waiting until my sister can let us know, one way or another, if she sent it out," Mr. Valera said. "There's no sense in having law enforcement officers spend time on a theft that might not have occurred."

This made sense. But if the Conti had been stolen, letting the trail go frozen cold was the worst thing possible. Of course, Mr. Valera knew that. In this age of criminal investigation television shows, pretty much everyone did, let alone an experienced circuit court judge. And maybe that explained his brief hesitancy. The management of the cottage and its contents were clearly controlled by numerous people with associated numerous opinions, and perhaps he was in the minority. That he could be bowing to the majority rule, even when he likely felt it was completely wrong, made me like him even more.

"I hope she gets better soon," I said. "Do you get to see her often?"

"Now that I'm north, yes. She's at Lake View Medical Care Facility."

I perked up a bit. "They do great work. Their long-term rehabilitation care for stroke patients is fantastic."

Mr. Valera zipped his coat. "That sounds like the voice of experience."

It was indeed. "A few years ago a good friend of mine had a stroke when he was only fifty-six. He did his long-term rehabilitation at Lake View and credits them with his full recovery."

"That is a fine testimonial." Mr. Valera nodded. "I'll share it with the family. We are looking forward to her improvement. We get reports of her restlessness and it's possible it's linked to the Conti. Either she wants to tell us where it is, or she's trying to tell us it's stolen and—"

He suddenly sagged, his right knee going out from under him. But before I could jump to help him, he'd recovered. And looked down. "My word,

Mr. Eddie. That was quite a head bump. You caught me completely unprepared."

"Eddie," I scolded. "Leave Mr. Valera alone!"

My cat, of course, paid no attention. He was too focused on circling the judge's pant leg, spreading black and white hairs as he went, purring all the while.

"Sorry," I murmured, moving to pick Eddie up. "He can be a pest."

"A cat's purr can compensate for much." Mr. Valera gave Eddie another scratch, which made my furry feline purr even louder. "Fare thee well, Eddie. Minnie." He nodded at Hunter, and when he was gone, my new clerk let out a long breath.

"So that was Mr. Valera. Wow. You weren't kidding when you said he was a presence."

I nuzzled the top of Eddie's head, murmured that he was a horrible cat, and let him ooze himself out of my arms and onto the floor. "He seems really concerned about that sculpture. Wonder if it's because of sentiment or value."

"Luckily, we have the rectangle of knowledge with us." Hunter pulled his cell phone from his pants pocket. "Wonder how you spell that sculptor's name. C-O-N-T, but then is it an I or an E . . . hang on . . . whoa."

He blinked. Blinked again.

"What's the matter?"

He handed me his phone and I felt myself do the double blink thing. "Vittorio Conti," I said slowly. "One of the most popular modern classic sculptors in the world." I looked up. "No kidding. Have you ever heard of him?"

"Nope."

We mulled over our general ignorance of twentieth—and twenty-first—century sculptors the rest of the bookmobile day. My sole contribution was Maya Lin, the architect and sculptor who designed the Washington, DC, Vietnam Veterans Memorial. Hunter added Frederic Remington, painter and sculptor of Western imagery, until we looked him up and found he did most of his work in the late 1800s.

Hunter drooped. "Zero for me."

"Don't feel bad. I could only come up with one."

"Not the point," Hunter said. "I have lots more testosterone than you do so I feel the need to win."

I patted him on the shoulder as we finished setting up for our last stop of the day. "Poor thing. Doesn't that get exhausting? To be in competition all the time?"

"You have no idea," he said feelingly.

"Mrr!"

"Exactly." Hunter gave Eddie a nod. "You're a guy, so you get it, right? It's not me, it's the—" He snapped his fingers. "Calder. The guy who did that big reddish orange thing in downtown Grand Rapids." He tapped quickly on his phone. "Born 1898."

I beamed. "Nice!"

"What's nice?" Pug Mattock, one of my favorite seasonal residents, bounded up the bookmobile steps. "You're not talking about this weather, are you?"

Clearly, weather was the topic of the day, but I was pretty sure nothing anyone said was going to change it. I spent a brief moment wondering what the world would be like if complaining about the weather actually did change things and gave it up quickly. Far too many possibilities. Fun for the short term, perhaps, but probably bad long term.

"You're up early," I said. "Don't tell me you got fooled by that warm spell last week."

He snorted. "Not a chance. I been around the block more than once. False spring, we used to call it. Now." Pug eyed Hunter up and down. "Who is this young man and what have you done with Julia?"

I made the introductions and the two men shook hands. "But, Pug," I asked, "why are you up this early? I've never seen you here before the end of April."

"That is about to change." Pug, a stocky man in his late fifties, grinned hugely. "I've been working remote for years. It's been harder for Sylvia, but she's finally there. We're moving up here year-round as soon as she does a last round of meetings."

Pug worked for a car-parts manufacturer as a project manager. Sylvia, his wife, was a partner in a very successful firm of business consultants. Her specialty was data analysis, and there'd been a time or two when I'd come very close to understanding what she did all day.

"My theory," he said, "is the more prepared the cottage is for her, the sooner she'll abandon ship. I've actually been here a number of times this winter, moving up this and that, which is why I—" He broke off and squinted at us.

"Why what?" I prompted.

His squint continued. "I know how things work up here. Half the people are related, and the other half went to high school together."

Not entirely true, but I knew what he meant.

Then he shrugged and laughed. "But if you can't

trust librarians, who can you trust? I'm up here right now because I made an appointment with that conservation officer. Jenica Thomas. I saw someone poaching last time I was up and want to make a formal report."

"Poaching?" My brain went immediately to eggs, but I was pretty sure that wasn't what he was talking about.

"Turkeys. Out of season."

The intricacies of fishing and hunting rules and regulations were way outside my scope of interest. Rafe, my fiancé, did an annual November deer camp with a group of friends, but I'd never been convinced that any of them actually left the cabin for anything except food and beer runs.

"Hunting turkeys out of season is bad?" I asked.

Pug and Hunter exchanged a look, the patently male one that said, Here we go. Now we have to explain all this to a girl. Who's going to go first?

"Never mind," I said, trying to stave off the pending condescension. "I hope you and Officer Thomas catch the bad guy and throw the book at him. Or her." Then, to change the subject as quickly as possible, I said, "Are you going to sell your house downstate right away, or—"

"Mrr!" Eddie bumped my shin. "Mrr!"

To keep him quiet, I bent down to pick him up. He immediately squirmed out of my arms and raced to the front of the bookmobile, jumped onto the console, and bounced from there to the dashboard.

The three of us silently watched, and when Eddie flopped down, smashing the length of his back and tail along the windshield, where it was extremely difficult for me to clean away the loose hairs that would inevitably result, I turned my focus back to Pug and Hunter.

"Sorry about him," I said.

Pug was still watching Eddie with a bemused looked on his face, but Hunter was focused on something farther away. "Is that Ryan Anderson?"

I looked out at the pickup truck in the parking lot and the figure climbing out, his brown hair mostly covered by a baseball cap. "Looks like it. He's often at this stop."

Ryan was a twentysomething young man who had wandered north a few years ago and hadn't left. He made a living by cobbling together part-time jobs of all sorts. Waitstaff, ski lift operator, custodial and security work, construction, retail; he was a hard worker and took any job that came his way. He'd become a regular bookmobile patron and we'd bonded after he'd checked out books by Dick Francis, Ursula K. Le Guin, and Bernard Cornwell.

Over the nearly three years of the bookmobile's life, I'd started to treat Ryan like the younger brother I'd never had. Our friendship had recently deepened when, over a pile of books we'd managed to mutually drop, we'd confessed to each other stupid things we'd done. His most recent was losing his wallet when he'd gone downstate last month and not noticing until the day before; mine was when I'd called my mom and, while on the phone, told her I couldn't set a date for wedding dress shopping because I couldn't find my phone.

"Do you know him?" I asked.

Hunter shrugged. "We play darts sometimes. At the brewpub. I didn't know he was into reading."

I folded my arms and looked fake sternly at the younger men as Ryan came inside. "So apparently you two know each other but don't know each other. Why is it that men don't talk?"

"All the important topics are covered," Ryan said, smiling.

I counted. "Sports, beer, and . . ." I looked at my two extended fingers. "And that's it, right?"

"Fishing," Pug said.

My finger arrangement didn't change. "Goes in the sports category."

The three men simultaneously sucked in sharp breaths. "Minerva Hamilton," Pug thundered. "You take that back."

"Not a sport," Ryan said.

Hunter nodded. "Religion. Didn't you ever read Norman MacLean? Izaak Walton?"

"On my list," I said automatically. Because surely, somewhere on my long mental list of To Be Read books were *A River Runs Through It* and *The Compleat Angler*. Way down on the list, but on there. Probably.

Ryan's eyebrows went up. "Is that so? How about a quiz on the *Angler* next week?"

I suddenly understood why my childhood friends had complained about their little brothers. But it wouldn't hurt me to read the thing. And if I was interpreting Ryan's smirk correctly, he didn't think I'd pick up the book at all. Hah. I'd show him. "Give me two weeks."

Ryan, Hunter, and Pug did a group knuckle bump. "We'll make her a fishing fan yet," Pug said, slapping Ryan on the shoulder.

Three men bonding over the possibility of me

becoming more like them. Outstanding. I shook my head, but on the inside every bit of me was smiling. This was a classic bookmobile moment. Things like this just didn't happen in a brick-and-mortar library, and this was why I loved the bookmobile so very much.

Eddie chose that moment to jump down from the dashboard and bump his head against my shin. Obediently, I scooped him up and watched fondly as the men chatted about the end of ice-fishing season. Sillies. Didn't they know you could buy fish in the store?

There was a muted chirp. Ryan slapped his hand to his back pants pocket and pulled out his phone. "Sorry," he said, reading. His face went still. For a moment he didn't move. Didn't breathe. He looked up and, though his gaze met mine, it didn't seem as if he saw me at all. "Sorry," he said again. "I have to . . . I have to go."

We watched Ryan rush out of the bookmobile and hurry across the parking lot to his truck, jump in, and roar off, all without looking in our direction even once.

"Well, that was odd," I said.

Pug cleared his throat. "Didn't mean to snoop, but I did see it was a long text from his mother."

"Hope everything is okay." It had looked like an emergency of sorts, and after the stop was done and we were driving back to Chilson, I tried to come up with reasons for Ryan's actions that weren't serious.

His mother's car was making funny noises and she wanted his advice. A long-lost girlfriend of Ryan's was in town for a few days, and had contacted his mother, wanting to see him. He'd scheduled a routine doctor's appointment, forgotten about it, and the doctor's office had called his mom to remind him.

There were so many possible innocuous reasons that I'd practically forgotten about the incident by the time we rolled into the library's parking lot and started unloading.

Holly Terpening, one of the library clerks and my good friend, showed up at the back door to help us lug the loaded crates into the room where we sorted the bookmobile books.

"Did you hear?" she asked, pushing her straight brown hair behind her ears, then taking the first crate from me.

"We hear lots of things out on the bookmobile," I said. "The sigh of the wind, the songs of birds, the lapping of waves."

"No, about that Ryan Anderson. He shows up on this bookmobile run, doesn't he? Did you see him today?"

"Sort of." I frowned. "What's the matter?"

Hunter stood at my shoulder. "Is he okay?"

"The police are looking for him," Holly said.

A shiver of unease went up the back of my neck. "What? Why?"

"There was a bank robbery. Downstate. They're saying he stole like two hundred thousand dollars. But what's worse," she said to our shocked faces, "is they think he killed a security guard."

Chapter 2

There was no way Ryan would have robbed a bank, let alone killed someone. They were looking for the wrong guy. That's what I told Holly and that's what I told the downstate detective who'd tracked me down and left a voice mail. Eddie was in his carrier, waiting for me in the car, so I hoped the call didn't take long.

"Yes, ma'am," he said. "I'm making note of your opinions regarding Mr. Anderson. Now, you've already said you saw him briefly this afternoon. Please tell me what time, as precisely as possible."

The man talked just like every other detective I'd ever met, which was a total of two local sheriff's office detectives. Two and a half if you counted detective-in-training Ash Wolverson. Ash hadn't completely succumbed to the short declarative sentence structure of his supervisor, but it was probably only a matter of time. I knew for a fact that Detective Hal Inwood talked that way on and off

the job and retired detective Devereaux probably
did, too. It was in Ash's future; I just hoped his girlfriend, Chelsea Stille, would be able to deal with it.

I told the downstate detective the location and
time I'd seen Ryan and described what he'd done,
which was nothing, really. I also rattled off to the
detective all the very reasonable explanations I'd
come up with for Ryan's actions. The detective
made murmuring noises that indicated he was listening to me, but I did not hear any keyboard clicks
or pencil scratchings that meant he was taking
notes. I decided he must be using a pen, which
would be silent.

The detective asked, "Was there anyone else on
the bookmobile who saw Mr. Anderson's movements?"

It was a question I'd expected. I gave him Hunter's name and cell number and Pug's name, which
was technically David. One of these days I'd get the
real story of why he was called Pug. So far he'd told
me three different versions, none of which I be-
lieved.

"No phone number for Mr. Mattock?" the detective asked.

There was none in our records, but there was an
e-mail address, which I gave him. "Hope you find
the guy who killed the security guard," I said. "But
I don't think Ryan had anything to do with it. I really don't."

"Thank you for your time, Ms. Hamilton. We'll
be in touch if we have further questions."

I returned my desk phone's receiver to its technological nest and leaned back in my chair, spin-

ning around to look out the window. It was still dull and dreary out there. Still March. Technically, sunset wasn't until eight o'clock, but it had been so dark all day I was half convinced the sun had never risen at all. "You could have made more of an effort," I told it, sighing. "Would have made a lot of difference to a lot of people."

But the heavy cloud cover had to end soon. After all, it was the end of March. April would start the very next day. Sure, we'd get some more snow, and we wouldn't see any serious green on the trees for weeks, but the daytime temperatures were way above freezing. The sap was running. Spring was on its way. I enjoyed winter, but there was a time and place for everything, and April was the time for this heavy cloud cover to clear off.

"Spring is coming," I said to the window, and said it again the next morning when I walked into the break room, coffee mug in hand. Though the library wouldn't open to the public for another fifteen minutes, I'd been at my desk for a couple of hours and was ready for more caffeine and some coworker conversation.

The three people in the room glanced up.

"You trying to convince yourself of that?" Josh Hadden, our IT guy, added a heaping spoonful of sugar to his coffee. This told me that Kelsey, one of our part-time clerks, had made the pot on the burner.

I opened the fridge, grabbed the jug of creamer, and added a healthy dollop to my mug before adding the black liquid. "Undeniable fact. Calendar says so."

"The term 'spring equinox' is stupid." He sipped his coffee, made a face, and added more sugar. "Equal day and equal night doesn't mean the grass is going to be green next week."

"But in the next month," I said. "So spring is indeed coming."

Donna Beene, another part-time clerk, laughed, tossing back her short and thick gray hair. Seventy-some and way fitter than a fiddle, Donna worked at the library to earn cash for trips to exotic locales so she could participate in feats of athletic endurance. Running marathons, mostly, but also bicycling, kayaking, and I thought I'd heard her mention snowshoeing. "So in Minnie logic," Donna said, "spring is always coming. Even when it *is* spring. Because there's always next year."

It made perfect sense to me. "Exactly."

My coworkers, however, ignored this positive life outlook in favor of grilling me about Ryan Anderson.

The night before, I'd told Rafe about Ryan's abrupt departure from the bookmobile, and that the police were looking for him. Rafe, a Chilson native and principal of the middle school, knew more about the investigation than I did. It was the last day of the school's spring break, and though he'd spent a lot of time working on the house, he'd also spent time hanging out with his friends, doing whatever it was that guys did.

"The bank that was robbed," he'd said, "is next to the second-oldest pizza place in the state."

I'd looked at him over the top of my vegetarian sub sandwich. "How do you know this stuff?"

He'd given me a fake-stern look. "Keeping my finger on the pulse of the community is my job."

Then he'd grinned, his teeth flashing white against skin that looked permanently tanned thanks to distant Native American ancestors. My heart went mushy and our talk turned to other things.

Now, faced with three curious coworkers, I realized an opportunity might be presenting itself. "Do any of you know Ryan?" Josh and Kelsey and I were roughly the same age, and what Donna didn't know about Chilson natives wasn't worth knowing. Not that Ryan was from here, but maybe one of them had run into him at the brewpub. "Hunter knows him a little from playing darts at Hoppe's."

But all three were shaking their heads. Josh said, "Sorry. Don't think I've ever met him."

"Could you ask around? I'm sure he didn't do anything wrong, and that detective from downstate seemed ready to put cuffs on him."

Donna gave me a look. "Minnie, dear, I know you want to believe that all library patrons, and especially your bookmobile people, are good, kindhearted folks who wouldn't walk across the street against a red light, but don't you think the police know what they're doing?"

I felt my face freeze into grim lines. In recent years, I'd had more than one very similar discussion with law enforcement. Though the people in law enforcement did indeed know what they were doing, it was my experience that they also tended to think in straight lines, always assuming the noise of the hooves was horses, and not accepting the possibility of zebras until the black-and-white-striped hides zoomed past them.

"Innocent until proven guilty," Kelsey said. "I'll ask my husband."

I turned to Josh. "And you'll ask Mia?"

Josh's square face turned soft at the mention of his wife. The two had been married not quite six months ago in a hastily planned ceremony arranged for the sole purpose of pleasing Mia's grandmother. In spite of the shortest engagement I'd ever heard of—three hours—the couple gave every indication of delirious happiness that would last for decades. "Sure," he said. "I can ask, but you know she doesn't get out much."

I did. Mia was also in IT and was the poster child for shyness. But there were signs that being married to the gregarious Josh was peeling back some of her social reluctance.

"Thanks," I said. Just then, something tingled in the back of my brain. "Say, isn't Mia's grandmother's last name Conti?"

Josh shrugged. "Guess so. Why?"

"Can you also ask Mia if her grandmother is related to a Vittorio Conti? He was a sculptor." I sped on to answer the inevitable questions. "This isn't anything to do with Ryan. It came up on the bookmobile, is all."

He shrugged again. "I can ask, but if Nana was related to anyone famous, everyone would know."

Since I'd met Mia's grandmother, I was sure he was right. "Thanks." Then, doing my duty as assistant library director, I reminded everyone that Graydon Cain, our boss, would be out of town the next week.

"On vacation, right?" Kelsey asked.

I nodded. "He and his wife are flying to Southern California."

"He's not combining vacation with a job interview, is he?"

"What?" I frowned. "Why on earth would you say that?"

"Just checking. He's the best director we've ever had. Other than you, I mean." She grinned. "It'd be a shame if he bolted after only a year."

During the brief time I'd been interim library director, more than one person had tried to convince me to apply for the permanent position. But I hadn't been ready to give up driving the bookmobile, and there was no way I would have had time to do both jobs.

I could almost hear the conversation. The library board president would have looked at me over the top of his reading glasses. "Minnie, you do understand the responsibilities of library director, don't you? That they will preclude you from so much dedicated time on the bookmobile."

The vice president would have chimed in, her face kind but firm. "Not that we'd keep you from ever going out, of course. But you just wouldn't have time to do the same amount of outreach. You'd have to hire an assistant. A new you."

I pondered the idea as my coworkers kept talking. What would the New Me have looked like? Taller, for sure. Shiny straight hair. A couple of kids in school. Would have been an assistant librarian downstate somewhere and looking to make a fresh start. Would have been thrilled to be working in Chilson. Would have had a to-do list starting with redecorating the bland assistant librarian's office.

"Minnie, you've heard that, too?" Kelsey asked.

"Sorry?" I asked vaguely, seeing paisley wallpaper rolling up my office walls.

Josh snapped his fingers. "Earth to Minnie. Come back from wherever you are."

The vision vanished. I breathed a sigh of relief. "Did I hear what?"

"Ash Wolverson and Chelsea Stille."

I smiled. "They're a great couple, aren't they?" The incredibly handsome Ash and I had briefly dated a couple of years ago, but it had been like hanging out with a brother. Fun, but no passion. We'd parted on friendly terms and I'd been thrilled when I'd started seeing Ash and Chelsea, the sheriff's new office manager, walking down the street, hand in hand.

Kelsey's eyebrows went up. "Then they're back together? Good."

"Wait." I shook my head, flushing out the last of my inane decorating daydream. "What are you talking about?"

"So many brains," Josh said sadly. "Yet she uses so few of them."

"More that she just doesn't pay attention." Kelsey eyed the mostly empty coffeepot and moved to start making another, ignoring the collective sigh. "You had your chance," she said. "Anyway, I was saying that I was at the Round Table yesterday, waiting to pick up lunch, and saw Ash and Chelsea, sitting in a booth and, you know, not talking. For ten minutes straight. They just stared at the table the whole time."

That wasn't good. "You think they broke up?"

She shrugged. "When they got up to leave, I heard Ash ask if there was any way she'd change her mind.

And she said, 'Only if you change yours.' Then she walked away. No kiss, no hug, no 'see you later.' Ash looked like the world had ended, and when Chelsea walked out, I could see she was crying."

It certainly sounded like a breakup. I walked back to my office, slowly as to not spill my topped-off coffee, and hoped that Ash and Chelsea could work through whatever it was that had pushed them apart. Every relationship was a mystery, though, and there were probably an infinite number of reasons why things could fall apart.

I entered my office, glanced at the walls—yep, still the same boring light beige they'd been fifteen minutes ago—and sat at my desk. But before I went back to updating the library's magazine subscriptions, I pulled out my phone and started texting.

Minnie: *Suddenly afraid.*

Rafe: *Of what*

Minnie: *Everything. But mostly that someday you'll stop loving me.*

Rafe: *Be not afraid. If that hasn't happened in the last 20-some years, it won't ever.*

Minnie (after a pause to wipe her suddenly teary eyes): *I love you.*

Rafe: *Took you long enough*

This, as he'd surely intended, made me laugh. I sent one more text, telling him that I'd pick up dinner on the way home that night, and turned my attention to my job.

At half past noon, my stomach let me know that it was time for lunch. A millisecond later, my brain let me know that I'd forgotten to pack any food. This gave me the options of: go hungry (not a chance), eat from the library's vending machine (see previous answer), walk home and make my own lunch, or walk downtown and buy a lunch someone else made for me.

Since both of the viable options involved walking, I slipped off my library shoes, pulled on my light boots and coat, and headed out. When I'd arrived in the morning, it had been dark outside and in, but now the building was bright with light from overhead fixtures and bits of scattered sunshine that were trickling in through the windows. I walked through the library, its beauty calming me as it always did when I took the time to look about me.

When I'd been hired as assistant director, the library had been a sixties-ish–era building of high functionality but zero charm. Happily, the voters had chosen to fund the renovation of an empty two-story school building into the glorious space we now occupied.

I smiled at it all. At the lovingly restored oak woodwork that outlined the ceiling, windows, doors, and floors. At the shiny metallic tile surrounding the drinking fountains. At the tall windows of the former gymnasium that shone soft light onto the main book stacks. And at my favorite place, the reading room, with its upholstered chairs, window seats, and working fireplace.

It was tempting to skip lunch and instead spend an hour with a book in front of the fire, but I'd promised my mother—via an e-mailed New Year's resolution for accountability—that I'd start eating like an adult and not a college student. After checking with my coworkers for any lunch order pickups I could do, I zipped my coat and headed out.

The chill air reminded me, once again, that I lived Up North, and that early April was no time to expect warmth and sunshine. I consciously pushed all longings for blue skies and newborn lambs to a back corner of my mind and instead focused on what was around me.

My walk through tree-lined residential neighborhoods, houses small and close together, quickly gave way to a quirky downtown. A stucco 1930s gas station turned restaurant here, a general store there, a fieldstone toy store here, a restaurant that was nothing but windows there. A statuesque bank. Retail stores in all shapes, sizes, and styles.

I looked from left to right, admiring the mix of ages and materials that combined to make a harmonious whole in a way that could never have been planned. This growth was organic, shifting over the years, and the result was the heart and soul of my adopted town.

A knock dragged my attention away from squinting at the twin stone sculptures that had been affixed to the roof of the jewelry store for at least seventy-five years—yep, there were still baby goats up there, and someday I'd learn the story behind that—and I turned to look at retailer Pam Fazio.

My friend Pam, who was smushing her smiling face against the inside of her front door, guaranteeing a need to wash the glass, had fled the corporate world of central Ohio a few years ago. Pam was in her mid-fifties, with short smooth black hair, and she had more marketing and graphic design talent in her fingernail clippings than I would have in the totality of my life. Upon leaving her corporate cubicle, she'd taken a vow that, every day from then on, she'd drink her morning coffee outside in the fresh air. That vow had been made a bit difficult when she'd moved north and had to face subzero temperatures, but she'd solved the problem by interpreting her glassed-in front porch as "outside," which I found perfectly acceptable.

Now she opened the door and poked her head outside. "Tomorrow!" she yelled, though I was only ten feet away. "Container Day!"

Those two words explained her goofily exuberant mood. During the depths of winter, Pam journeyed overseas to find summer goods for her eclectic store, Older Than Dirt. The fruits of her labors were put into a semitruck container and shipped to Chilson.

The day the container arrived—cleverly dubbed Container Day—was like Christmas for her. She dragooned friends far and wide to help unload, and we were happy to help out. It was fun seeing what she'd purchased, and the pay of as much pizza as we could eat was more than enough compensation.

I gave her a mittened thumbs-up. "I'll be there."

"How about Rafe?" she asked. "Because I'll need to order an extra pizza if he's coming."

"Count on it," I said confidently, because we'd been looking forward to it for weeks. "First thing in the morning?"

"The coffee shop is delivering coffee boxes at seven."

"If we're not there at seven, do we get penalized?"

"In a way. You'll get less coffee."

"Then we'll see you tomorrow at seven." I waved and headed to Shomin's Deli. Mindful of my New

Year's resolution, I strong-mindedly stayed away from my favorite of Swiss cheese and green olives on sourdough bread, and instead ordered a salad with grilled chicken, light dressing on the side.

Oddly for the time of year, I didn't recognize any of the other diners, so I sat by myself at a small table. In my coat pocket was a paperback I'd picked up at the local used bookstore, so after texting Rafe about Container Day, I settled down to *War of the Roses: Stormbird*, by Conn Iggulden.

I was deep in the Lancaster versus York saga when my attention was caught by the conversation of two women who'd sat in the booth behind me.

"Mrs. Anderson," one of them said, "I don't know what to do. I mean, what *can* we do?"

"There has to be something," said the other woman. "Every day he's missing takes a year off my life."

I half turned. The first woman looked to be in her twenties, the second in her fifties. Despite the difference in their ages and their physical differences—the older woman had short graying hair and a shape that spoke of many meals and not many hours spent exercising, while the younger woman had long dark blond hair with a purple streak and arms the diameter of a stick—their faces matched each other, showing concern and anxiety. And fear.

"Sorry to interrupt," I said. "And I didn't mean to eavesdrop, but are you talking about Ryan Anderson?"

The older woman gave me a hard look. "This is a private conversation."

"Wait." The younger woman put out a hand.

"Mrs. Anderson, I think I know who she is. She's on the bookmobile. Ryan is always talking about Eddie. You know, the bookmobile cat?"

"Minnie Hamilton," I said, nodding. "Eddie's mom." So to speak. I looked at the older woman. "Are you Ryan's? Mom, I mean?"

She was, and with her was Keegan Kolb, who rented the second floor of an old farmhouse where Ryan was renting the first floor. The two women had met when Mrs. Anderson came north to find her son after she'd been contacted by that downstate detective.

"There's no way he did what they say he did." Keegan was emphatic.

"Of course not," said Mrs. Anderson. "He's a good boy. I never would have raised someone who could . . . who could do all that."

I nodded again, more slowly this time. Not in complete agreement—because how could you ever be totally and completely one hundred percent sure of anyone other than Rafe?—but I agreed with their basic premise, that Ryan did not rob that bank. And that he didn't cause the death of that security guard.

When I told them so, their faces lightened the slightest bit. Which broke my heart a little and encouraged me to say, "Matter of fact, I'm so sure Ryan didn't do anything wrong that I'm going to work on a plan to prove his innocence."

Mrs. Anderson clapped a hand over her mouth. "You'll do that?" she asked through her fingers. "For my Ryan?"

I'd do the same thing for anyone I was convinced

was innocent of a crime, but sure. "I'll do what I can," I promised.

Mrs. Anderson rushed over and gave me a huge hug. "Thank you, thank you, thank you," she whispered into my hair. "You don't know how much that means to me."

Keegan said, "Thanks so much. It's great knowing you're on our side."

"I can't promise anything," I cautioned.

"Of course not," Mrs. Anderson said. "But you're a librarian, so you have to be smart. If you think Ryan's innocent, then others can't be far behind."

"Plus you have Eddie." Keegan smiled. "And I know he likes Ryan, so that has to be good, right?"

"Sure," I murmured, trying hard not to laugh hysterically at the notion. "You bet it is."

And then I started to make a plan.

Chapter 3

It was Sunday night, and I was sitting in the kitchen of Three Seasons, the restaurant owned by my best friend, Kristen. My feet were swinging back and forth and back and forth because the stools were sized to fit the six-foot Kristen and not the five-foot me. Every once in a while the toe of one of my feet would bump the side of the stainless-steel island, which normally would earn me a steely blue-eyed glare. Tonight, however, Kristen was preoccupied with two tasks: finishing our traditional Sunday dessert of crème brûlée and complaining about her physical state.

"How did I get this big?" she asked, slapping her very pregnant midsection with the hand that wasn't wielding a small flamethrower. "I'm huge! The size of a house."

I held up my thumb and eyed it, pretending I was an artist making precise perspective measurements. "Have to be a small house."

She triggered the flame and waved it about. "A cow, then."

"Cows weigh over a thousand pounds." At least I was pretty sure they did. If I remembered, I'd look it up later on. "Last I checked you were nowhere near that big."

"You're not going to let me wallow in my extra-large-sized despair, are you?"

"Nope."

She made a rude noise and focused on melting the sugar in a pair of ramekins. I breathed a small sigh of relief. Kristen was an extremely talented chef. Her restaurant was a rousing success, thanks in part to a spot on the nationally syndicated television show *Trock's Troubles*. She'd never once cut off one of her fingers, seared away her eyebrows, or burned down any large structures. Still, there was always a first time, and her cavalier attitude could be interpreted by those unsavvy in the ways of kitchens—say, me—as her not paying enough attention to what she was doing.

"I have to be as big as a car, at least," she said. "One of those adorable little ones."

"Mini Cooper?" Though there were probably dozens of small-car manufacturers, it was the only one my brain could summon quickly.

Kristen patted her belly again. "That's it. Got my own personal Mini Cooper, right here." She squinted at the ramekins and gave them one last wave of fiery heat. "Hope you're okay with no fruit garnish tonight."

I thumped the stool next to me. "Have a seat, O Pregnant One. I would have been okay with eating ice cream out of our own special tub."

Hitching herself onto the seat, she asked, "What, and mess up our reunion? Not a chance."

I slid over a spoon and napkin. "It is a reunion, isn't it? I never thought of it that way."

"Silly." Kristen inspected her crème brûlée with a chef's eye, shaking her head at a flaw invisible to everyone else in the universe. We dug in, and for a few moments there was nothing but the crackle of sugar and the scooping of spoon into custard.

Before she married Scruffy (not his real name) Gronkowski, Kristen had split her time between Chilson and Key West. Her restaurant was named after the Three Seasons it was open: spring, summer, and fall. After she closed down in October, she bade a cheerful good-bye to northern Michigan and skedaddled for the warmth of Florida before the snow fell. Kristen did things flat out or she didn't do them at all, and she expended every bit of energy she had on the restaurant. Down in Florida, she watched old movies and tended bar and spent a lot of time napping in hammocks.

At least, that was what she used to do. Now that she was married to Scruffy, things had shifted. The Scruff was the producer of *Trock's Troubles*, and the son of Trock Farrand (not his real name). Kristen still ran Three Seasons and still spent some of the winter in Key West, but more and more she was traveling with Scruffy and the production crew. Trock himself, large and round and full of exuberant life, had begun hinting that retirement was starting to hover and that the show would need a new face.

"So," I said. "Has there been a decision? About the show?"

Kristen scoffed. "Trock is never going to retire. That show is his life. What would he do with himself if he wasn't gallivanting around the country half the year?"

The premise of Trock's show had originally been solving common kitchen cooking problems by first making them on camera. His comic genius had caught the nation's attention and quickly turned his show into a phenomenon. Over the years, the show had morphed to feature restaurants of every stripe, and each one creatively solved a "trouble." Three Seasons had been featured on an episode two years ago, which was how Kristen and Scruffy met. The rest, as they say, was history.

"Are you even listening to me?" Kristen demanded. "Don't waste your breath trying to deny it. You were a zillion miles away."

"I was thinking about how you met Scruffy."

She laughed. "Back then I thought he was an uptight corporate drone with no sense of humor."

The ironic nickname had been bestowed upon him by his loving father. Trock could come out of a manufacturer's clean room covered in dirt. His son could come out of a mud bog without a drop of muck on him, his pants still with a knife-edge crease.

"Where is he, anyway?" I asked.

She rested one hand on her stomach. "At the house, putting the crib together. I tried to help, but the Mini Cooper here makes getting down on my hands and knees more than awkward."

"I'm glad you're here," I said softly.

"Well, I wanted to give birth here at home. My

gynecologist back east has been talking to my gyno here, so it's all good."

Most of Kristen's family lived in Chilson and Trock had owned a house on the outskirts of Chilson for years, but Trock's signature restaurant and the show's home base were in New York City. Warily, I'd been watching for signs that the bright lights would become "home" to her. So far, so good, but you never knew.

"How did Container Day go? What was the best thing Pam brought back?" Kristen asked. "I would have gone, but the drive from New York kind of conked me out."

"Fun, like always," I said. "But you'll have to go see for yourself. Pam found this old-fashioned French baby buggy, a what-do-you-call-it, a perambulator. The thing is huge. She said it called to her." I grinned.

"Yeah? What did it say? 'Buy me and take me to Chilson for my pregnant friend to spend a fortune on'?"

Probably. Pam's store was very successful for a reason. "You'll have to ask." I scraped the last bit of custard out of my ramekin. "Speaking of asking, do you know Ryan Anderson?"

She frowned. "Isn't he the guy who robbed that bank downstate? And killed a security guard?"

"He did not!"

My voice came out louder than I'd intended and Kristen looked at me, speculation writ large on her face. "Okay," she said slowly. "Isn't that the guy the police are looking for? Because *they* think he robbed a bank and killed that guy?"

I put my spoon down. "The police can be wrong. It's been known to happen."

"Fair enough." Kristen nodded. "I've heard the name, but I don't know him. I think one of my sous-chefs does, though."

"Can you send him a text? About Ryan?"

She shrugged. "Sure, but he's working in Utah, finishing up the ski season, and he might not pay attention to a text from me until the end of April. I told him he didn't have to be here until May first."

Kristen had a solid core of loyal staff. She browbeat them for months, worked them mercilessly—and they loved her. Sure, she paid them well, but the reason they kept coming back and coming back was that she loved them, too. Even if how she showed it was through commands shouted at the top of her lungs.

"But you could try?" I persisted.

"What exactly do you want me to ask? If Ryan Anderson thumped Mr. Plum over the head with a candlestick in the drawing room?"

I returned to my last bite of custardy goodness. "Pretty sure that's a reference to some board game I've never played."

"Duh." She elbowed me lightly. "For someone who's smart, you're pretty dumb sometimes. But I mean it. What should I ask my guy in Utah? Because I can see you're shifting into investigative mode, even though there are professional law enforcement officers working on this."

"They can get things wrong," I said. "And as for what you should ask him . . . oh, I don't know." I sighed.

"Hey, don't go all sad on me." Kristen elbowed

me again. "This is Sunday night. Pathetic sighs are not allowed. What we need," she said firmly, "is a plan. So that's what we're going to do."

"We?" I echoed. "But you're . . . really pregnant. And I'm already working on a plan." Hadn't gotten very far, but I'd started. In my head.

"Of course, 'we.'" She rolled her eyes. "You don't think I'd let you do this by yourself, do you? Because you obviously need help."

"Is this what friends are for?" I asked, my eyes suddenly blinking with moisture.

"Duh," she said again.

And, after I surreptitiously wiped my eyes, we got to work. The two of us together would surely come up with something.

Rafe opened our front door as I hurried up the porch steps. "About time you got home," he said. "I was going to start without you."

"You were not." I toed off my boots, shucked my coat, and put it all in the front closet, handy for tomorrow morning. Maybe next week I'd be comfortable wandering around outside in regular shoes and a light jacket, but then again, maybe not. Last year a foot of snow had dropped on us in mid-April. Even though the upcoming forecast didn't indicate anything like that, I wasn't sure it could be trusted to stay that way.

"Yeah, you're right." Rafe pulled me into a hug and kissed the top of my head. "Eddie would have made my life miserable. He hates it when his routine is messed up."

I nodded into the shoulder of Rafe's plaid flannel shirt and asked, "Where is he, anyway?"

"Mrr."

Detaching myself, I looked around. "What, exactly, is he doing there?"

"No idea. I wouldn't have thought he'd fit."

Eddie, a good-sized cat of thirteen pounds, was sitting in the middle of the stairway. Sort of. He was halfway up the wooden steps but, for a reason known only to him, was sitting on the three inches of step outside the stair balusters. Much of him flowed either inward through the balusters or outward over the edge of the step. Though his perch looked precarious, Eddie gave every indication of poise and unconcern.

I gestured at my cat. "Is this the definition of sangfroid?"

Early in my life, my parents had taught me that intelligence and education weren't necessarily the same thing, and my life experiences had shown me how right they'd been. But then there was Rafe, who managed to take advantage of both sides of that coin. He acted the part of an Up North hick when it could get him out of doing something he didn't feel like doing, but had used his bachelor's and master's degrees to become Chilson's middle school principal. The school board loved him, the school superintendent loved him, his teachers loved him, the parents loved him, and his students adored him. Of course, none of them ever had to deal with his horrific tendency to forget to buy coffee or his penchant for leaving wet towels on the bathroom floor.

Rafe considered my question. "Not sure if it should count that he's really exhibiting cool composure in a dangerous circumstance if he got himself into the situation."

"Hear that, Eddie?" I went forward and reached up. "You're not as cool as you think."

"Mrr!"

"I know, that shouldn't be possible, because cats are always cool, but think about it," I said, lifting him off the step. "You're the exception to the Cats Are Always Cool Rule, and how cool is that?"

"You realize that doesn't make any sense, right?" Rafe asked.

"Shh." I covered both of Eddie's ears with the hand that wasn't struggling to hold on to him. "Not in front of the children."

Rafe nodded solemnly. "Understood. Are you ready, or do you want to change first?"

"Change." I handed Eddie to Rafe. "Be down in a flash," I said, running up the stairs. In the bedroom, I changed quickly from the jeans and sweater I'd worn for dessert into the coziness of fleece pants, an old T-shirt, and a fleece sweater.

Dressed in my regular Sunday night attire, I went back downstairs, my hand skimming the oak handrail Rafe kept muttering about. He was insistent that it wasn't quite right and that one of these days he'd replace it. I had no idea what he was talking about—to me it was fine, even better than fine—but Rafe had milled, finished, and installed it, so it was understandable that he could find flaws that no one else would ever notice.

This, I'd found, was the downside of renovating your own home. Years ago, soon after I'd moved permanently to Chilson, Rafe had purchased a fixer-upper to end all fixer-uppers. It was Shingle-style and had a great location, right next to a marina, but it was also large, a century old, run-down, and chopped up into multiple apartments. Oddly, I'd just purchased an adorable little houseboat and moored it at that same marina, where I used to live from May through mid-October. When it got too cold, I moved up to stay with my aunt Frances in her boardinghouse.

But everything was different now. Aunt Frances had married Otto Bingham, a very nice man, and sold the boardinghouse to our cousin Celeste. Rafe had proposed to me; I'd accepted and moved into a gorgeous house. Just a few months ago, he'd told me he'd been renovating it with me in mind all along, and I still got sniffly when I thought about it.

In the living room, Rafe was already settled on the couch under a blanket, his long legs stretched out on the ottoman. Eddie was on top of Rafe's legs, and a fire crackled in the fireplace. Everything was set for our Sunday night: Netflixing the next episode of a ten-year-old Australian television show we'd gotten hooked on in December.

"How is The Blonde doing?" Rafe patted the space on the couch next to him, carefully not dislodging Eddie. "Still pregnant?"

"As pregnant as I've ever seen anyone." And her pregnant status had overridden our planning session for helping Ryan. Indigestion, she said, but her green face concerned me enough to call her husband. Scruffy said it probably was indeed indigestion, but he told her to get home and, shockingly, she did, proof that miracles happened.

Rafe tossed the right half of the blanket over me and I snuggled in, wondering how I'd gotten so lucky.

More than twenty years ago, I'd been sent north by my parents to spend the summer with my dad's sister. Aunt Frances had taken me to the city's beach on Janay Lake on a sunny afternoon. Kristen had been there all by herself, something that the city-raised Minnie had found shocking.

My amused aunt had introduced us—though she wasn't a local, her long-since-passed-away first husband had been, and my aunt knew virtually everyone in town—and Kristen and I became fast friends in the space of five minutes. Rafe had wandered down to the beach soon afterward, and we'd been a summer trio for years. Our friendship had waned when we'd graduated from high school and gone our separate ways, but Kristen moved back to Chilson about the same time I got the library job, and it soon seemed as if we'd never been apart.

Rafe and I were ten minutes into the show when I made the time-out signal. "Forgot to tell you," I said after he'd paused the TV, freezing the characters in unflattering poses. "About our wedding date. Kristen wants us to wait until she's recovered from the Mini Cooper."

Rafe felt my forehead. "No fever. Yet you still made a car reference." He glanced ceiling-ward. "Is the sky falling? The apocalypse upon us?"

I pushed his hand away. "Not as far as I know."

After I explained the new nickname, he nodded. "Got it. So, wedding-wise, that means what?"

"She's hoping we'll wait until August, at least. I know, I know. It's hot and it's still in the summer season, parking will be horrible, and it'll be next to impossible for anyone to find reasonably priced hotel rooms. So I'm thinking September. But only if that works for you." Rafe was always busy the first month of school.

He squinted, thinking. "I can make late September work," he said. "Shouldn't be a problem."

"Third Saturday?"

"Sounds good."

He looked at me and I looked at him. "That was easy," I said. "Why did it take us so long to figure this out?"

"Sometimes things just fall into place," he said, putting his arm around my shoulders. "Once again, procrastination pays off."

I looked at him curiously. "Is that what you tell your students?"

"No, I tell them to do what I say, not what I do."

I snuggled in next to him. He probably did. And they probably thought he was hilarious when he said it.

"There's only one thing about September," he said. "And it's going to be tough. But I want you to know I'll be behind you every step of the way. And I do mean behind."

I sank deeper into the couch. "Yeah, I know." For months my mother had been pushing for a June wedding. I wasn't sure why I'd resisted, other than the fact that since birth I'd resisted my mother pushing me to do pretty much anything, but now that it was April, planning a reasonably sized wedding in June was outside the realm of reality. Maybe Rafe was right about that procrastination thing.

"Tomorrow," I said. "I'll tell her tomorrow."

Or if not tomorrow, then at least the day after that. This week, for sure.

Rafe picked up the remote, but I reached out and put a hand on his arm. "One more thing," I said. "I could use some help. With finding Ryan Anderson."

The next morning, sun streamed in through the kitchen windows, making every surface gleam. Oak floors, pine ceiling, cream-colored cabinets with glass knobs, and hanging light fixtures that looked like something from an old boat; it was a beautiful kitchen, even to someone like me, who had the cooking skills of masking tape. Rafe and I sat side by side at the kitchen island, me in wet hair and a bathrobe sipping coffee, him in his school clothes spooning cold cereal into his body faster than should have been possible.

"What's the rush?" I curled my hands around my mug, letting its warmth ooze into me. Rafe had a school board meeting that night, so I'd scheduled myself to work at the library until it closed and didn't have to technically be at work until noon. "You don't normally leave for half an hour."

"Mmph," he said through a milky bite of toasted oats. He swallowed. "Sorry, just got a text. We had a substitute all lined up for Bob Rivera's class. Bob's out, remember? He fell in the grocery store parking lot, hit shoulder-first, and now he's on medical leave for at least six weeks. Anyway, the sub called in, saying she has to take her dad to the emergency room because *he* slipped and fell on some ice."

I hoped that both her dad and Bob would be okay, but I still wasn't sure why this meant he had to leave early, and said so.

"Because this means"—he picked up his bowl to drink the last of the milk and I hastily averted my eyes while he did so—"that I have to take over the class until we get another substitute."

I laughed. "'Have to'? Or 'want to'?"

Rafe pulled on his cold-weather board-meeting jacket, tweed complete with elbow patches. In summer he sported a navy blue jacket with bright brass buttons. I kept threatening to take him shopping so he could get out of the 1980s, but he told me that he'd picked a style decade he liked and saw no reason to change.

"Tomato, tomahto," he said. "Does it really matter?" He gave me a quick kiss. "I'll text you when the board meeting is done. Love you!"

And he was out the door.

The room, which had up until then felt warm and comforting and cheerful, suddenly felt empty and cold. It was always like this when Rafe and I parted; something in me was just . . . gone.

"Mrr?"

"He'll be back," I assured Eddie, who had apparently just decided that his new favorite kitchen spot was the deep sill of the window that looked over the backyard.

"Mrr."

Without getting out a tape measure, I guessed the amount of Eddie overhang was a good two inches. "This is just like the outside of the stairs last night," I told him. "You didn't fit there and you don't fit here."

He wriggled his shoulders and didn't say anything.

"Right. Well." I swallowed the last of my coffee.

"Hope you can manage all by yourself today. I'm off to investigate." Last night, Rafe and I had come up with a couple of ideas, and it was time to put the first one into action.

"Mrr!"

"Of course I'm going to get dressed first." I put my mug in the dishwasher and patted Eddie on the head. "And no, you're not going with me. It's not a bookmobile day."

"Mrr!"

"What is with you?" I gave his head one last pat. "Do that too much and you're going to lose your little kitty voice, and then where will you be?"

I went upstairs to change, and when I came down my fuzzy friend was nowhere to be seen. I looked in his typical favorite spots, but all were vacant. No Eddie on the back of the couch. No Eddie on any of the floor heating vents. No Eddie on the dining room chairs. And no Eddie where he shouldn't be—kitchen counters, fireplace mantel, or the top of the refrigerator.

Well, he was somewhere. I'd just have to leave without knowing where. "Eddie, I'm headed out," I called. "It's going to be hours and hours before I get back, so if you want one last snuggle, you'd better come now."

He'd never once fallen for that trick, and he didn't fall for it now. But as I shut the back door, I did hear a faint "Mrr."

"Silly cat," I muttered, getting into my small sedan and backing out of the driveway. All the way out to Bowyer Township I thought about all the places Eddie might possibly have fit himself into, and as I pulled into the gravel driveway of an old two-story farmhouse with a big barn out back, I'd created a mental list of 147 places.

I shut my car door and walked across the muddy drive. The house had, at one point, been sided with wide white aluminum. But that had been a long time ago and now the metal was dusty and flaking. The roof's shingles were starting to curl with age and the wooden window frames needed some serous maintenance. Still, the place was clean and tidy, and even though large snow piles lingered everywhere, I could tell the yard had been raked free of leaves in the fall and mowed one last time before the snow fell.

Inside, a curtain twitched and the front door was open by the time I'd climbed the warped porch steps. The older woman I'd met at Shomin's Deli stood in the doorway, her face working its way into politeness. "Hello, Minnie. What are you doing way out here?"

I smiled. "Hi, Mrs. Anderson. I was just wondering if you've heard from Ryan."

"Oh, honey, call me Danielle. And I'm so sorry, but I'm headed out. I've been up here for days, and my boss needs me back at work. There's only so much time I can take off."

"You're headed back downstate?"

"It's time for me to go," she said. "There's nothing I can do here, and it won't do anyone any good for me to lose my job." She paused, then tacked on, "Thanks so much for wanting to help. But I really don't think there's anything you can do from here on out."

"Um, sure." I searched in my coat pocket, found my wallet, and pulled out a business card. "I wrote my cell number on the back, so you can text me yours. If I learn anything about Ryan, I'll let you know right away."

She thanked me again, murmured that she really had to get going, and shut the door.

It wasn't until I was halfway to Chilson that I realized she'd never answered my question about hearing from her son.

Chapter 4

The first step in the investigative plan had been to sit down with Ryan's mom and share absolutely everything we knew, taking notes all the while. The second step had been to talk one-on-one with Ryan's upstairs neighbor, Keegan Kolb. I'd been prepared for her being at work, so I'd left another of my business cards in her roadside mailbox, complete with handwritten cell number and a note asking her to call. Maybe she would and maybe she wouldn't, but if she didn't, I knew where she lived. If I didn't hear from her in a day or two, I'd figure out a non-stalkerish way to connect with her.

And maybe it was good that Danielle Anderson was on her way out of town. After our extremely short chat, my suspicions were strong that Ryan had, in fact, contacted his mother, and that she wasn't about to say anything to anyone about it.

While the law-abiding side of myself objected to that possibility, the empathic side of myself understood completely. I wasn't a mother, but if, say,

Kristen was accused—wrongly, of course—of theft and murder, what would I do? What would I do if Rafe was accused?

By the time my thoughts got to this point, I was standing on my aunt's front porch, finger pushing the doorbell. She opened the door and I said, "Just so you know, if the police want to haul you in on suspicion of murder, and I don't think you did it, I'll probably be okay with hiding you until things get sorted out."

Aunt Frances didn't blink. "Good to know. Coffee? You sound undercaffeinated."

I wasn't sure that was a word, but if it wasn't, it should be. "Coffee would be fantastic." As we walked through the house, its thick carpets making our footsteps *swoosh* lightly, I looked around. No Otto in the front parlor–type room. No Otto in the study or anywhere that I could see. "What did you do with your husband?"

"Meeting with Cody Sisk, the young man from your bike and kayaking shop. They're finishing the winter financials and polishing up the summer plans."

Calling it "my" shop was a huge stretch. All I'd done was connect a business owner who'd expanded a bit too fast with Otto, a retired accountant and financial wizard. At the time, I'd already dragooned Otto into giving the occasional free personal finance workshop at the library and it had taken only a minor nudge to get him to meet with Cody. Otto had subsequently invested in Cody's business and the shop was now thriving. All this had started from me popping into the shop one day and chatting. Which went to show, you just never knew what could happen.

I plopped myself in the big kitchen's cozy breakfast nook. Aunt Frances slid two mugs onto the nook's butcher-block table and sat across from me. "Don't you have a job?" she asked. "Don't tell me you've been fired and are coming to me for sympathy. I'm fresh out."

As if. Aunt Frances was the most empathic person I'd ever had the pleasure to know. She hid it under a thick layer of wry humor, but her true colors were obvious to anyone who knew her longer than five minutes. Sometimes I was staggered that we were blood relatives. She was tall, and I was . . . not. She had those Katharine Hepburn cheekbones and I didn't. Her hair was miles from the unmanageable mess that mine was, and her mechanical aptitude was legendary. In my dad and brother, those genes had translated into engineering professions, but they'd skipped me altogether. Which was fine with me. Why did I need any mechanical skills when I had Aunt Frances, Rafe, a host of friends, and a cell phone?

Months ago, Aunt Frances had declared her intention to retire at the end of the school year, but lately she'd started to say things like "I'm not sure what I'm going to do with myself this fall." I wasn't sure if she was planning ahead, or having second thoughts about retiring, but I had decided not to poke my nose into the topic.

"Working noon to eight," I said, explaining about Rafe's board meeting. "Did you see my text about the wedding date?"

"Inked in on my calendar." She waved a hand at a wall calendar featuring scenic photos from around the world. "We'll delay our trip to Door County. You can thank me now."

"Thank you," I said automatically.

"You're welcome." She shoved her mug against mine, making a quiet *tink*. "Congratulations. You're getting married."

"Too far away to get excited."

Aunt Frances laughed. "You realize mid-September is only five and a half months away."

I nodded. "Weeks and weeks and weeks. Like more than . . . um . . . twenty. And way more than twenty days. Lots of time. Oodles, even."

"Mmm." My aunt gave me a look.

"I'm trying to be like you," I said.

"Which part? The arthritic hands or the gray hair?"

"The part where you don't worry about hardly anything."

"Oh, that." Aunt Frances continued to look at me in a way that made me want to squirm like a five-year-old caught in a blatantly obvious lie about puppies and peas left on a plate. "You do realize that while worrying about things over which you have no control is pointless, worrying about things you *can* control *is* appropriate."

My hand that wasn't clutching the coffee mug made a rolling get-on-with-it motion. "Moving forward. I'm here because my plan for deep background research on Ryan Anderson didn't work out. I'm moving on to Plan B." Which was almost always the same thing: Ask Aunt Frances.

"Who is Ryan Anderson?" she asked.

Huh. Plan B had hit an unexpected snag. "Mid-twenties," I said. "Five nine or ten. Short-ish brown hair. Not fat, not thin."

"Sounds like more than half of men in that age range. Is there anything else I'd remember about him?" She tapped her nose. "Rings or studs any-where you'd notice? How about tattoos?"

I shook my head and considered the point she'd made, that the general description I'd given her of Ryan wasn't very useful. "You know, I've never thought about it this way, but you're right. He's not one of those people who is instantly memorable. He's a blends-in-with-the-crowd person."

Aunt Frances laughed. "Sounds like the perfect spy. Is that why you're looking for him? Maybe he's hiding in plain sight." She glanced around the room.

This made me smile, just a little. "There are downstate police looking for Ryan. They think he robbed a bank down there and killed a security guard. But"—I added hastily—"there's obviously some sort of mistake going on. Ryan is the nicest person ever. There's no way he did any of that."

My aunt put down her mug and gave me the Full-On Aunt Look. "You know that how, exactly? And don't tell me it's because he's a regular library visitor, has never had any overdue fines, and do-nates to the Friends of the Library."

"Okay, I won't," I said, because I had no idea if he donated to the Friends. The nonprofit group was important to the library, but they operated inde-pendently. Sometimes more independently than Graydon and the library board preferred. "Ryan is a regular bookmobile visitor, though, and he only once was late returning a book."

"Minnie—"

I held up my hand to stop the objection I knew was coming. "Plus, Eddie likes him."

She rolled her eyes. "Then that settles it. Why haven't you told the police about the feline stamp of approval?"

"If I'm asked, I will." I imagined the scene. I'd be in the small interview room at the same table where I'd sat many times before, facing Detective Hal Inwood and detective-in-training Deputy Ash Wolverson. They'd have their notepads out and pens clicked, waiting to take down my information. I'd tell them that Eddie liked Ryan, so they could stop the search, and neither one of them would move a muscle. I'd get irritated; they'd put on their patient voices and tell me to stop wasting their time and to go away and not come back until I had something real to tell them. In an excruciatingly polite way, of course, but that would be the general gist.

Aunt Frances made a tsking noise. She was probably imagining the same scene. "This Ryan isn't from here?" she asked. "What does he do?"

I summarized what I knew of his story. He was from the Livonia area. Moved north a few years ago after a weekend trip with some friends, made ends meet through a series of short-term and part-time jobs. Lived out in Bowyer Township on the first floor of an old farmhouse.

"Hmm." My aunt put her elbows on the table and cupped her chin with the palms of her hands. "Do you know any of the places he worked?"

Other than Nub's Nob, where he'd worked as a ski lift operator, I did not.

"That's not very helpful," she said. "If you figure

out any others, text me. If I know any of them, I'll do some digging."

I thanked her and looked at my phone for the time. A few more minutes, then I had to get going. "Have you heard from Celeste lately?"

Aunt Frances glanced in the direction of the boardinghouse. Which she couldn't see, because she didn't have X-ray vision to allow her to see through walls. The boardinghouse, where she'd lived for decades, was directly across the street. It had been empty since October, when our cousin had abandoned Chilson and made like a snowbird, off for warmer and sunnier climes.

With Celeste gone, the boardinghouse was dark and cold. To see the place empty of life was more than a bit sad. My aunt and I had spent five winters there, popping popcorn and sitting in front of the fieldstone fireplace. And now . . . no one was there.

Aunt Frances turned back to face me. "She'll be here soon. The place will come back to life in no time."

"Absolutely," I said, but I didn't sound convincing, even to myself.

My aunt half smiled. "Life goes on, Minnie," she said. "Nothing stays the same forever."

"I know. And I wouldn't want it to. It's just . . ." My voice tailed off.

"Yes," she agreed. "It's just different."

We sat there for a moment, each thinking our own thoughts. Then I thanked her for the coffee, put our mugs in the dishwasher, and headed to the library.

I walked into the library board's meeting room fifteen minutes before the official meeting time to make sure the room was ready, but more than half the board was already there.

The room itself intimidated me, with its wood-paneled walls, coffered ceiling with magical hidden lighting, and an imposing conference table and chairs that looked like they'd been ordered from a furniture manufacturer that catered primarily to Fortune 100 companies.

But the women and men sitting in the high-backed leather chairs intimidated me even more. They looked perfectly at home. Like they belonged. When I sat in one of those chairs I felt like a grade school urchin who'd been hauled into the principal's office and was waiting to learn what punishment would be handed down.

"Minnie, good to see you."

I twitched at the sound of my name being called out by Trent Ross, the library board's president. The principal himself.

"Nice to be here," I said, trying not to sound awkward or uncool, and undoubtedly failing.

"Have a seat," Trent said, waving down the length of the table, which seated twenty. "Anywhere is fine."

Nice of him to say, but he was absolutely wrong. Not all the board members were here yet, and if I sat where one of them usually sat, I'd look like a clueless newbie. If I sat at the far end of the table, leaving empty chairs between myself and the board members, I'd look like a supplicant, pleased to get any scrap of favor the board might bestow.

"Minnie!" A large hand slapped me in the middle of the back, sending me staggering. "Haven't seen you in dog's years."

I summoned the strength to stand up straight and smiled up at Otis Rahn, who was probably my favorite board member. If I had favorites, that was. Because if I had favorites, I'd also have non-favorites, and it wouldn't be smart to place the board president at the bottom of a list like that. Trent was a retired attorney from the Chicago area, smart and observant and financially astute, but he had a city polish that wasn't wearing off. That might have been fine if I'd understood his sense of humor, but we laughed at completely different things.

Otis, who was nearly eighty, ushered me toward a chair. "This is where Graydon sits. Say, have you heard from him?"

At the sound of Graydon's name, the atmosphere in the room changed instantly. The casual chitchat of people who met once a month came to a screeching halt, and the seated board members turned as one unit to look at me.

And not just a plain old look. These were piercing stares that wanted to peel off my skin and drill down to my bone marrow. Trent put his elbows on the glossy tabletop and steepled his fingers. Linda Kopecky, the board's vice president, took off her reading glasses, the better to see me. The other two board members, Sondra and Bruce, had expressions that reminded me of eagles about to swoop down on their prey.

"Um," I said, sounding as clever as I felt. "I got a text on Saturday, saying that they made it to California safe and sound." I intentionally let my voice rise at the end of the sentence, making it almost a question. No one took the bait. I summoned all the courage I could muster and asked, "Why do you ask? Do you think something has happened to him?"

Trent leaned forward. "Not at all. We're just interested to know the level of contact you have with him when he's out of town."

I tried not to look as puzzled as I felt. Why did they care? "He told me to text or call him if there's an emergency."

His actual words upon departure had been a laughing "Call me only if the building is burning. On second thought, don't. Call nine-one-one instead." But I wasn't about to say that to the board. Graydon hadn't been serious and Trent might take it the wrong way.

Linda tapped her glasses on the table. "So he's responsive if you have to contact him outside of normal working hours?" *Tap-tap-tap.*

I stiffened. Why was there suddenly an anti-Graydon feeling in the room? If a majority of the board was unhappy enough, they could vote to fire him, something that didn't bear thinking about. "Yes," I said. The short word didn't seem like enough, so I added, "He's always there when I need him."

Bruce nodded. "If you'd taken on the position of library director, what would you be doing differently from Graydon?"

I desperately wanted to laugh and say, Buy more bookmobiles, but I had a feeling that in this situation humor wasn't the card I should be playing. What could I tell them but the truth? "Absolutely nothing major," I said. "And hardly anything minor, either. Just the other day the staff was saying he's the best director we've ever had."

"Hmm." Trent looked at me over the top of his steepled fingers, then past me. "Good morning," he said to the final two board members, who were just coming in the door. "Nice to see you both."

The meeting started exactly on time—something that Trent insisted upon—and they went through the agenda item by item. But even as I fielded their various questions, a question of my own kept running through my head.

Were they going to fire Graydon?

The next day was a bookmobile day, and Julia was scheduled to ride along. Hiring her as a part-time clerk had been an idea of my aunt's, and like most of her ideas, it had been a fantastic one.

Julia Beaton, mid-sixties, typically had her long enviably straight strawberry blond hair in a braid that she slung over one shoulder when she wasn't using it as a prop for whatever persona she happened to be inhabiting. There were days when she was Julia from dawn to dusk, but thankfully those days were few and far between because her former life as a Tony Award–winning Broadway actress had given her the ability to be the best-ever story reader the library was ever likely to see, and a deep well of roles to draw from.

She also had a penchant for making up personalities to suit her mood. I was never sure which was which and I'd decided long ago to stop trying and enjoy the ride.

"They're not going to fire Graydon," Julia said.

I glanced over at her. Nothing but crystal-clear confidence showed in her face and body language. "You can't be sure of that," I said. "There could be lots of things going on we don't know about." The board had seen a lot of turnover in the last couple of years. Otis had been on the board forever, but most of them were still new to their roles. What if they wanted to take the library in a completely different direction? What if one of them had a niece or nephew who'd just graduated with a library science degree and thought she or he would fit perfectly in Chilson? Would the new library director love the bookmobile as much as Graydon did? Or would the new director feel bookmobiles were anachronisms and convince the library board to sell ours?

"And you can stop that right now," Julia scolded in a thick Southern accent, her vowels long and round and almost echoing inside themselves.

"Stop what?" I asked.

"Ah can see what you all are doin' and it's not good for your complexion. Stop that worryin' right now."

I peered through the windshield and eased off the gas pedal, slow to navigate around a series of massive puddles left after the previous night's heavy rain. "Is there any G you wouldn't drop?"

"Not in this accent, mah dear. And we're talkin' about you."

Many times in the past I'd privately and publicly vowed to be more like my aunt Frances, and never worry about anything. I'd yet to do that, and I also hadn't mastered the ability to keep my face blank. Rafe had long ago declared that he would only play cards against me, never as partner, and I didn't blame him.

"Okay," I said. "But what I'd really like to talk about is Ryan Anderson. You've heard about him, right?"

It turned out that she hadn't, so I spent the next ten miles explaining what had happened at the bookmobile stop, that I'd met his mother and his upstairs neighbor, but that his mother had returned downstate.

"Interesting," Julia said, abandoning the Southern accent. "You're right, it does sound like Mom has heard from him. Wonder if the neighbor—Keegan?—knows anything about that."

"Exactly what I was thinking," I said. "But even if his mom has heard from him, that doesn't mean he's safe." Or that he was warm and dry and getting enough to eat.

Julia nodded. "And since we both know that nice young man couldn't possibly have stolen that money or killed anyone, it makes sense to talk to Keegan as soon as possible."

I smiled. "Do you realize that at the end of today's route we'll be within a couple miles of the house where Ryan and Keegan live?"

She did indeed, and also had no problem with a later-than-expected return home. Thus it was that at six o'clock, I parked the bookmobile on the road shoulder in front of the farmhouse, not wanting to risk getting it stuck in the muddy mess that was the driveway. An SUV sat next to the house, near a tall set of wooden stairs that led to an upstairs door.

Julia eyed the long expanse of brown. "Minnie, my dearest ever librarian, you do realize that I did not bring the proper footgear for a trek such as this." She pointed at her nonseasonal ballet flats.

"That's okay," I said, pulling on the bright red rain boots I kept in a cabinet. "You and Eddie can keep each other company."

"Mrr," Eddie said sleepily. He'd been snoring most of the day, which was not a Good Thing because that inevitably meant he'd be awake most of the night.

"He wakes!" Julia said, delighted, and I fled, because I was pretty sure a lengthy Shakespearean monologue was about to begin. Though I liked and appreciated the Bard and his work, Julia had a tendency to flit from play to play as it suited her, and afterward I would spend too much time trying to figure out what play and which character.

My boots and I squelched up the drive and up the stairs, which would qualify as rickety within the next year. Up at the top, I knocked and Keegan's surprised face appeared through the winter-dirty window.

She quickly opened the door. "Minnie? What are you doing here?" Then she looked past me and laughed. "You and the bookmobile! How cool!"

I explained that we'd been in the neighborhood and that I'd stopped to see Ryan's mom.

Keegan nodded, tucking her long hair behind her ears. "She's gone, though. Had to go back to work, even if Ryan is still missing."

"Do you . . ." I hesitated. At this point I'd been hoping I'd have been invited inside, but that was apparently not to be. "Do you think she's heard from Ryan? And that was why she was okay going home?"

"Oh, wow. I never thought of that." Keegan pinched her lower lip. "You know, that makes sense. It explains a lot."

"How's that?" I asked.

"The night before she left, I was down there and she was looking through Ryan's stuff. Just to see if she could find anything that might tell us where he went. She'd asked me to help, but it felt weird, you know? Okay for his mom, but Ryan and I, we're"—she turned a light shade of pink—"we're friends, is all."

Hmm, I thought.

"Anyway," Keegan went on, "I was in the living room and she was in his bedroom, talking to me about how cute Ryan had been as a baby, when she stopped talking. I asked if she was okay, and she didn't say anything. I went to see if something was wrong, but she came out of the bedroom with her phone in her hand and a really funny look on her face."

"She got a text from him," I said, guessing.

Keegan shrugged. And nodded. "Maybe. But why didn't she say anything to me about it?"

To me, the answer was obvious. Danielle Anderson was a mother and she was protecting her son.

But before I could say so, Keegan's phone trilled and she pulled it out of the pocket of her fleece hoodie to silence it. "Sorry, but I have to go. I have a project at work I'm way behind on. I just came home to get something to eat. If I hear from Ryan, I'll let you know, okay?"

She kindly gave me a ride to the end of the driveway, and when I was almost back to the bookmobile, Julia opened the door.

"Thanks," I said, climbing the stairs. I stood on the plastic mat and pulled off my boots, which, instead of red, were now the color of early April. "I didn't learn much, but—"

"Minnie," Julia said quietly. "You need to sit down."

I blinked. Her tone was more serious than I'd ever heard. I sat on the carpeted step that ran in front of the bookshelves and served as both a ladder to reach the top books and as seating.

"What's wrong?" I asked, trying not to think of all the possibilities.

"It's Pug Mattock," she said.

I blinked again. "Pug? What about him?"

"He was found at his house. He's dead."

"That can't be right," I said. "He was on the bookmobile just the other day. He was fine. You must have . . ." What? Confused him with some other guy who went by the name Pug? "You must be wrong."

But she shook her head, saying, "My husband just called." She held up her phone, then let her hand fall to her side. "Pug was shot. He was murdered."

Chapter 5

Over a dinner of grilled chicken on spinach with toppings of the few vegetables we had in the refrigerator, I told Rafe what I knew about Pug Mattock. Which, as it turned out, wasn't all that much.

"He was basically a sales guy," I said, inspecting a piece of red pepper for signs of old age. "Most of his career he worked for a company that made car parts. Something for the interiors, I think it was. Liners? Is that a thing?"

"Headliners?" he asked.

Could be. All I knew about cars was that I had to put gas in mine every so often to make it go—and take it to my mechanic friend Darren every once in a while. Though this was something I often forgot to do for my own vehicle, the bookmobile followed a rigorous maintenance schedule. Why I was willing to do that for the library's vehicle but not my own I wasn't sure. But then again, now that I was engaged and about to be married, maybe I could get Rafe to take over car maintenance. I made a mental note to bring that up soon.

"Pug and his wife, Sylvia, didn't have any children," I said, "but there's a large extended family on the Mattock side. He had a bunch of siblings and there are nieces and nephews all over the place."

Rafe aimed his fork at a particularly large piece of chicken. "There are a few Mattocks around town."

"Might be related. But most of them live downstate. Pug said that's one of the reasons he wanted to move north full time, to get away from all the relatives."

I smiled, remembering. His direct quote had been "I love my family, but getting them to call ahead before showing up on our doorstep is harder than sneezing with your eyes open."

My eyes suddenly started misting. Poor Pug. Poor Sylvia. They'd had so many plans. So many things they'd planned to do together, so many places they'd planned to go. And now they wouldn't be able to do any of it because someone had fired a bullet into Pug's heart, ending his life with a—

"Here." Rafe handed me his paper napkin.

Dutifully, I took it. Wiped my eyes, blew my nose. Blew again. "Thanks," I said, wadding the napkin up into a ball. "I didn't expect to do that. It's not as if Pug was a close friend or anything."

"But he was still a friend." Rafe got up and stood behind my chair. He leaned down and hugged me from behind, kissing the top of my head and letting his warmth, his strength, his love, flow into me.

I sniffed one more time and felt myself relax against him. "Love you," I whispered.

"Back at you," he said into my hair.

"Mrr."

Rafe gave me another squeezing hug and stood. We looked at Eddie, who was sitting in a statuesque manner in the doorway between the dining room and kitchen.

"What did he say?" Rafe asked.

"And what makes you think I know?"

"You've known him longer."

While this was true, I wasn't sure how much help it was. "He's a cat. Mostly he's asking for one of three things. For treats, to go outside, or to have the kibble in his bowl mounded properly."

"Mrr!"

Rafe walked over to Eddie and crouched in front of him. "What's that you have there, buddy?" he asked, reaching down. He extracted something from between Eddie's front paws and held it up. "Do you know what this is?"

I eyed the item. "A small piece of brown plastic in a vaguely human shape. Looks like something from a game."

"Not just any game," Rafe said, handing the object to me. "Giddy Giants, a board game of skill and talent that requires great intelligence to win."

From which I assumed he'd been good at it in his misspent youth. The figure had two legs, one missing arm, and a helmeted head. "Never heard of it," I said. "An army game of some sort?"

"From a local company." Rafe plucked the figure out of my hand and slid it into his jeans pocket. "They went out of business years ago."

"But where did Eddie find it?"

Rafe and I turned to ask him, but he'd vanished.

Then we heard the unmistakable noise of cat kibble being crunched by sharp teeth. Not so much vanished as teleported, then.

"Anyway," I said, picking up my fork. "The sheriff's office hasn't arrested anyone for Pug's murder. I wonder . . ." I put my fork down.

"Wonder what?" Rafe asked, sitting. "And I know that look. You've thought of something about Pug and now you're wondering if you should tell Hal or Ash."

I nodded. "It probably doesn't matter, but Pug was up here earlier than normal. By a few weeks. He never came up this early. So maybe he saw something he wasn't supposed to."

"Or someone," Rafe added.

"And was killed so the secret could be kept a secret." I sighed. "Looks like I need to stop at the sheriff's office tomorrow morning."

"Look at you, doing your civic duty." Rafe grinned. "You are an admirable person, Minnie Hamilton."

Not hardly. An admirable person wouldn't be dreading the encounter. And a truly admirable person would be happier about the next two hours of her life. "Time for me to go." I pushed my chair back.

"Have fun," Rafe said. "Eddie and I will take care of the dishes, right, buddy?"

"Mrr!" came a distant voice.

I rolled my eyes but smiled as I grabbed my coat from the front closet and hurried out the door.

A five-minute walk later, I met up with Aunt Frances. She was leaning, arms and ankles crossed, against downtown's newest retail store. "You're nearly late for a very important date," she said.

"You and the White Rabbit have as much in common as I do with"—I searched for an analogy and came up so empty that, in a slight panic, I looked at our surroundings—"as I do with that clock." I nodded up at the massive Victorian-style four-sided timepiece used by locals and visitors alike as a meeting spot. "Anxiety just isn't your thing."

"Lucky for you." She levered herself off the wall and glared at me. "What was it I said the other day about this event?"

I grinned and quoted her. "Don't make me go alone."

"True then and true now." She put her hand on the shop's doorknob. "You do realize that there are friends of mine inside."

"Yes, ma'am."

"You will not sit in the corner, saying nothing. You will be social."

"Yes, Aunt Frances."

She started to open the door, then shut it again. "And you will not laugh at inappropriate times."

"Cross my heart and hope to die, stick a needle in my eye."

She nodded. "You are my favorite niece."

"I am your only niece."

"Let us not split hairs." She took a deep breath. "Now or never, yes? Yes," she said, and opened the door.

A wash of female laughter flowed over us. My aunt took a deep breath. Then another. I reached out, put the flat of my hand against the small of her back, and gave her a firm push.

"Get in there," I commanded. "You know you'll have fun once we get started."

"Yes, but what if . . ." She took one step and stopped.

I gave the back of her head a good talking to. "Remember what you told me? That you're getting closer and closer to retirement, and that you need to develop some new interests and hobbies, and maybe find more friends. That you've been woodworking most of your life and maybe it's time to try another medium." I gave her another push.

"Yeeees," she said, managing to make a complete sentence out of a one-syllable word. "But . . ."

"But nothing. You're the one who found that new blog *The Chilson Diversion.* You're the one who saw the notice about this event and saw who was hosting. You're the one who said, 'Don't make me go alone.' In spite of the stupidity of your anxiety, because these are your friends and the last thing you need is my support, I agreed to come with you and you will not back out. You. Will. Not." I gave my aunt one last shove, which propelled her the rest of the way into the wine store.

Inside, among the racks and racks of bottled wine, were three large rectangular tables, the kind that were ubiquitous at book sales and family reunions. The tables themselves were covered with newspapers, and on top of the newspapers were rolling pin–like objects, knifelike objects, small tubs of water, and piles of gray blocks that were two to three times the size of ice cubes.

I swallowed, suddenly intimidated. What I'd agreed to attend was a fun night learning how to do a little pottery while drinking a little wine. "Pottery and Pinot," my aunt had said. "Drink a little wine, make a little something. It'll be great." But . . . this? I didn't understand the function of a single thing on the table, other than the wineglasses, and those were at the far end, miles out of my reach.

What I did understand was my aunt's uncharacteristic hesitation at the door. I started to back up. Maybe I could fake a library emergency. Or maybe Kristen would go into labor and need me to drive her to the hospital because the Scruff was too freaked out. Or—

"Frances!" A fiftyish woman with salt-and-pepper hair and a friendly face waved madly. "We were just wondering if you were going to make it. And I know this is Minnie." She smiled at me. "We haven't met, but I've heard all about your bookmobile and your Eddie. So much fun."

She introduced herself as Lisa and rattled off the names of the other women at the tables too fast for anything to stick in my head. "Pull up an empty chair," Lisa said. "We'll get started in just a minute."

Aunt Frances and I shared a glance.

"It'll be fun," she said softly.

"Of course it will be." I paused. "You go first."

My aunt grabbed the sleeve of my coat and hauled me forward. "Patsy," she said to a seated woman with short, tightly curled hair. "You've met my niece, haven't you?"

Patsy nodded. "Minnie, how are you?"

I was pretty sure Patsy was an intermittent library patron, but not super sure, so I nodded and let Aunt Frances sit next to her while I took the chair farther away. This sat me next to a fortyish woman with long jet-black hair, someone I didn't recognize at all.

When I introduced myself, however, her face took on an odd expression. "I know who you are," she said. "You're the bookmobile librarian. With that cat." She almost sneered as she said the word "cat."

The evening was suddenly a lot less fun. "That's me," I said politely, and cast about for an empty chair I could move to. The lighting wasn't right here, I could say. But the chairs were all occupied, so I turned my attention to the instruction sheets in front of me.

"Have you heard about that Ryan Anderson?" my new neighbor asked. "Do you know him?"

"Yes," I said. "Ryan's a good guy. Is he a friend of yours?"

She made a sour face. "No, I've never met him, but I've heard everything I need to know."

What I knew was that he'd been a loyal bookmo-biler for years. That Eddie liked him. That I liked him. That the only time he'd had an overdue book was when he'd had a horrible case of the flu. That he always offered to carry heavy book bags for other patrons. That he held the door for everyone.

"Oh?" I asked. "What's that?"

"You haven't heard?" Her eyes were wide. "He robbed a bank. He killed a security guard. And I bet he's the one who killed that summer guy!"

The insides of my stomach suddenly clenched tight. "No one has proven anything," I said. "The police are looking for him, yes, but at this point no one can say for sure what he did or didn't do."

"He ran," she said loudly. "Only guilty people do that."

Actually, I could think of lots of reasons to run,

but I doubted my temporary neighbor would listen to the list. "He's innocent until proven guilty."

She snorted. "Don't be naive. He ran and they'll catch him. And then they'll put him in jail where he belongs."

"How can . . ." I stopped. I'd been about to say that Ryan reread the entire Jan Karon series every year, and that no one who did that could possibly be a hard-core killer, but what was proof to me probably wouldn't have convinced anyone except book lovers.

I nodded vaguely and picked up the top sheet of instructions, and she started talking to the person across from her.

After breathing a small sigh of relief, I let the type on the page fuzz in front of my eyes. So the town gossips had already tried, convicted, and jailed Ryan, for robbery and two murders, had they? I sat up straight and put my shoulders back.

Well, then I'd have to work even harder—and faster—to prove Ryan's innocence.

The next morning was a typical early April day in northern lower Michigan: too warm to ski but too cold to do anything else outside.

"What are you talking about?" Deputy Ash Wolverson asked. "Just above freezing is a great temperature for lots of things."

The two of us were in my favorite interview room at the sheriff's office. Nothing had changed since the last time I'd been there: same rectangular fluorescent light fixture, same scratched and scarred table, same worn chairs. I'd been first in the room and I'd made sure to get the one chair that didn't wobble. If I'd been stuck with the worst-wobbling one, I would for sure have started to rock back and forth, making an irregular *tink-tink-tink* noise that would have driven Ash crazy. And since he was a good friend—and former boyfriend—I didn't want to do that to him.

Once again, I idly wondered about the oddities of personal chemistry. Ash was smart, funny, and incredibly good-looking. Yet there'd been no spark between us. Being with him had been nice enough but had completely lacked the skin-prickling fireworks that exploded when Rafe's hand touched mine. Maybe a sparkage lack had pushed him and Chelsea apart? But, no. I'd seen them together too many times. The electricity between them was almost visible. I shook my head and turned my attention to the topic at hand.

"Lots of things are good at just above freezing?" I asked. "Really? Name five."

Ash held up his index finger. "Collecting maple sap."

Okay, he had me there. I gave him a nod. "That's one. Four more."

He held up a second finger. "Snowshoeing." Finger number three. "Running." Number four. "Fat-tire biking." He grinned and held up his thumb for number five. "Beer drinking."

I made a rude noise in the back of my throat. "You can't count drinking beer."

"Sure I can," he said. "Tell you what. How about I text Rafe and ask him? He can be the tie breaker."

That was ridiculous, because of course Rafe would agree with Ash on the appropriateness of beer drinking. "Back to your number four. Fat-tire biking. Are you doing much of that? I hear it's fun, but I haven't talked to anyone about it who isn't trying to sell me something."

His face, which had been cheerful, fell into blankness. "Earlier this winter I was getting out three or four times a week. Now, not so much."

I could have kicked myself. My tiny little memory had remembered too late that Ash and Chelsea had done a lot of fat-tire biking together. "Sorry about that," I said. He shrugged and toyed with the edge of the table. I watched this for a moment, then said softly, "I was sorry to hear about you and Chelsea. Do you want to talk about it?"

"No."

His response had been so fast, I'd barely finished the question. I waited a beat. "If you ever want to talk, I'm here to listen."

"Thanks, but it's not like that. It's . . ." He shook his head and pulled a notepad and pen from his shirt pocket. "Never mind. You didn't stop by to talk about my personal life. As I recall, you have information about Pug Mattock's murder."

Clearly, he wanted the Ash-and-Chelsea conversation to be over. Since we were friends, I moved on. For the time being. "What I said was that maybe I have information." Which I could have given him over the phone, but I'd wanted to talk to him about Chelsea. "It's just that Pug had come north weeks earlier than he normally did."

Ash's pen didn't move. "And?"

"That's pretty much it. No, don't go all Hal Inwood on me," I said, because his face was starting to take on the distant and disinterested look of his superior officer. "Listen. You know how it is up here in the winter on most lakefront properties. Hardly any of those places are lived in all year long. What if Pug, by coming up earlier than he ever had, saw something he shouldn't have? Or someone."

The pen continued its imitation of an immovable object. "Give me five examples."

I held up my index finger. "He saw a vehicle in a driveway, a vehicle owned by someone robbing an empty house. The owners are still south, so they don't even know they've been robbed."

Finger number two went up. "He saw an illegal drug sale."

Number three. "Without knowing it, he saw evidence of human trafficking."

Four. "He saw two people who shouldn't have been together, say, CEOs of two companies that are in the middle of a merger and aren't supposed to be exchanging information."

And five. "Um . . . he saw someone hauling beer into a house when the guy had sworn to his wife that he'd never touch the stuff again."

Ash's eyebrows went up. "And you think any of those scenarios could have incited someone to commit murder?"

I leaned back and crossed my arms. "Anyone can be a murderer. It just takes a certain set of circumstances."

He sort of smiled. "If I didn't know better, I'd say you were quoting Hal."

"She is."

In the doorway was Detective Hal Inwood himself, sixtyish, tall and lanky, and devoid of any charm whatsoever. How he and his perpetually happy wife, Tabitha, had managed to make their marriage such a long-lasting one was a complete mystery.

"What brings you to the sheriff's office this morning?" the detective asked. "No, let me guess. You have ideas on how we should conduct our investigation into the murder of Pug Mattock."

Since he'd just heard me talk about a murder, I didn't give him any points for mind reading. "Last night," I said, "I heard someone say that since the police are looking for Ryan Anderson, that Ryan must have killed Pug, too. Is that true?"

Detective Inwood sat, continuing his facial expression of nothing. "Every avenue of investigation is being pursued."

Of course it was. Just like always. But I was getting the distinct impression that the detective would be very willing to tag Ryan for the murder of Pug Mattock. Two murders, one murderer. How tidy for him. How conveniently easy. Clearly, I had to make sure all those other avenues were just as wide and well traveled.

"Pug and Ryan barely knew each other," I said. "Pretty sure they only met the once."

"When was that?" the detective asked.

Ash's pen was now at full attention, and I internally berated myself for talking too much. "On the bookmobile. A few days before Pug was killed. They hadn't met before, and even then it was only a short conversa—"

I came to a full and sudden stop.

"Ms. Hamilton," Detective Inwood said sharply. "You remembered something. What is it?"

"Um. Nothing. I'm sure it was nothing."

"Minnie." Ash's voice was gentle. "You know you have to tell us."

But did I? I thought about it and sighed. "Okay, you're right. I do have to tell you, just in case it meant something. I'm sure it doesn't, so you'll be wasting your time, but Ryan got a text message on his phone. Pug was standing right next to him, and he might have read the text."

The detective leaned forward. "Do you think Mr. Anderson recognized that Mr. Mattock could have seen the text?"

"Can't say for sure," I said. A stray thought about George Washington and cherry trees zipped through my brain. "But," I added reluctantly, "probably. Maybe probably."

Hal asked the exact time and date and, after pulling out my phone for the bookmobile's schedule, I told him.

Ash's eyebrows went up. "That's the last text he got, isn't it?"

"Deputy Wolverson," Detective Inwood said, and even I could tell it was a rebuke. Ash colored and slumped slightly.

I, on the other hand, sat up tall. "There's no way Ryan would have killed Pug over a text message!"

"Wouldn't it depend on the contents of the text?" the detective asked mildly.

"Tell me what the text was and I'll let you know." I stared at him. "But you're not going to tell me, are you, because it's an active investigation. Then I won't waste any more of your time," I said, standing.

Ash got up to walk me out and I asked, "New question. I would have asked Hal, but I don't think we're on speaking terms right now. How's Tabitha? I haven't seen her around lately."

"No," he said. "And you won't for two or three more weeks."

"Is something wrong?"

"Not with her." Ash shook his head. "She's downstate, taking care of her sister, who fractured her wrist snowboarding. Needed surgery, lots of pins and screws, sounded like."

"Um, a younger sister?" Like her husband, Tabitha was in her early sixties.

"Vanessa is seventy-one." He left me at the front door and headed back to his office.

I smiled. Not that I was happy about Tabitha's sister having such a bad accident, of course, but that she had a sister who was snowboarding in her seventies. Yet another positive role model for me.

Then my smile faded. A few months ago, Tabitha had been a huge help on a different murder investigation. Unless I got Rafe more involved, this time I was on my own.

Chapter 6

As I left the sheriff's office and started my walk up to the library, I thought about Ryan. Hoping that he was okay, afraid that he wasn't, and laying plans for proving that he had nothing to do with the downstate robbery and murder, and certainly not Pug's murder.

When I was halfway through downtown, I had a brilliant idea: If I could help find whoever killed Pug, that would go a long way toward establishing Ryan's innocence. Maybe not in a court of law, but at least in the court of public opinion. Not that I had any genius ideas on how to do that, but surely something would come to me. Rafe would help with the brainstorming (especially if I agreed to eat at Hoppe's Brewing that night), and if I kept my ears, eyes, and mind open, all sorts of ideas would pop up and some of them might even be good ones, and—

"Hey, Minnie!"

I jumped. To my right, Tom Abenaw, owner and

proprietor of Cookie Tom's, who had to be the skinniest baker in the history of bakers, was laughing.

"You were going to walk right past me without saying hello, weren't you?"

Of course I was, because I was so busy thinking about keeping my ears and eyes open that I hadn't been keeping my eyes and mind open, which might be the definition of irony. "Would I do that to my favorite cookie maker?"

"Sure. You do it all the time."

One of these days the habit of being completely lost in my thoughts was going to get me into serious trouble. "But never intentionally. You know that, right?"

"No worries. Everybody knows what you're like." He laughed again, nodded, and headed back inside his shop.

I hesitated, thinking. Everybody, he'd said. Hmm. It just so happened that I knew where "everybody" went on a Wednesday morning in early April. I made a personal U-turn, walked a couple of blocks, and went into the Round Table, local diner extraordinaire.

A uniformed waitress, her long gray hair wound up in a bun, coffeepot in hand, gave me a raised-eyebrow look as I slid into a back booth. "What are you doing here?" she asked.

"Nice to see you, too, Sabrina." I turned over the mug that was sitting there waiting. "Just coffee, please."

The pad that she'd been pulling out of her apron pocket slid back home. "You've had breakfast?"

"You realize you're acting like my mother."

She snorted and filled my mug. "You realize that

you need one? Even if you had breakfast, it wasn't enough to keep a bird alive. A blueberry muffin should be just about right."

When Sabrina was in this kind of mood, it was best to accept the inevitable. "Sounds good," I said.

"Anyone joining you?" she asked.

"Not as far as I know." Since she didn't move, which could only mean that she was waiting for an explanation, I added, "With Graydon gone this week, Kelsey's been in early to make coffee. I'd really rather have yours."

She smiled and nodded. Now my solo presence on a Wednesday morning made sense. All was right with the world. "I'll bring you a to-go cup with the muffin."

The muffin I didn't want, didn't need, but would enjoy to the last crumb. "Thanks!"

I busied myself with cream and spoon and tried to make myself invisible to the group at the nearby table. It was my theory that every small town had a place where men gathered in the morning to have breakfast and coffee and to pat one another on the back for how much better the world would be if only it would listen to them. In Chilson, this group gathered around the restaurant's round table and was a blend of retired and not, farmers and not, locals and not. Given that I'd seen Pug, every once in a blue moon, sitting with this group of self-appointed wisdom dispensers, it stood to reason that his death would be a topic of discussion.

Of course, being men, they didn't talk about Pug at all. They talked about the weather, the new city manager, the hockey playoffs, the upcoming baseball season, and circled back to the weather.

I dawdled over my coffee as long as I could, but there came a point when I had to abandon my plan and get to work. In theory it was possible for me to break into the conversation, but in practice I lacked the courage to breach the broad backs that faced me.

Internally grousing about men and their reluctance to talk about anything resembling an emotion, I grabbed my check and to-go cup and headed to the front counter. I waved the check at Sabrina, who was taking the order of an elderly couple. "I'll leave cash at the register," I said.

"Tip big," she called. "Bill and I want to go to Hawaii."

Shaking my head at such a comment from a person who not so long ago had declared that only boring people traveled, I murmured, "Who are you and what have you done with Sabrina?"

"But she's happier," a large male voice said.

Blinking, I looked up. "Hey, Cookie." As far as I knew, the name of the Round Table's longtime chef was indeed Cookie. When the kitchen was slow, he often came out front. "You think marriage makes Sabrina happy?"

Cookie shrugged and took my money. "When it's marriage to the right person, sure. Marriage to the wrong person will make your life seem ten times longer."

I watched as he counted out my change, thought he was probably right, and then, on a sudden impulse, asked, "Did you know Pug Mattock? He and his wife were married more than thirty years. Losing him is going to be hard on her."

"Sure, I knew Pug." Cookie handed over my change and put his elbows on the counter, crossing his arms. "He was in here just last week, buying something for his wife."

That was odd. "Everyone loves the Round Table," I said, "but unless he was buying the restaurant, I'm not sure gift cards would be super great for a present."

Cookie grinned, revealing a small dark gap in his upper teeth where an incisor should have been. "I ain't selling until I can't cook. What would I do with myself all day, eh? Sit around and watch soap operas? No, Pug was meeting somebody. The guy was selling and Pug was buying.

That made more sense. "Buying what?"

Cookie shrugged. "An artsy-fartsy sculpture by some guy. Sounded Italian."

"Italian?" The hairs on the back of my neck prickled. "Do you remember his name? The sculptor's I mean?"

Another shrug. "First name started with a V is all I remember. Last name was Cottey, or something like that."

"Conti?" I asked.

"Yeah, I guess so. Why, is he somebody famous?"

Not to me, but apparently to lots of other people. I hurried to the library, trying to keep from being late, my head suddenly spinning with information overload. First, how was it that I hadn't known Cookie actually owned the Round Table? But mostly I was wondering if there was any connection between Herb Valera's missing Conti sculpture and Pug's murder.

* * *

Rafe, Kristen, Scruffy, and I were at the long shiny wooden bar in Hoppe's Brewing, waiting for a group of late-season skiers to vacate the table of choice, which according to Rafe and the Scruff was the one table equidistant from the dart board, pool table, bar, and restrooms. I'd made the comment that any table would be fine, really, but I'd been ignored and here we were, perched on high chairs, awkwardly trying to have a conversation among four people sitting in a long row in a space where sound bounced around in ways so odd that it was sometimes easier to hear the conversation at adjacent tables than the voice of the person next to you.

"You have got to be kidding." Kristen glared at her husband, at me, at Rafe, at her mug of diet root beer, which hadn't done a thing to deserve it, and back at the Scruff. "You have seriously lost your marbles if you think I'm going to do that!" Her voice had increased in volume, and at the end of the sentence, she was in full-on Diva Chef Mode.

"Do what?"

The four of us turned. Ash was standing behind us. I nodded a hello to his companion, his buddy Tank, and Ash, Tank, and Rafe exchanged fist bumps.

"Excellent timing," I said. "We need law enforcement on our side."

Ash, sadly, did not immediately agree with me. "What side is that?" he asked, and once again I thought he was starting to sound way too much like Detective Inwood. Couldn't he, just once, agree with me on something without needing every single fact? Couldn't he, just once, trust that I was intelligent enough to be right about something?

"The dumb side," Kristen said. "These three think I need to stay out of the restaurant until the end of this." She slapped her huge belly. "What am I going to do, sit around and eat bonbons all day? I'm already as big as a car. You want me to get even bigger?"

Ash, having known Kristen for some time, murmured that he saw someone on the other side of the room he needed to talk to, and beat a hasty retreat.

"Coward!" Kristen called after him.

Tank shrugged. "See you guys later," he said, and followed Ash.

There was a moment of non-conversation. Then: "Don't," Kristen said. "Just don't. I am fine. There is no earthly reason for me to stop working."

I could see Scruffy start to open his mouth, to start listing all the reasons—fatigue, back pain, swollen ankles, foot pain, et cetera—and leapt into the breach, sacrificing myself to save their marriage.

"Please think about it." I wanted to add, We just want what's best for you and your baby, but left that part unsaid. In her present mood she would take that all wrong, and an irritated Kristen was never a good thing, let alone an irritated and very pregnant Kristen.

She gave me a mulish look and laid a hand across the mound of future baby. "Fine. I'll think about it," she said as she looked at the three of us. "I promise I will."

If Kristen promised something, it was as good as done.

"Thank you." Scruffy reached out, took her hand, and kissed the back of it. "I love you, you know."

"Whatever," Kristen muttered, but the look she was giving him was filled with love and much, much more.

"Get a room, you two." Rafe rolled his eyes and picked up his beer mug.

"We did," Scruffy said, putting his own hand on Kristen's stomach. "That's what got us into this situation in the first place."

Rafe laughed, spitting beer across the bar in the process. While he and Scruffy used their napkins to clean up the small mess, I leaned over to Kristen. "Let me guess. You've thought about it already and decided that you're going to keep on doing what you're doing."

The corners of her mouth curled up in a slow, Grinch-like smile. "Let's just say it may take some time to think it all through."

And by the time she was done thinking, the baby would be long born. I was about to commend her on her cleverness when the *thunk* of a dart hitting a dart board caught my attention. In the back corner of the room, Ash and Tank had started a game.

"Darts," I said out loud.

"What's that?" Kristen asked.

"Hunter said he played darts here with Ryan. I wonder if he was in a league." I made a come-hither gesture to the bartender, who'd just filled a tray of beer mugs and was wiping her hands with a towel. She bustled over, polite smile on her face, and asked, "What can I get you?"

Something that didn't taste like beer. "Do you have dart leagues here?"

"Sure. Tuesday nights."

Last night. Timing was not my friend. "My fiancé

there is thinking about getting into a league"—
unlikely to be a complete lie, as I was sure he'd
considered it at some point—"but I want to make
sure my ex-boyfriend isn't on a team, if you know
what I mean."

The bartender grinned. "Boy, do I." She reached
under the bar, pulled out a three-ring binder, and
slid it over. "The names of all the people on the
teams are listed in here. Don't tell anyone I showed
you, okay? Someone might get uptight."

"Promise," I said, and thanked her. It didn't take
long to see that Ryan's name wasn't in there. I slid
the binder back across the bar and it disappeared
from whence it came. So much for finding Ryan—
or even for finding out more about Ryan—through
one of his dart team buddies.

Rafe bumped my elbow. "What was all that
about? You have a sudden interest in darts?" After
I explained, he said, "Good idea. Too bad it didn't
work out."

I glanced back at the dart board. Ash was laughing uproariously. Trying a little too hard to have
fun and not think about Chelsea, perhaps?

"You're doing that thinking thing, aren't you?"
Rafe tapped my forehead. "There's a moral di-
lemma going on in there. I can tell."

I made a face. "Can everyone read me so easily,
or is it just you?"

Kristen, who'd been talking to Scruffy, said over
her shoulder, "Everyone," then went on talking to
her husband.

"Everyone who knows you well," Rafe said, patting my hand in an avuncular manner. "What's up?"

I told him what Cookie had said, that he saw Pug

buying a Conti sculpture, and that Herb Valera thought his family Conti might have been stolen. "But he wasn't sure," I finished. "So is this important enough to tell Ash? Maybe there's a tie between Pug's murder and the sculptures."

Rafe took a swig of beer to help him think, then said, "You know what, I'd leave it until we know whether or not the Valera sculpture was really stolen. If it wasn't, if his sister did send it out to get cleaned, then there's nothing to tell, right?"

I nodded. "So obvious when you say it out loud."

"Captain Obvious, that's me." He slapped his shirt front. "Besides, do we know if Pug ever finished buying the sculpture?"

It was an excellent question. Unfortunately, I had no idea how to get the answer.

Thursday was a bookmobile day, one of Hunter's. The roads were clear and dry, so after our normal preflight check of the vehicle, I summoned all the courage I possessed and told Hunter he could drive.

"You sure?" He asked the question casually, but the inside of his skin seemed to twitch with excitement.

I laughed. Sort of. "You know and I know that you've been ready since the day you started. It's me who has a little problem letting go."

"Mrr!"

"Didn't ask you," I muttered, settling into the passenger's seat and buckling up. "Hunter, start her up. Let's roll."

And roll we did, smoothly and confidently. After a few miles, the muscles in my shoulders started to relax. A few miles later, the rest of me started to relax, and a few miles after that, I began to enjoy myself.

Because when you weren't driving, you could look around and take in the rolling, forested, and lake-strewn countryside. You could look through the trees, still winter-naked of leaves, and see things you'd never see in summer. Ponds. Houses. Trails. And, off in the distance, deer gathering in their spring herds.

"Should have done this ages ago," I said, peering at a fieldstone barn I'd never noticed before.

"What's that?" Hunter asked.

"You're doing fine," I said happily, and sat back for the ride.

The day went quickly, as most days did on the bookmobile. During our drive time, we exchanged thoughts on Ryan's whereabouts—Hunter figured Ryan was long gone, but I had the feeling he was still close by—and spent a lot of time talking about Pug.

"Wish I'd known him longer," Hunter said, looking left and right past the empty intersection of two lightly traveled roads before proceeding past the stop sign. "I only met him that one time last week. He seemed like a good guy."

Had it really been just a week ago? I ticked off the days in my head, and sure enough, it had been exactly seven days.

"Do you know Pug's wife?" Hunter asked.

"Sure. Not as well as Pug, but Sylvia always came north for a month every summer. Pug would always bring her to a stop." I smiled, remembering. "And every time he'd tell her there was nothing like the bookmobile where they lived downstate, and when she moved north she could visit it all the time."

"Do you think she's going to move up now that Pug's gone?" Hunter asked.

"No idea." And Sylvia probably didn't know yet, either.

"Are you going to the visitation?"

I turned to look at him. "It's scheduled already?"

"Saw it online this morning. Set for tomorrow, I think it was."

Huh. I pulled out my phone and ran a search for Scovill's Funeral Home. After a few taps and some scrolling, there it was. Visitation for David "Pug" Mattock was scheduled for the next afternoon. Paying my condolences to Sylvia was the important thing, of course, but maybe, just maybe, I could also learn something about the sculpture.

And so, the following day, I took a late lunch and arrived at the funeral home just before the visitation started. Signs directed me to a large room to the right, so I went that way, my feet noiseless on the deep carpet. Inside, a fortyish man I recognized as one of the Scovill brothers was talking to Sylvia. Her white-blond hair was cut in a short pixie, and she was wearing a dark navy blue dress that looked almost military, with brass buttons down the front and at the cuffs. From the ankle up she looked poised and elegant, but her shoes told another story. She wore scuffed tan loafers that might have been older than I was.

Of course, there was the possibility that the shoes had some sentimental meaning, but I'd never seen Sylvia anything but perfectly attired, even on the hottest day of summer.

"Minnie?" She'd seen me and was coming across the room, arms outstretched. "It's so good of you to come."

We embraced, and as she released me I said, "Sorry I'm early. If you're not ready, I'll come back later."

"Don't be silly. We're all set here." Sylvia glanced at the Scovill brother, who nodded and glided away. "And I know what you're going to ask: why are we having a visitation now, when Pug . . . when he won't be released for some time." She sighed. "I'm in town, some of his relatives are in town, and it just seemed to make sense. We'll have a big memorial service this summer. You'll come, won't you?"

I promised to do my best, and gently maneuvered her to a smoothly upholstered couch and sat us both down, as up close, she looked pale and trembly.

"Pug was at the bookmobile last week," I said. "He tried to explain turkey-hunting season to me."

She managed a small smile. "He did that to me, too. I just wish . . ." Her voice trailed off.

I was sure she wished many things, but I was mostly wishing that whoever killed Pug had never been born.

We sat quietly for a moment, then I said, "I heard Pug was giving you a fantastic present."

She gave me a startled look. "Where did you hear that?"

Uh-oh. "Um, well, at the Round Table. Pug was

in there a couple of weeks ago, meeting with a guy to finalize the details."

"Details of what?" When I hesitated, she leaned forward and spoke with low urgency. "Minnie, you have to tell me. You know Pug, he'd been trying to convince me to move north for years. Last month he promised me a wonderful present when I 'did the deed,' as he kept calling it. But I don't know what it was."

"Okay," I said slowly. "This is secondhand information, you understand. You should really talk to Cookie. But it sounded like Pug was buying you a sculpture by Vittorio Conti."

Sylvia's hands flew to her mouth. "A Conti? He was buying me a Conti? That man, that dear, dear, man." A single tear trickled down her cheek, followed quickly by another. And another.

I reached for a box of tissues I'd already spied on a nearby table and pulled one out for Sylvia.

"Sorry," she said, dabbing at her face.

I murmured that she had no reason to apologize. "I'm the one who should say sorry. I assumed you knew."

"Pug liked to surprise me." She took another tissue and blew her nose. "He could keep a secret better than anyone. If only I'd moved north last year, but I kept saying I wasn't ready. Why was I so stupid? Why did I think work was more important than spending time with my husband?"

Just then, more people came into the room. Sylvia blew her nose one last time, thanked me for coming, and got up to speak to the newcomers.

I stood, too, thinking furiously.

Sylvia didn't know about the sculpture. Had Pug

actually bought it? Or had he only considered a purchase? And if he had bought it, had he been killed because he got in the way of a thief? How much could these sculptures be worth, anyway?

I had no idea, but I knew how to find out.

Chapter 7

Russell "Cade" McCade and his wife, Barb, sat across from me at Corner Coffee. It was Saturday morning, and they'd just returned to Michigan after spending the winter in Arizona. Two things made them stand out from the other coffee shop patrons; their tanned skin contrasted sharply with everyone else's white faces, and their heavy parkas didn't come even close to the spring coats everyone else was wearing.

I'd made fun of them, of course, for thinking that near-forty-degree temperatures meant hauling out winter gear, and received baleful looks and dire warnings of things that would happen when I got to be their age.

Since the McCades were about ten years younger than my parents, who never wore winter coats unless it got below freezing, I ignored their cautionary tales and asked what they knew about sculpture in general, and Vittorio Conti in particular.

"Nothing," Cade said promptly. "I know as much

about sculpture as I do about the aerodynamics of jet design."

I put my coffee mug down. "But you're an artist." An internationally famous one, to boot. How could he not know?

He sighed heavily. "I smear acrylic paint on canvas, my girl. Different world entirely. Do you know anything about running a bookstore? Hah, I see from that dazed expression that you don't. Same principle."

"Vittorio Conti is an acquired taste," Barb said.

Cade's eyebrows went up. "Good heavens, woman. Don't tell me you've gone out and become a sculpture fanatic when my back was turned."

"Not yet, but you never know." She smiled at her husband of many years. "Minnie, if you want to learn about sculpture, Gallery 45.3 carries more than anyone else in the area. I'd talk to them."

Accordingly, an hour later, after getting caught up with the McCades, I walked into Chilson's newest art gallery for the first time. And probably the only time, I thought, as I noticed a price noted oh so discreetly on the white wall next to a painting of something that might have been a sunset over Lake Michigan, or might have been an egg sunnyside up. Though my job was the best possible job in the world, no one went into library science for the money. The gallery's white walls and white pedestals featured paintings, sculptures, jewelry, and weavings that were far beyond my fiscal reach. Which was just as well, because if he'd felt like it, Eddie's claws would have made mincemeat out of almost everything in the gallery, and I was pretty sure insurance didn't cover cat damage.

"May I help you?"

I turned away from my inspection of a gorgeous necklace that looked like it could have come from an Egyptian tomb. "Hi," I said, smiling at the tall and thin thirtyish man. He wore a black turtleneck, black pants, and bright lime green running shoes. His dark hair was pulled into a ponytail, and if I had to guess, the last time he'd trimmed his beard had been for Christmas dinner.

After introducing myself, and learning that his name was Skyler Ellison, I said, "I've been told that this is the place to learn more about sculpture. And, um, about sculptors." I held my breath, waiting for him to ask why. If he did, I'd have to fumble for a fast reason that held some semblance of sense, and I wasn't sure I'd be able to come up with anything close to sensible.

"Then you're lucky. You've come to the right place," Skyler said, looking down on me.

He must have had a different definition of personal space, because he stood a little too close. I edged away and pointed at a nearby sculpture, something that looked sort of like the Leaning Tower of Pisa but maybe more like a giraffe. "This is interesting. How do you think it was made?"

Skyler smiled into his beard. "You have very good taste, Minnie. That's a work by one of our finest local sculptors. It was made through an additive process. A casting."

Additive? Sounded like a math problem. "Ah." I thought about trying to fake my way through the conversation, then decided that (1) it wouldn't work, and (2) I would likely learn more by admitting my complete ignorance.

"Skyler," I said, "here's the thing. I'm thinking about getting my fiancé"—I pointed at my engagement ring—"a sculpture for a wedding present, and I know nothing about the sculpting process. Do you have time to give me a quick crash course?"

It turned out that he did. I learned about the four basic sculpture techniques: carving, casting, modeling, and assembling. That carving was a subtractive process (because of the whole carving-out thing), and that casting, modeling, and assembling were all additive. Then I learned about the classic materials. Bronze, ceramic, marble. Then he started talking about the different periods of sculpture, starting with the Paleolithic era and rolling on to Mesopotamia and Egypt. When he'd rocked back on his heels and started in on the Renaissance, I waited until he took a breath and jumped in.

"That's just fascinating," I said, nodding eagerly. "And you know what? I just remembered the name of a sculptor. Have you heard of Vittorio Conti?"

Skyler's mouth sagged open. "Sure. Everyone in the art world knows how important Conti's work is."

Not quite everyone. "Oh? How important is it?"

My instructor sailed into a deeply technical discussion, complete with hand and arm gestures, none of which meant anything to me. When he started to wind down, I jumped into a space and asked, "So does that mean his works are expensive?"

Skyler's face instantly lost its animation. "Art isn't about money," he said shortly. "Popularity is fleeting. Ephemeral. It doesn't mean anything. It's the importance of the work that matters. Standing the test of time." He took a deep breath and sighed it out. "But to answer your question, some of his pieces have sold in the six figures. Not all, but some."

"Do you have any here?" I asked, looking around. "I'd love to see one."

Skyler laughed. "You and me both. We had one last summer, but not for long."

"It sold fast?"

He snapped his fingers. "Like that."

"If you get another one . . ." I gave him my card. "You never know, a Conti might be just the ticket for a wedding present." Might, but almost certainly wouldn't be.

I thanked Skyler for his time and headed out. Yes, I'd learned a lot about sculpture, but was any of that useful in finding Pug's killer? I had no idea. Not yet, anyway.

Rafe and I had a Saturday lunch at home: grilled cheese sandwiches (made by Rafe) with salad (assembled by Minnie) eaten at the kitchen island while discussing our mornings.

He told me about the progress he'd made on planning our spring and summer landscaping projects, and I told him what I'd learned about the world of sculpture and how it might or might not relate to Pug's murder.

"Oh, and if anyone asks," I said, "I briefly considered buying you a Conti sculpture for a wedding present."

"Did you consider how much you were willing to pay?"

"Still exploring possibilities," I assured him. "No dollar amounts were mentioned."

"Good to know. So this Conti was a somebody in the sculpture world?"

"According to my new friend Skyler, absolutely. Influential, was what he said." More than once, if I recalled correctly.

"Mrr!"

Rafe looked down at Eddie, who was sitting on the floor, glaring up at us humans. "Great balls of fire, cat. My ears are less than five feet away from your mouth. Do you really need to use that much volume?"

"Mrr!"

"Could have told you that's what he'd say," I murmured into the edge of my sandwich. "What are you doing this afternoon?"

"Helping a buddy of mine move, remember? I told you the other night at Hoppe's."

I vaguely recalled him saying that he might be gone on Saturday afternoon, but I couldn't remember details. "Anyone I know?"

Given that Rafe was a lifelong resident of Chilson, except for his college years, and also given that he was a gregarious sort who found it nearly impossible to make enemies, his list of friends was far deeper and wider than mine. That he would be helping one of those friends on a weekend do something or other was part of who he was, and I'd long ago come to accept it. And what went around came around—all those friends had helped him finish the house not long ago, and moved all my possessions in one surprising evening.

"Nope. Guy from Petoskey I knew from high school hockey. He's moving to Chilson and I said I'd give him a hand at this end."

Rafe's ability to resurrect a twenty-year-old friendship at the drop of a hat was one of the things I loved about him.

"Something funny?" he asked, picking up our empty plates and taking them to the dishwasher.

I put my elbows on the counter, my chin in the heels of my hands, and enjoyed the sight of my beloved doing the dishes. Could there be a luckier woman in the history of the world? "Just happy. You know I love you, right?"

"That's what you said the other night when I did all the cooking and cleanup for dinner. Did you agree to marry me just so you could stay out of the kitchen?"

"No," I said. "Your cooking isn't that good."

"Fact." He added some silverware to the dishwasher. "What are you and the Edmeister up to this afternoon?"

I looked around for Eddie, but he was either absent or invisible. "My guess is Eddie's on the bed, hoping for naptime. But I'm meeting Keegan Kolb for coffee to talk about Ryan. And I'm going to do some background on Pug."

Rafe pushed some mysterious buttons on the dishwasher's control panel and popped the door shut. Whooshing water and mechanical noises started immediately, giving the reassuring impression that all was right with the world.

"Tonight," Rafe said, drying his hands on a kitchen towel, "you can tell me everything you learn. We'll figure out what to do next."

I nodded. Because even though the dishwasher was giving me the feeling that things were okay, Pug was dead, killed by an unknown assailant, and

Ryan was still missing. Things were definitely not right.

Half an hour later, I was back at the Coffee Corner, and Keegan was saying the same thing. Today, her hair's color streak was lavendar, matching her fingernail color. I wondered which had come first, the nail polish or the hair color, but decided this wasn't the time to ask.

I'd just told her that public opinion was moving against Ryan and she'd put her chin up and said, "That's just not right. What happened to 'innocent until proven guilty'? He hasn't done anything!"

"You don't think so," I said, "and I don't think so. But until we can find proof, the police will still be looking for him." The stubborn look on her face didn't fade, so I kept talking. "Have you found out anything that could help? Anything at all? You never know what might turn out to be important."

She shook her head, her long straight hair flowing over her shoulders as she did so. "How do you prove a negative? There's nothing to find because he didn't *do* anything!"

And we were back to denial. Which was loyal of her and all, but wasn't exactly useful.

I listened to her describe how Ryan helped a neighbor of theirs round up horses that had wandered through a broken fence, citing that as proof of his innocence of anything and everything, and began to wonder at her vehemence.

How could she be so sure? Was it pure trust? Or did she know something she wasn't telling me? Or . . .

A brand-new idea crept in, one that I didn't like in the least.

What if . . . maybe Keegan herself was involved with the robbery and death of the security guard. Could that be why she was so sure Ryan was innocent? Could Keegan be the link between Ryan's disappearance and Pug's murder?

Maybe I needed to find out what Keegan had been doing the day Pug was killed.

Sunday evening, I was back at Three Seasons, back on my stool, back watching an extremely pregnant chef finalize dessert preparations.

"You sure I can't do something?" I asked.

She snorted. "I can't believe you asked that question in a serious way. What makes you think I'd let you touch anything in my kitchen other than that stool?"

"Temporary insanity," I said. "I'll get over it soon."

Kristen, who had been glaring at me with an intensity that had reminded me of Eddie when the water in his dish had a cat hair in it, stopped staring and nodded. "Nice to know you've given up on making me take it easy."

"Oh, I haven't. We haven't. Just taking a break, is all."

My best friend sniffed and went back to sifting sugar on top of the custard-filled ramekins. "Back to what you were talking about. After coffee with Keegan, you went online and stalked Pug. What did you find out?"

I wasn't sure "stalking" was the right term, given the circumstances of his being dead, but it was close enough. "Like I told Rafe last night," I said, "there wasn't a bad word to be found about him."

"Of course not." Kristen rolled her eyes. "The poor guy is dead. No one disses a dead guy."

"Sure, but I went back to before he died. Found posts from when he was still a manager with that car-parts manufacturer. And not just social media—from those job-seeker sites where people rate their former employers."

Kristen smiled in a sharklike manner. "Yeah, I check those every once in a while for here. But no one gives real names on those sites, so how does it help you?"

"Given the dates and Pug's job title, it wasn't too hard to figure out which of the people posting might have worked with him."

"And?" Kristen fired up the scary blowtorch tool.

"And I reached out to them." It had been easy enough, thanks to the fact that most of the sites allowed a method of anonymous contact. Once Pug's former coworkers heard that he'd been murdered, they'd been more than happy to e-mail me with information. "They all said he'd been a great guy to work with, and that whoever killed him must have been a stranger, because no one who knew him would ever want to do something like that."

"Really." Kristen aimed the pointy flame at our future dessert. "What's that thing you say? That anyone can kill, given . . . whatever."

"A certain set of circumstances," I said under my breath, not wanting to distract her. I'd grown used to Kristen wielding knives of all shapes and sizes, but Kristen with a flamethrower—and extremely pregnant to boot—wasn't in my comfort zone.

She inspected her work and must have considered it good, because she turned off the frightening device, slid the desserts over, and, groaning, sat on the stool next to me. "Cheers," she said.

We tinked spoons and dug in. For a few blissful moments, there was nothing but sweet crackling goodness and a friendship that had stood the tests of middle school, high school, college, adulthood, careers, and marriage. And now . . .

"It's okay," I said, "if we can't do Sunday dessert after the baby is born."

"What? Of course we will. Why wouldn't we?"

I slid her a look. "Do you really need me to start counting reasons?"

"Don't you dare," Kristen said in a near snarl. "I need to know that one thing will stay the same after . . . well, after. Knowing we'll be together at least once a week is an anchor in my life. I need this, Minnie. I need you."

I blinked. Kristen did not do heart-on-sleeve emotions. "Well, okay then," I said. "We'll figure it out."

"Okay," she said, and I thought I detected a watery sniff.

My spoon went after the last of my custard. "I need you, too," I said to the ramekin, because I didn't do heart-on-sleeve very well, either.

"I know," she whispered.

"It'll work out," I said, not sure exactly what I was talking about, but knowing it was true. "Whatever happens, we'll make it work."

After a sniffly pause, she said, "Okay."

And I was suddenly sure that it would be.

* * *

By design, I arrived at the library before anyone else the next morning. I checked the entire building, top to bottom, front to back, inside and out, making sure that everything was in order. Graydon had been gone a week and the last thing I wanted was for his return to be marred by an unexpected problem.

Things happened, after all. Pipes burst. Vandalism happened. Roofs leaked. Janitorial crews used the wrong cleaning fluid and ruined carpets. I'd heard of all those things happening to other libraries and I didn't want any of them to happen on my temporary watch.

My last inspection was in the break room, where everything looked fine, so I blew out a sigh of relief and started making coffee.

"You're here early."

I looked up and smiled at my boss, who was standing in the doorway. "Hey, Graydon. I could say the same to you. How was your vacation?"

"Great, but I never did get the hang of the time difference. Next time my wife and I go somewhere, it has to be in the same time zone."

Laughing, I filled a mug and held it out. "Here. Have a non-Kelsey coffee on me."

"Thanks. How did things go last week?"

I caught him up with a few minor personnel issues, said that Holly had casually introduced two library patrons who had ended up making a romantic dinner date, and told him Hunter had done well in his first bookmobile driving run.

"Sounds like a good week," he said cheerfully,

sitting in a chair and gesturing for me to join him. "How did the board meeting go?"

"Oh. That." I paused. "Um, it was fine." True enough, because the actual meeting had gone as expected. No surprising questions or unsettling discussions. Those had all happened before the meeting started.

"Fine?" Graydon repeated. "If it went so fine, why do you look as if you've lost a winning lottery ticket?"

I hesitated. Did I owe more loyalty to the board, or to Graydon? But shouldn't being loyal to one mean being loyal to the other? Then again, with all those questions that Trent and the others had asked, not once had they said to keep it confidential. Then again . . . I sighed.

"Before the meeting," I said, "some of the board members asked my opinion. About you. About your job performance."

At that particular moment, Graydon was drinking coffee, so I couldn't read his expression. When he lowered the mug, he looked completely unfazed. "That's completely understandable," he said. "They're working on my one-year performance review."

"You're okay with them asking me questions about you?"

He smiled. "I asked them to do that. I'm doing my own, too. It's called a 360-degree review, so stop frowning. It's fine."

Maybe. But he hadn't heard how pointed the questions seemed. Still, if he wasn't going to worry, I wasn't. "Okay. Thanks."

"Good. Anything else?"

I knew full well I'd skipped over the worst of it, what had happened to two of the library's own, so I took a deep breath and told him about Ryan Anderson's disappearance, and the murder of Pug Mattock.

Graydon fingered his coffee mug's handle. "That's odd about Ryan, but hard news about Pug. I met him last summer, here in the library. He and his wife came in together to take a photography workshop. They seemed like one of those couples who fit together just right."

I'd thought the same thing myself, many times. "She's having a rough time," I said, remembering her tears at the funeral home. "They'd been married more than thirty years."

"You said there was a visitation already?" Graydon asked. "I would have gone if I'd been in town."

"Sylvia said they'll have a memorial service this summer. When I hear the date, I'll let you know."

Graydon nodded. "Thanks, I'd appreciate that. Even though I barely knew the man, I'd like to tell her that I found him memorable. In a good way, of course," he said, smiling.

"Of course," I said. "She'd like that, I'm sure. You can never have too much support. Just like you can never have too many friends."

"Time for me to face my e-mail." Graydon stood and toasted me with his coffee mug. "See you in a few hours. Send up food if I don't come out at lunch."

"We can probably get Shomin's to deliver," I called after him. But I hadn't called very loudly, because I was mostly thinking about what I'd just said. That you can never have too many friends. Which made me wonder how many friends Ryan had. What we'd found so far was acquaintances, but not any deep friendships. A small town, with its established and entrenched relationships, could be a tough place to make new friends. Who did Ryan talk to? Did he have anyone? And if he didn't have anyone to turn to, where was he hiding?

Dinner that night was a quick meal of Rafe-cooked hamburgers on the griddle I'd bought him for Christmas and a salad tossed together mostly by the grocery store.

"What's on your agenda tonight?" he asked.

"The weather's so nice I was thinking about a bike ride. Want to come?" Late that afternoon, a light wind had swept away the low, gray cloud cover, bringing us a temperature of nearly fifty degrees and revealing a deep blue sky that held a promise of good weather for weeks and months. It was a lie, of course. Early April was no time to put away the snow shovels and haul out the garden hoses, but there was every reason to take advantage of the evening.

Rafe, who had been about to eat a final bite of hamburger, put it down. "Somewhere in there I heard an ulterior motive. Have you heard something about Ryan?"

"No." The man was getting so good at reading me it was a little scary. "This isn't about Ryan at all. More about Pug. And Sylvia."

"Minnie." The hamburger stayed on the plate, a sure indication that the perennially hungry Rafe was being flat-out serious. "Pug was murdered. The idea of you poking around into how he died is not a comforting one."

Put that way, it didn't make me feel all that good, either. "All I want to do is take a look at Pug and Sylvia's house. To follow up on my theory that maybe Pug saw something or someone that he shouldn't have. Maybe that'll help me remember something he said, that day he was on the book-mobile."

Rafe looked only partly convinced, so I went on. "And what could be more innocent-looking than a young couple out on their bicycles? Way more inno-cent than one person, right?"

And so, half an hour later, with the dishes done, bicycles hauled out of the back of the garage and their tires pumped, the two of us were tootling along the lakeshore road that led to the Mattocks' house, enjoying the scents and sounds of early spring.

"Watch that—"

With an *"Ooff!"* I hit the pothole that Rafe had tried to warn me about. My bike's frame shuddered under the impact and so did I, from teeth to toes. I braked to a stop.

"Are you okay?" Rafe had already made a U-turn and was wheeling back to me.

I got off my bike, popped its kickstand, and stood back to assess the damage. Other than poten-tially loose fillings, I was fine. "All good," I said. Because my bike also looked fine, although after a thump like that, a trip to the bike shop to get the wheels trued up was probably a good idea.

"Three times," said a gravelly voice.

Rafe and I looked up to see a seventyish man stalking down his driveway toward us. "What's that?" Rafe asked.

The man nodded. "Three times I've called the road commission in the last week about that pothole, and look what they've done. Not a thing. All the taxes I pay for lakefront property, and what do I get for it? Nothing."

I wanted to tell him that he got an exceptional school system, a fine library, and an amazing bookmobile, but this wasn't the time or place. "Thank you for trying," I said politely.

He gave me a glance, then turned his attention to Rafe. "You look familiar. Can't place you, though."

Rafe introduced me, then himself.

"Niswander?" The man scratched his bristly chin, then absently rubbed the left side of his chest. "Could be your dad I'm thinking of."

"Could be," Rafe said cheerfully. "I'll tell him I met you, Mr. . . . ?"

"Pinnock," he said. "John Pinnock. My family's been here since 1879."

"Homesteaders?" I asked.

"My great-great-grandpap," he said to Rafe, "came up here in a wagon with his wife and five kids. Homesteaded a farm on the lake for years, kept every acre in the family until the property taxes went so high."

He gave me a short look, then turned his attention back to his fellow male. "Came a day when the family had to sell lakefront lots. And now look." With a jutting chin, he gestured at the mailboxes dotting the roadside as far as the eye could see. "People. Everywhere."

Rafe and I exchanged glances and started to edge away. "Well," Rafe said, "people do tend to have children."

"Summertime, it's nonstop noise," Mr. Pinnock growled. "Used to be I could count on nine months of peace, but now these people come up weekends and holidays all year long." He gave an annoyed grunt. "And then I hear those Mattocks are moving north. Going to be here full time."

I stopped. "Pug was a neighbor of yours?"

John Pinnock gestured with his chin to the adjacent cottage. "There's someone there now, no idea who. So much for having winters to myself. Used to be I could walk the original Pinnock property October to April and not see a soul. With what the hospital and heart doctors keep saying and you people everywhere, there's not much left to take away from me."

He gave me one last searing glare, then stalked off down his driveway.

Rafe took my hand. "That was . . ." His voice trailed off. Rafe, rarely at a loss for words, had come up dry.

"Interesting," I supplied. Because though uncomfortable in all ways, meeting John Pinnock had, in fact, been interesting. And it had given us a real suspect for Pug's murder.

After the encounter with Mr. Pinnock, we biked slowly past Pug's cottage, where a yellow and very expensive-looking car was parked in the driveway. Sylvia drove a silver-colored SUV, so I assumed the yellow car owner was some other relative. Rafe and I continued on a mile or so farther along the lakeshore, then headed inland, which meant up. And up. Then even more up. Part of me was enjoying the physical work, but the other part of me—the much larger part—was wondering why I'd ever thought this might be a good idea.

"You coming?" Rafe asked over his shoulder.

I gave him a Pinnock-category glare. He hadn't even sounded out of breath. How could that be? I was no elite athlete, or any kind of athlete at all, but I got a decent amount of exercise. I went for walks. Lots of them. Did some biking. Some skiing. On occasion, I'd even been known to run. Unless Rafe was sneaking out at three in the morning for clandestine training, he got less exercise than I did. How was it I was the one sucking wind while he was zipping to the top of the hill as if he'd been doing this every day for months?

After we got home, I posed that exact question.

When I asked, Rafe had his head in the refrigerator, and I heard enough rattling noises to know that he was pushing various bottles and cans of beer around in search of the one that most closely fit his mood.

"What's that?" he asked, emerging with a can of Pabst Blue Ribbon. He popped the top and took a long swig.

I hadn't realized we'd had any PBR in there, which made me wonder what else might be back there. One of these days we really needed to do a thorough cleaning of the fridge. Maybe next week. Or month.

"How is it," I asked, "that even though you never work out and I get a reasonable amount of exercise, you can bike faster and longer than I can?"

Rafe lowered his beer. "You sure you want to know? Because you're not going to like it."

I braced myself for a lecture on body mass, muscle weight, testosterone, estrogen, and fast-twitch and slow-twitch fibers, something about which we both knew very little. I put on a look of eager anticipation. "Tell me."

"You have to promise not to share, as I'm about to break the male code of silence. I'll take your suddenly blank look as agreement. The secret is . . ." He muttered, "I can't believe I'm breaking the code. Ash is going to have a cow," and threw his shoulders back and put his chest out and chin up. "The secret is . . . beer!" He held his can of PBR up high, like the Olympic torch.

"How could I not have guessed?" I asked. Actually, halfway through his performance, I had guessed, but I hadn't wanted to spoil the show. "Is this true, Eddie?" Because my cat had joined us in the kitchen. His yellow eyes shifted from focusing on me, to Rafe, then back. "Is beer the secret to male prowess in certain specific, but very limited, aspects of life?"

"Mrr," he said, and sauntered over to whack Rafe's shin with the top of his head.

"See?" Rafe crouched down to pull lightly on Eddie's tail, hoisting his back legs off the floor, then suddenly released to let the furry back feet go *thud*. Eddie, who would have hissed at anyone else who did that, purred.

Rafe grinned and stood. "He agreed completely."

"Sure he did." I seated myself at the kitchen island and nodded when Rafe held up a bottle of red wine. "What do you think about John Pinnock? Do you think he knows your dad?"

"Could be." Rafe opened the cupboard and took out a wineglass. "Dad knows lots of people."

Rick, Rafe's dad, worked for a regional power company. He'd started as a lineman, moved into management, and was now a vice president at Northern Energies. I had no idea what he actually did on a daily basis, but the same was true of my brother, Matt, who was an Imagineer at Disney World. Every so often I'd ask Matt or Rick a question about their jobs. They'd tell me, speaking in acronyms and multisyllabic terms that sounded completely made up, and I'd walk away knowing less than when I started.

I thanked him for the wine. "Are you going to ask?"

"Ask who what?"

"Your dad," I said. "Are you going to ask him if he knows John Pinnock?"

Rafe leaned against the kitchen counter. "Sure, if I remember."

Which meant probably not. I reminded myself that I loved this man very much. Reminded myself again. "Okay, then I'll do it."

"What for?" Rafe put his beer on the countertop and leaned down to swoop Eddie up in his arms.

"Because," I said patiently, "John Pinnock clearly couldn't stand the idea of Pug and Sylvia living there full time. Pinnock seems like a really angry kind of guy, and I think it's within the realm of possibility that he could have killed Pug."

Rafe held Eddie up by his front end, letting his back legs dangle. "You really think so?" he asked, moving Eddie from side to side.

"All I'm saying is it's a possibility. And if we talk

to your dad, if he knows Pinnock, maybe we'll learn something important. I'm not saying he'll know any specifics about how much John Pinnock knew Pug, but maybe he'll know something useful about Pinnock himself."

Eddie, his hind legs flowing back and forth, looked up at Rafe in apparent adoration. If I'd done the same thing to him, I would have ended up with burst eardrums and scratches up my arms. Life truly was not fair.

"Knock yourself out," Rafe said. "But I bet you're wasting your time. Sure, Pinnock didn't want to see any year-round residents near him, but practically everyone feels the same way. If that was a motive for murder, there'd be a lot more deaths up here."

I saw his point. But still. "He seemed so angry," I said. "It practically vibrated off him."

Rafe shrugged and continued his Eddie swings. "Some guys are just like that."

Not just guys, I thought. There were women whose personalities twanged like a taut wire. "It's one for and one against John Pinnock as a suspect. Eddie, we need a tiebreaker. What do you think?"

Midswing, Eddie rotated, stretched out his back legs, used Rafe's belt as a launching pad, and jumped to Rafe's shoulder. "Mrr!" he said, leaning against the side of Rafe's head. "Mrr!"

Fantastic. The males in the house were ganging up against me. My future was bleak. But I was still going to talk to Rick. If we were going to find Ryan and salvage his reputation, we needed all the information we could get.

Chapter 8

"Sure, I know John Pinnock," Rick said.

I sat up straight. "Really? How well do you know him? What is he like? Someone you'd invite to dinner, or not? Do you think he's a decent guy?" I ran out of breath before I ran out of questions, but in my pause to suck in air before I fainted dead away, Rafe's dad spoke up.

"How about if I tell you what I remember, and then, if you still have questions, you go right ahead and ask."

That seemed like a sensible plan, so I nodded at him to go ahead.

It was now Wednesday morning. I wasn't scheduled to be at the library until noon, so I'd arranged for Rafe and me to meet Rick at the Round Table for breakfast. The only downside of this was he had to be in his office by seven, so here we were, digging into scrambled eggs, hash browns, and bacon at oh dark thirty.

I wasn't sure I'd ever been here so early, and the clientele was vastly different. Normally I saw chatting families, couples, and the group of men. At this time of morning, the vast majority of my fellow restaurant eaters were singles. Silent singles at that. A scattering of women and men sat in their booths or at their tables, staring at their coffee or their phones, not interacting with anyone except for Carol, the diner's non-Sabrina forever waitress, and even then only to grunt for refills.

It was a bit surreal. How could the same place feel so different in the space of a couple of hours? I tucked the thought away to think about later, and looked across the booth's table to Rick. He was in his early sixties, and if you squinted just a bit, imagined black hair instead of mostly gray, and erased some laugh lines, you saw Rafe. No wonder John Pinnock had noticed; you'd have to be completely blind to family resemblances to miss the connection.

Rafe's elbow bumped mine. "Bet you there's a classic coming," he whispered.

I automatically reached into my purse for my wallet, pulled out a five-dollar bill, our long-standing betting amount, and surreptitiously slid it under my place mat. The bet was on.

Rick had been taking a long slug from his coffee mug. "It was an easement request, back about ten years. A lakefront owner a few doors down from Pinnock wanted to put up a pole barn on a nearby vacant parcel he'd bought. For working and storing his antique cars, I think it was. Anyway, to run the electrics underground, he needed to get easements from a bunch of other property owners, and Pinnock wouldn't agree."

"So he didn't get his electricity?" I asked.

"Oh, he got it, but he had to run it aboveground, on poles, and we charge up the wazoo for that. Trying to encourage underground installation, don't you know." He upended his coffee mug. "And now I need to get going. See you kids later." He stood, bumping fists with Rafe and squeezing my shoulder on the way out.

I switched around to the other side of the booth, because it was just too weird for the two of us to sit on the same side, snatched my money from under the place mat, and held out my hand. "Five dollars, please. No way did that meet the threshold of a classic Rick Story."

Rafe did not immediately open his wallet. "He's not done. You heard what he said. 'See you later.' He's going to continue the story. This was the end of a chapter, is all."

I thumped the back of my hand on the table and wiggled my fingers. "A classic is told at one sitting. If it's spread out over time the impact just isn't the same."

Rafe's mouth opened, then shut. There was no denying the truth. His dad's storytelling abilities were legendary, and one of the prime reasons for their legendariness was sheer length. Half an hour was not uncommon, and I'd known the hunting dog story to run twice that long. On one momentous occasion, the Las Vegas story ran three hours. Bathroom breaks had been needed.

My beloved bowed to the inevitable and pulled out his wallet.

"Thank you," I said, taking his money and trying not to sound smug, but not trying all that hard.

"And even though the story wasn't a classic, it did give us some insight into John Pinnock's character."

"Yeah, now we have proof that he's a complete jerk. Giving an underground electric easement to a neighbor is a normal thing around here. But it's a huge jump from that to murder."

Though I knew he was right, I also had the itchy feeling—call it a gut feeling, an instinct, whatever—that John Pinnock could be violent.

"What's your plan for the rest of the morning?" Rafe asked.

"Oh, just a little online research." And, after he left for the school, I headed back home and fired up the computer. After three failed attempts to get Eddie to settle on my lap and be cozy, I reconciled myself to working without the comfort of a purring cat.

A couple of hours later, I sat back, thinking.

Using the county's website, I'd looked up the property owners up and down the lakefront from the Mattocks' cottage. For half a mile in both directions, all of them except John Pinnock had downstate or out-of-state addresses for their tax bills. This essentially guaranteed that they were not year-round residents. Then I'd done some mild social media stalking on all of those folks. I hadn't been able to track down one hundred percent of them, but the ninety-nine percent that I had found online had posts indicating downstate (or out-of-state) locations at the time of Pug's death.

"Well, there you go," I said out loud.

To me, this meant one very important thing. Odds were extremely good that John Pinnock was the only person around when Pug was killed.

Which could mean two things.

The first scenario was that Pinnock could have seen something that would help track down who killed Pug. The second scenario was that, if Pinnock had pulled the trigger, there would have been absolutely no one around to see.

Or hear.

All afternoon, I mulled over what I'd learned. At first it had seemed like a lot of information, but once you distilled it down to its essence, it was really only one thing; that John Pinnock was not a nice person.

Well, that and the fact that he was the only person who lived on that stretch of lakeshore all year-round. But those two points mushed together added up to a total of nothing that got us any closer to finding out who killed Pug, which was the only thing I could do that would rescue Ryan's reputation. Because if we couldn't do that, he would never find a job in this small world of northwest lower Michigan.

"Um, hello?" a quiet voice asked.

As I was doing a stint at the reference desk, I should have been prepared for people to come ask me questions, but it had been a slow day and other than a couple of queries about the location of the computer lab and restrooms, I'd had time to work on ordering new books with a side order of cogitating murder suspects.

"Hi," I said, putting on a smile and looking up. "What can I do for . . . um . . . you?"

The woman standing in front of the desk was maybe my aunt Frances's age, was about my height, and had dark red lipstick and hair so brightly gray it couldn't have been natural. She wore a pink pea coat over a sweatshirt glittering with silver sequins, and the top few inches of her pants, which were all I could see over the reference desk, were orange. Extremely so.

I must have blinked, because she grinned. "A day like this"—she pointed at the tall windows, which had been letting in very little light due to the thick cloud cover—"needs some brightening up, don't you think? I wanted to do my part, that's all."

Laughing, I nodded. "Absolutely. How can I help you?"

She introduced herself as Mary and said, "My grandmother was born in 1900 and grew up in San Francisco. She's been gone for years, of course, and now my sister is suddenly claiming there was a newspaper picture of her in an article about the 1906 earthquake and fire. I did what I could at home, online, but couldn't find anything."

I shifted a bit. "So, um . . ."

"Do I want to prove my sister right, or do I want to prove her wrong?" She chuckled. "Didn't know myself, at first. But after some thinking, what I really want is to find a picture of Nonna as a child. We don't have any, not a single one."

She sounded so sad that I silently vowed to dedicate the rest of my day to the needle-in-a-haystack job. "If it's there," I said firmly, "we'll find it."

And, three hours later, our necks and backs aching, we did.

Mary gasped and pointed at the monitor to an adorable image of a little girl with two long braids and ears sticking out from her head. She was standing in front of a tent, holding a dented metal bucket, and almost, but not quite, smiling. "That's her," Mary said excitedly. "Those ears? Has to be her. And that pail. I'd know that dent anywhere. It's what my parents used for a Christmas tree stand for years."

I wrote down the website's URL and handed it to her. She clutched it to her chest as if she'd been drowning and I'd thrown her a rope. "Thank you, thank you, thank you. I never would have found this without you. I can't wait to show my sister!"

Mary gave me a huge hug, and as I watched her hurry off, I thought about the benefits of persistence. Anyone could have helped her find that photo; I'd just happened to be the one who did.

At five o'clock, when the reference desk technically closed, I wandered back to my office, shut the door, and hunted for something I was sure I'd seen, once upon a time. And there, underneath files and catalogs and annual reports, it was.

"Hah!" I extracted the telephone book and started flipping pages. Sure, the publication was out of date, but my guess was that John Pinnock was a landline guy through and through, and sure enough, there he was, between Pinney, T, and Pintel, J.

Before I could think too much about it, I picked up my cell phone and dialed the number. Five rings in, Pinnock picked up. "Hello," he said gruffly.

"Hi, Mr. Pinnock, this is Minnie Hamilton. My fiancé, Rafe Niswander, and I met you the other night when we were out on our bikes."

Silence from the other end of the phone.

Okay, then.

"Anyway, I was wondering if you'd contacted the road commission again about that pothole. It is a nasty one."

"Got that right," Pinnock said. "Yeah, I called them again, for all the good it did."

"So it hasn't been fixed? I guess that's what I was wondering"—not a complete lie—"so I'm going to give them a call, too. Maybe if more people complain they'll actually do something about it."

He snorted. "Good luck. Seems like you got to have political connections or money to get anything done in this county."

If he was so sure his complaint calls wouldn't improve anything, I wasn't sure why he made the effort, but whatever. To keep him chatting, I said, "We met with Rafe's dad, Rick, this morning. He remembered you from an easement issue a few years back."

Pinnock grunted. "Some dang downstater wanted to run his electrics across my land so he could light up his fancy garage for his fancy antique cars. Why would I want his wires running across my land? Of course I said no."

I made soothing and agreeable noises. "I see what you mean. Those downstate people are taking over, aren't they? Changing everything." I kept quiet about the fact that I was a downstater myself.

"It used to be," Pinnock said, "you could count on peace and quiet up here except for maybe the Fourth of July. Now there's nothing to count on."

"Things are changing all the time," I said, sighing heavily. "Like the Mattocks moving up to be year-rounders."

He grunted again. "And people bring more people.

Mattock was north early this year, and that was bad enough, but the day after he shows up, there's even more traffic. A man can't hear himself think anymore. If this wasn't family property, I'd pull up stakes and head north. Canada, maybe."

Many people had said the same thing, and hardly anyone ever actually moved. "More traffic?" I asked. "Like a handyman? Or an electrician?" I didn't remember Pug saying anything that day on the bookmobile, but that didn't mean much.

"Don't ask me," Pinnock said curtly. "All I know is when I was getting more firewood from my shed that morning, a truck rattles into Mattock's driveway and out gets a guy with hair so red it was almost orange. He called to Mattock in a voice so loud it scared up a deer."

"Red hair?" I asked slowly. And a big voice. "Was it a silver pickup?"

"Don't remember. Don't care. All I know is I went inside and when I came back out, he was gone."

I thanked Pinnock for his time, wished him success with the pothole elimination, and hung up.

Bright red hair, a booming voice, and a pickup truck. There were probably hundreds of men in the world who fit that description, but how many were likely to be in this particular corner of the country?

"At least one," I said out loud.

Because I knew exactly who fit that description.

Ian Breece was about forty, and he and his wife were one of the many local suppliers Kristen used. Kristen's vow to use only local and only fresh ingredients had stalled her business plan, because fresh was hard in the depths of winter. Eventually she'd decided to be open three seasons (hence the restaurant's name) and head to Florida in the fourth.

If I recalled correctly, Ian and his wife, whose name I wasn't sure I'd ever learned, grew all of Kristen's leafy and root vegetables. I'd never known I liked parsnips until Kristen had basically force-fed me some she'd roasted with her magical mix of herbs and spices. It was possible that someday I'd learn to cook them myself, but at this point I didn't see any reason to learn since I had Kristen to do it for me.

I tapped my phone to send her a text, then stopped. There was no reason to involve her in this. I moused my computer screen to life and launched a browser. Thirty seconds later I had the phone number for Breece Farms and was dialing.

"Breece Farms," a male voice said. "This is Ian."

"Hi, Ian," I said breezily. "This is Minnie Hamilton. I don't know if you remember me, but I'm a friend of Kristen Jurek's. Well, Gronkowski, technically."

"Sure. You're the librarian, right? With the bookmobile. And the cat."

The fact that he put the librarian part first and the cat part last gave me a small warm fuzzy. But only a little one, because a truly good person would have been fine to have her cat be more famous than she was.

"That's right," I said. "I was contacting you because now that she's back in Chilson, I'm thinking about throwing her a party."

"Now?" he asked, surprised. "I thought she was due any day."

Great thinking, Minnie. "No," I said, "the party

would be after. The timing didn't work out to have one before. I'm just trying to get an idea of how many people will want to come."

It sounded stupid, but Ian didn't hesitate. "Count us in. It was Kristen's orders that made the difference to our farm. She's great."

I beamed at the compliment for my friend. "She is, isn't she? Okay, I'll put you two down, and if this party actually happens, you and your wife will for sure get invitations."

"Sounds good. Thanks."

It was a natural end to the conversation, so I jumped in fast with a new topic. "I assume you heard about Pug Mattock; he was killed about a week ago, out at his place on Trout Lake."

Ian didn't say anything for a moment, then, slowly: "Yeah. I heard someone was killed out there. Horrible thing. Do they know who did it?"

"Not that I've heard. Did you know Pug?"

"Me? Why would I know him? He was a snowbird, wasn't he?" There was a beat of silence. "I mean, that's what the obituary said, right?"

It had been, but Ian hadn't answered the question. "So you didn't know him?" I pressed.

"No," he said. "I didn't."

"That's weird. Because a neighbor of Pug's could have sworn he saw you at Pug's house right before . . . before he died."

There was another short silence. "I don't like what you're implying." Ian's voice went tense. "Whatever you think you know, you're wrong. I didn't know Pug, I was never at his place, and if someone said they saw my truck out there that Saturday, they're lying."

After he said a terse good-bye, I lowered my phone. I intentionally hadn't said the type of vehicle John Pinnock had seen, and I certainly hadn't said what day of the week, because Pinnock hadn't said.

"The whole thing was odd," I said out loud, and I said the same thing later that night to Eddie. The two of us were cuddled up together on the couch, and we were about to start watching the *Buffy the Vampire Slayer* movie, something I'd been planning for this particular night for weeks. Since Eddie was on my legs and I couldn't possibly move, Rafe was in the kitchen, making popcorn on the cooktop using the whirling popper my aunt and Otto had given us for Christmas. The popping noise was already going and I hoped he remembered to use the garlic-flavored popcorn salt.

"Mrr," Eddie murmured. His whole body was burrowed into the blanket I'd tossed over my legs, and the only visible part of him was two-thirds of his tail, which was twitching back and forth in an uneven rhythm.

"Marching to the beat of your own drummer, are you?" I patted his tail, trying to make it go still, but he pulled it out of my grasp and sent it twitching again. Cats. "Anyway," I said, "the more I think about it, the more I'm sure it had to be Ian out at Pug's house that day. The odds are super against it being anyone else. There just aren't enough people up here."

Eddie's purrs stopped, then started again.

"But what was he doing at Pug's cottage?" I asked. "If he'd stopped by to talk to Pug about taking a share of the Breece Farm CSA, why wouldn't he just say so?" The Breeces' community-supported agriculture program had been one of the first in the area. People bought full shares or partial shares of a summer's worth of vegetables, paid ahead, and got boxes of produce for weeks. Rafe and I were even considering it. To do someday.

Eddie rolled over, squashing my kneecap painfully. Oh so slowly, I eased my leg out from under him to avoid a future need for surgery.

"So why did he lie?" I asked, going back to Eddie's tail. "That's question number one. Question number two is what was Ian doing out there in the first place? If it was to finalize the sale of a Conti, why wouldn't Ian say so?"

I stopped abruptly, remembering. That day on the bookmobile, Pug had said he'd had an appointment with a conservation officer to talk about turkey poaching. Thomas? No, that had been the last name. Jenica Thomas, that was it.

Maybe the poacher Pug had reported on should be considered a murder suspect. Or maybe Officer Thomas had seen Ian, too, and didn't realize the significance.

I shivered, because I'd thought of a question number three.

Should the conservation officer herself be considered a suspect?

Chapter 9

Rafe looked at me over the top of the popcorn bowl. His hand was frozen in midair and his mouth was slightly open. It wasn't often that I saw him at a loss for words, but my brand-new theory that I was adding Conservation Officer Jenica Thomas to my mental suspect list had done the trick nicely.

"You're kidding, right?" he asked.

I shook my head.

"Sure you are. You must be. Jenica is . . . well, she's Jenica. You've met her, haven't you?"

"Once. We barely said half a dozen sentences to each other."

Rafe smiled and started digging into the popcorn. "That's about all you'll ever get out of her. Talking isn't her thing. But obeying the law is. Even the ones everyone breaks."

I frowned. "If there's a law that everyone breaks, it must not be much of a law."

"Speed limits."

Oh, those. Technically, I supposed those really were laws. The bookmobile's speedometer had never once needled over the limit, but I wasn't going to swear on a stack of anything that I'd always driven my car at or below the posted numbers. "You're telling me Jenica Thomas has never broken a speed limit?"

"What I'm saying. She sees things in black and white. There's not a single shade of gray in her world."

"Huh." Eddie was on my legs and I wiggled my toes to make sure I still had circulation. So far, so good. "Does that make her an excellent law enforcement officer or a difficult one?"

Rafe went in for more popcorn. "Probably depends on the situation. She's all about going by the book, but she's also whip smart. Could probably be sheriff someday if she wanted."

"I still think the sheriff's office needs to know that Pug was talking to her just before he was killed."

"Jenica being Jenica, she's probably already told them. Do you want me to check?"

I did, and he pulled out his phone to text Ash. Seconds later, his phone dinged and he turned the screen so I could see the reply.

"'She told us the day Pug was killed,'" I read out loud. "Then, okay, I'll cross her off the suspect list." I held up my hand and made the motion. "You seem to know her pretty well," I said, eyeing him. "Did you ever date her?"

"Couple of times, about twenty years ago." He shrugged. "She's nice enough, but I'm not sure she knows how to laugh."

I felt a pang of pity. The poor woman. There were days when the only thing that saved me from spiraling down into a dark hole was laughter. And lots of it. "And you, too," I murmured, reaching out to pat Eddie's head.

"What's that?" Rafe asked.

"That I love you." I leaned over and gave him a huge smack on the cheek. "What did I ever do to deserve you?"

"Maybe you were really bad in a previous life."

I tipped my head to the side, resting it against his shoulder. "Possible."

He reached up and stroked my hair with his non-popcorn hand. We sat like that for a moment, our breathing and Eddie's snoring the only sounds. I held the moment in my head, in my heart, storing it away forever.

Finally, I said, "Do you know why I insisted on watching *Buffy* tonight?"

"Because you want to be prepared for vampires."

"Wouldn't it be funny if I said yes? But, no. That's not it. I wanted to watch this tonight because it's the movie I saw the night I signed my first student loan."

"You're saying you're going back to college?" Rafe asked. "What degree? No, don't tell me. Has to be one of two things. Veterinary science, so you can figure out what makes Eddie tick, or criminal justice, so you can start your second career in law enforcement."

As if anyone would ever be able to determine what went on in Eddie's head. And I wasn't sure I'd be a good candidate for law enforcement. I understood the chain of command and all that, but I didn't always keep my mouth shut when I should.

"Wrong and wrong," I said. "Today I got written confirmation that my last student loan has been paid off."

"That's great!" Rafe wrapped his arm around me. "We need to celebrate. What night? Tomorrow? If The Blond is still pregnant and not a mom, let's do something with those two. It'll all be different as soon as that kid comes out, you know? And maybe Ash will come along. And Josh and Mia, right? How about my parents?" He pulled out his phone and started texting.

"Sounds good," I said. And it did. But more than celebrating, I wanted to talk about paying my housing share. I'd tried to broach the subject over and over, and he'd always waved me off, saying that we'd talk about it when my student loans were paid off. He'd paid his off ages ago, thanks to a higher salary and better college summer jobs, and invested all his money in the house.

The movie was almost over by the time his phone stopped pinging with incoming text messages, and I was mostly asleep, anyway. The next morning he was out the door for an early meeting before I was out of the shower, and I talked to Eddie about the Money Issue as I put him in his carrier, then drove him up the hill to the library and into the bookmobile's parking lot.

In spite of all my explanations, Eddie didn't have any solutions—or even suggestions—for me.

"Really?" I asked as I lugged the carrier across the parking lot. "Not a single word? Are you sure you're okay?"

"Just fine. Honest."

I looked up to see my boss smiling at me from the bottom step of the bookmobile.

"Morning," I said. "What brings you out so early?"

"Wasn't sleeping, so I thought I might as well do something useful." He shrugged. "And I haven't been over to the bookmobile for a few weeks, so when I saw you, I thought I'd walk over."

"Mrr!"

"When I saw you and Eddie," Graydon corrected himself. "Sorry, Mr. Hamilton. It won't happen again."

"Mrr," Eddie said quietly.

I rolled my eyes and Graydon laughed. A little.

Peering at him, I said, "Sure you're okay? You look . . . tired." What he actually looked like was preoccupied and unfocused. It was an unusual look on him and so was easy to recognize.

"Jet lag," he said. "I'm getting too old to fly one day and come to work the next."

"You sure that's it?" I asked uncertainly.

"All hale and hearty." He stood straight and saluted me and Eddie. "Carry on, Captain Hamilton. First Mate Hamilton."

I laughed and wished him a good morning. But as I watched him walk across the parking lot, I wasn't sure he would be having one. Maybe he had some family issues going on, and that's why he'd seemed preoccupied. Or, perhaps more likely, he was more troubled about the board's odd questions about his job performance than he'd let on.

"Rats," I muttered.

Because I knew what I should do, which was talk

to the one person who might know what the board was thinking. I needed to talk to the president of the Friends of the Library.

I needed to talk to Denise Slade.

After much texting to a group that grew to include more than twenty people, my impromptu celebration party wound up being held in the main dining room of Three Seasons. Kristen's formal opening wasn't for another week, and at one point in the text circle, location proposals had gone from the reasonable suggestion of our house to the sort of reasonable suggestion of the bowling alley, to the ludicrous suggestion of the city's pavilion.

The pavilion suggestion had been from Ash, who apparently thought standing around in thirty-nine-degree weather would be fun, and that was when Kristen ended the conversation.

Kristen: *3 Seasons. 7 pm.*

Holly: *We can't do that—too much imposition.*

Barb: *Generous, but we'll find another place.*

Kristen: *3 Seasons. 7 pm.*

Tom: *What about the Round Table*

Pam: *If I do a little cleaning, there's a room in the back of my store we could use.*

Josh: *How about one of the community rooms at the library?*

Kristen: *3 Seasons. 7 pm. Anyone who mentions another location will be banned from the restaurant for life.*

Kristen (again): *And also will be banned from babysitting privileges.*

Kristen (again): *Forever.*

Thus, at seven o'clock, nearly all my Chilson

friends and colleagues were gathering together in Three Seasons. The building itself was a renovated former cottage of a Chicago-based family. "Cottage" being a loose term, of course. To me, a cottage was cute and bungalow-ish, with one bathroom and everyone was okay with that, because everyone was in the lake most of the time anyway. But back a hundred years or so, to some people the term "cottage" had apparently meant seven bedrooms, multiple bathrooms, formal and informal dining rooms, a morning room, a parlor, and servant quarters in the attic.

Kristen had added a new kitchen and a new entrance, but other than that, she'd done mostly cosmetic work to the interior. Tonight we were in what had been the library—how appropriate!—with a spread of hors d'oeuvres conjured up from nowhere.

My coworker Holly glanced through the front windows. "Are you sure this is going to work?" she asked. "With all the cars out there, people are going to think the restaurant is open."

Kristen folded her hands on top of her belly. "Sign says we're closed. Door is locked. We're good."

My coworker didn't look convinced. "Maybe we should tape up a Private Party sign."

Kristen shrugged. "Have at it. Paper and tape is in my office, somewhere."

"Oh, good," Holly said, sighing in relief, and scurried off.

"I could have gone to the effort of taping up a Private Party sign," Kristen said, watching her go, "but it didn't seem worth it. Not sure why she needs to fix something that doesn't need fixing."

For reasons that I hadn't been able to figure out, Kristen and Holly—who'd been one year apart in high school—had never gotten along. They weren't exactly enemies, but certainly not friends. I'd given up long ago on ever reconciling them to each other. Sometimes people just didn't get along and there was no point in trying to force things.

"Well," I said, "you did go to a lot of trouble for tonight, with less than a twenty-four-hour notice. Thank you."

In addition to the food, which was laid out across three long white-linened tables, there were balloons and streamers and laser-printed letters taped over the tables, one each to a full sheet of paper, that read, FROM MINNIE TO MY STUDENT LOANS: GOOD-BYE FOREVER!

Kristen smiled. The sharklike version. "Worked out great for me. My staff is back, and after that comment from Trock last fall, I told them they had to work on appetizers."

That didn't explain the time spent on the celebratory decorations, but Kristen had never been good at accepting thanks. "What comment?" I couldn't imagine that Trock, her loving father-in-law, had ever said anything negative about Three Seasons. He'd welcomed Kristen into the family with open arms that were both metaphoric and very real.

She glared at a plate of something on the middle table. "Trock said it wouldn't hurt to add more sugar to the balsamic glaze we use on the antipasto skewers. I can't let a comment like that go unanswered."

I could have. Easily. But then I wasn't a chef at a

high-end restaurant. There was nowhere I wanted to go with this subject, so I diverted. "Have you thought any more about staying out of the kitchen until the baby is born?" I asked, more for form's sake than anything else, because I knew full well that she'd work until she physically couldn't. Unfortunately, I'd asked my question during one of those odd conversational lulls that happen, even in large groups, and everyone turned.

"You're still working?" my aunt Frances asked.

"Seriously?" Pam Fazio stared at Kristen. "Why on earth aren't you letting your husband wait on you hand and foot?"

Kristen calmly looked from one to the other. "Like I said the other day. I'm thinking about it."

"Are you nuts?" Holly asked.

Uh-oh, I thought. Kristen would tolerate pregnancy questions from my aunt and from Pam and from almost anyone who wasn't Holly. My best friend's eyes narrowed as she turned on my co-worker. Quickly, before this situation could escalate, I jumped in to prevent the fray. "Do any of you know John Pinnock?"

Kristen eyed me. We'd been best friends for decades and she knew exactly what I'd done. Half smiling, she said, "No. Why?"

Good question. And if I had a minute—or ten—I'd think of a good answer. "That day it was nice out, Rafe and I went for a bike ride. I hit a pothole in front of Pinnock's house, and he came out and said he'd complained to the road commission about it three times last week."

"I know who he is." My aunt nodded. "He's one of those perpetually disgruntled people. He used to show up at county board meetings to complain about things the commissioners didn't have any control over."

Hmm, I thought. *Very hmm.*

The others moved off toward the dessert table, but Kristen didn't move. "Do you want me to get you something?" I said.

"No. When you asked about John Pinnock, you almost said something else. I want to know what it is."

There were times when knowing someone so well was inconvenient. But since she was eleven and a half months pregnant, I told her. "I've added him to the suspect list for Pug Mattock's death."

She nodded. "You'd better solve this fast. I might give birth any second."

"On it. Because it really is all about you."

"Me and my Mini Cooper here." Kristen grinned and patted her belly. "Do you have any other suspects? Oh, hang on. No inching away from me. I can tell it's someone you don't want to talk about. Who is it? The Dalai Lama?"

I sighed. "Ian Breece," I said, and explained how he'd lied about being at Pug's house.

"That's weird." Kristen frowned. "I know they've been having financial issues. Their main irrigation well went bad last fall and a new one cost them thousands of dollars. But I don't see how that could have anything to do with Pug."

"Did Ian know Pug?"

"No idea."

We mutually shrugged. Kristen buttonholed Otto to talk about tax advantages for college tuition savings plans and I wandered over to the desserts.

But I was thinking about Saturday. Because I was suddenly sure that what Rafe and I needed was a trip to Breece Farms.

Saturday morning dawned bright and clear and—for Up North in mid-April—positively balmy at forty-five degrees with a promise of the day's high reaching the dizzying heights of sixty. The warmth wouldn't last, we knew the truth of that deep in our bones, but that was all the more reason to get out and enjoy the feel of the sun on our skin.

The prospect lightened my heart, and I bounded out of bed, into the shower, and down the stairs with an energy that I hoped would last the rest of my life. In the kitchen, I displayed my cooking skills by pushing the button on the coffeepot with one index finger and the start button on the microwave with the other index finger at the exact same time. "Ta-da!" I said. "See what I did there?"

Eddie, who was sitting in his new favorite spot on the wide kitchen windowsill, yawned in my general direction.

Rafe's attention was ninety percent focused on yesterday's sports section, five percent focused on his bowl of cereal, and one percent focused on Eddie, leaving about four percent for me. "What did you do?" he asked vaguely.

He hadn't looked up during my culinary accomplishment, so I felt free to make a face at him. "Never mind," I said loftily. "It was a one-time thing. Not to be experienced again in your lifetime." The microwave beeped. I took out my oatmeal, added a small spoonful of brown sugar, then another because if I wanted my energy to continue I had to feed it, and topped the whole thing with blueberries.

I added cream and coffee to my mug and took mug and bowl to sit next to my beloved, whose face was still buried in the newspaper. "Hey," I said, poking at the newsprint with my elbow. "Pay attention to me."

"Me who?" he asked. But he tossed the paper aside. "What's your plan today?"

"Well . . ." I glanced at him sideways. "You still planning to work on drywalling the basement?"

He nodded. "I can do the walls myself, but I need help with the ceiling. Once trout season starts up, we're out of luck for getting help."

That "we" was a little inclusive for my taste. Though I enjoyed doing most home improvement projects, drywalling was a notable exception. I did wonder, given that fishing season dates were set in stone and therefore completely foreseeable, why Rafe had waited until two weeks before the trout opener to buy drywall. Then again, there were things I was better off not knowing, so I nodded and said, "Since you're not going to need my help, I think I'll head up to Breece Farms."

"Minnie—"

I cut across Rafe's objections. "Last night when I told you what I'd learned about Ian Breece, you said that no way could he have killed anyone. That he was too nice a guy. So how can you say I shouldn't go up to the farm and buy some fresh . . . um, some fresh . . ." I tried to think of something a northern Michigan farm might sell in mid-April. "Maple syrup. And maybe they have some early lettuce. We should eat more greens, right?"

Rafe gave me a long look. "Fine," he said, sighing. "Just be careful, okay? And no saying that you always are, because I know you're not."

Like he was one to talk. I smiled, gave him a kiss, and half an hour later, I was standing in the Breece Farms retail barn. Given the season, I'd expected to see only a handful of things for sale. "Wow," I said softly, blinking at the offerings. "You guys have a lot going on."

I wasn't just saying that to make conversation. I really was surprised. In addition to the expected maple syrup and early lettuce, there were radishes and tiny carrots. There were also all sorts of cheeses, yogurt, milk, and cream. Plus there were cooked products: breads in all shapes, sizes, and flavors. Quiches. Muffins. Brownies. I found myself so drawn to a bag of no-bake cookies that it was clear they were coming home with me. Not that one hundred percent of them would make it all the way back to Chilson.

A fortysomething woman at the register, who I took to be Ian's wife, smiled. "Wish more people would say that. And you look familiar. You're from around here?"

Two short introductions later, I handed her my cookies and obligatory bag of lettuce for her to ring up. "The produce you and Ian supply for Three Seasons is outstanding. Or at least that's what Kristen says."

Felicia, for that was her name, smiled again. "Kind of her."

"Do you make home deliveries?" I asked, nodding at the two silver pickup trucks just outside.

She shook her head. "No, we don't have the staff

for that. We have a few pickup locations, though, if you're interested in subscribing for a season of fruits and vegetables."

"I'll talk to my fiancé." Because it was a good idea. "So Ian doesn't make any deliveries out to Trout Lake?" To the Mattocks' cottage.

Felicia gave me the "I already told you this" look and said politely, "Sorry, no. Matter of fact, I can't think of the last time we were out there. It's a pretty drive, but we don't have any reason to go that way, if you know what I mean." She bagged my goodies and ran my credit card. "Speaking of pretty, you should take a walk out back. We made a trail that circles our property and last year we planted a zillion crocus bulbs all along it. They're at peak bloom right now."

Since the day was fine and I still had no desire to help with drywall, after putting my purchases in the car—all except for the one cookie that I took to provide sustenance during my hike—I followed the arrows that said TRAIL.

It was a beautiful morning. Sun shone bright through the trees, their branches just beginning to show green pips. The short flowers were strewn along the trail with wild abandon, glorious in white and gold and purple. I walked quietly, marveling at the Breeces' efforts. "It's wonderful," I whispered, staring at the ground, not paying much attention to anything else, because how could I, when the flowers deserved my full concentration?

And it was because I was staring at the flowers that I noticed a smaller trail joining the one I was on. I stopped, frowning.

That was odd. Felicia had told me there was "no

way you can get lost." That there was only the one looping trail that went around the eighty acres of their property. So . . . where did this go?

I took one hesitant step onto the theoretically nonexistent path. Then another. It wasn't much of a trail, but it was certainly there, and too straight to be something deer would create. Puzzled, I kept walking. I needed to find out where this was going. Felicia clearly didn't know about it, and needed to, because she'd need to give out different directions, but surely there was some reasonable explanation. Maybe one of their employees had created a small path to a brush pile?

The narrow trail curved around the base of one hill and crested another. From there I could see a small cabin. An old one that looked as if it had been created out of logs 150 years ago. Mesmerized, I went closer, because the trail was leading directly to the front door. Maybe I was still on the Breece Farm property, and they used the place for storage. Or—

The door opened and a man walked out. My mouth dropped open and I must have made a small squeak of surprise, because he jumped and turned to face me. Yes, my first impression had been correct.

It was Ryan Anderson.

Chapter 10

Ryan started to go back inside the cabin, then suddenly changed direction. He rushed straight toward the deep and dark woods, straight into more fear and pain, running with panicked, frantic movements that broke my heart.

"Wait!" I shouted. "Ryan, it's me! Minnie Hamilton!"

The explosive run eased to a trot, then a walk, then nothing. He stood still, his shoulders heaving, and even from where I stood, I could hear his heavy, panting breaths.

"It's okay," I said, moving toward him slowly. "It's just me. Julia and Hunter and I have been worried about you." I spoke calmly and softly, a lot like I had a few weeks ago to Eddie after a friend had stopped by with an energetic golden retriever puppy. "We just want to know you're okay."

Ryan half turned. "You're not going to tell the cops where I am, are you?" His face, rather than showing its customary cheerful humor, was instead lined with tension and wariness.

"Did you steal that money?" I asked. Still moving slowly, I wandered across the small clearing until we were only a few feet apart.

"No," he said flatly.

"Did you hurt that security guard?"

"No," he said, flinching a bit.

"Did you kill Pug Mattock?"

"Pug? From the bookmobile?" Ryan's face went slack with surprise. "He's dead? What happened? The poor guy. And his wife, oh, man."

I'd already been convinced that Ryan was blameless, but his shocked look would have convinced all but the most hardened of cynics.

"Okay, then," I said, after giving him a short synopsis of Pug's death. "I'm not going to tell the cops where you are. I'm not going to tell anyone, not unless you say it's okay." I studied him. His brown hair was twice as long as I'd ever seen. But his frame didn't look any leaner than it had the last time I'd seen him, two and a half weeks ago, the day he'd vanished. "Your mom knows where you are, doesn't she?"

He quirked up one side of his mouth in a partial smile. "I left my cell back at the house, in case they could track me with it, but I picked up one of those prepaid burner phones to text with. Mom ships food and toothpaste and stuff to a summer place I know is vacant."

"So you're okay? But don't say you're fine, because no one who's been hiding out in an honest-to-goodness log cabin with no hot shower could possibly be anything close to fine."

His partial smile turned into a full-fledged version. "It's really not that bad," he said. "Kind of like living in one of those reality shows."

Sure, only without any backup if something went wrong. Though camping was all well and good, it wasn't how I'd want to live for very long. But his spirits seemed high enough, so I said, "How did you find this place, anyway?" By this time we were both standing by the cabin's front door. Technically probably the only door, but still.

"Ian and Felicia hire me to do seasonal work. I helped clear this trail last fall. One day I went off trail to . . . to use the bathroom," Ryan said, reddening, "and I found this place. Pretty cool, isn't it?"

He pushed the door open and I peered in. There was room for his small sleeping bag, a collapsible chair, a couple of cardboard boxes of food and supplies, a battery-powered lantern, a camp stove, a small kerosene heater, a bicycle, and absolutely nothing else.

After a moment, I said, "And now you're going to tell me what this is all about."

"Yeah," he said, sighing. "But it'll take a while. Hang on." He went inside, brought out the collapsible chair, and set it up, gesturing for me to sit. After I'd settled comfortably, he perched himself on the flattish rock that was the cabin's front porch.

"Remember a few weeks back?" he asked. "We were talking about dumb things we've done?"

I nodded. Since the conversation had been so long ago, I could have added to my own list, but we could talk about that later. Or not. Not would be fine.

"And you remember that my stupid thing was losing my wallet when I was downstate and not realizing it for a while?"

Again I nodded. These days, if you wanted to use fancy phone apps, you hardly needed a wallet at all.

He looked at me, then away. "Well, it turns out that someone found my wallet right after I lost it."

I was getting a bad feeling about this.

"Well." His voice went quiet. "I never got around to changing my driver's license address from my mom's house to Up North. The cops showed up at my mom's, looking for me. That's what Mom was texting me about, that day on the bookmobile. The real robber dropped my driver's license at the bank."

Yup. This was bad.

"The guy has been using my credit card, but not enough for the credit card company to flag the purchases as out of line and contact me. He made a trail that puts me right at the time and place of that bank robbery." Ryan banged his fist to his forehead. "How could I be so stupid?"

It was all making a sad sort of sense. "Now I see why you ran," I whispered.

"No way will the police believe me. I mean, *I* barely believe I didn't notice my wallet was missing for three weeks. And it's not like I have an alibi. The robbery was on one of my off days; I was ice fishing by myself. And now they're trying to pin Pug's murder on me?" His voice cracked. "I've been hanging out here, figuring they'll eventually find the right guy, but what if they don't? What if they really think I did it?"

I wanted to give him a huge, sisterly hug. I wanted to tell him that the detectives with the Tonedagana County Sheriff's Office were experienced, skilled, and more than competent. That they wouldn't rest until they had the right person in custody. But I remembered that Hal's investigation avenues all seemed to lead to Ryan, and I wasn't so certain. I was mostly sure, but I couldn't risk it, not with Ryan's freedom on the line.

And I remembered how the court of public opinion had already indicted, convicted, and sentenced Ryan to prison. How could people so easily believe in someone's guilt? How could people so easily think badly about someone they'd never met? How could—

I pulled in a deep, calming breath. Ryan didn't need to know any of that. But he did need to know one thing.

"You're going to clear your name," I said, putting conviction into every consonant and every vowel.

"Sure, but . . . how?" he asked in a voice so soft I almost didn't hear it.

"I'm going to help."

Rafe pulled the cordless drill from a loop on his tool belt and, with the other hand, extracted a small handful of screws from a leather pouch. "Hang on," he said. "Let me make sure I've got this right."

There was a pause while he inserted the screws into his mouth and positioned the big and heavy chunk of drywall against the wood furring strips he'd installed months ago. Since I was no help with this kind of work, I took the time to wonder about the primal appeal of tool belts. Sure, my beloved was toward the happy end of the physical bell curve, but that didn't explain the odd boost of attraction I felt in a certain part of myself whenever I saw his hips circled with—

Rafe, who had apparently fastened the drywall without my noticing even though I was staring right at him, waved his hand in front of my face. "Are you in there? Blink once for yes. Okay, good. Nice to have you back. So about Ryan Anderson."

"Oh, right. Ryan." I tried to remember what I'd already said. Couldn't, not quite. "Um, what do you think?"

"That I wish I'd gone with you up to Breece Farms. I don't like the idea of you approaching a guy who's hiding out from the law."

"It's not like he's a stranger," I said. "I've known Ryan for years." Plus, I knew Ryan read books that didn't contain a single bit of gratuitous violence. Of course, that wasn't going to convince Rafe of anything. Silly man. "Enough to know he's not a killer. Or a bank robber," I said firmly.

"Hmm." Rafe rubbed his face, leaving a smudge of white dust on his cheek. "Nice that you're loyal to your friend and all, but please promise me one thing. Let me know next time you go. And don't tell me you aren't already planning another trip. I bet you've already started a box of stuff for him."

I grinned. "Nothing that you'll miss. And yes, I promise." I blew him a kiss. "Thanks for trying to take care of me."

"Full-time job." He pulled another handful of screws from his tool belt.

Leaving him to his work, I climbed the basement's

ancient wooden steps, not a single riser the same height as its nearest neighbor, and up in the kitchen saw Eddie curled up on the stool where Rafe usually sat. He briefly opened his eyes before shutting them again. Two seconds later, he was snoring.

"Right," I said. "Well, now what?"

I didn't need Eddie, or anyone, to tell me what I needed to do, because that was to find a way to clear Ryan. Since I couldn't do anything about finding the wallet thief, I needed to work on finding out who killed Pug Mattock.

What I needed was a plan. Step one could be talking to Ryan's friends, neighbors, and coworkers to help establish an alibi. Detective Inwood and Ash were surely already doing that, but not everyone was comfortable talking to law enforcement, so maybe I'd come up with more information.

I looked at my cat. "What do you think?"

Eddie picked up his head and yawned. I averted my eyes so I didn't have to see the unsightly roof of his mouth, and my attention was caught by a hand-thrown pitcher Pam Fazio had given us as a housewarming present. Its almost-too-pretty-to-use swirl of green and blue made me, once again, marvel at the skills some people had—

"Conti," I said out loud. Maybe learning more about the sculptures of Vittorio Conti would help. But I'd already talked to what's-his-name, Skyler something, at the art gallery. And Barb and Cade said they didn't know much about Conti. Though they'd been the ones to point me in the direction of Gallery 45.3, so maybe they knew something . . . else.

Sighing, because I was about to start another

conversation in which I was going to sound stupid, I pulled out my phone.

"Hey there," Barb said. "What's up?"

"I wanted to thank you for sending me to Gallery 45.3. I learned a lot about Vittorio Conti."

"Well, you're welcome. But you never said, why were you asking in the first place? Are you thinking about buying one? Because if you are, Cade and I can ask around and find you something cheaper than a gallery price."

I kept my snort to myself. Barb clearly did not realize that assistant librarians in small towns did not make the sort of money that allowed for the purchase of True Art, even at reduced prices, even if all their student loans were fully paid.

"No," I said. "Conti's sculpture came up in . . ." I hunted for a quick reason that was truthful, that would answer Barb's question, and that wouldn't give away that I was working on a murder investigation, because she would get worried. ". . . in a conversation on the bookmobile and I got curious."

"That bookmobile," Barb said, laughing. "A lot goes on there, doesn't it?"

It certainly did. "So I was wondering. If Cade doesn't deal with sculpture at all, how did you know that Gallery 45.3 was the go-to place for information on Conti?"

"Because Sterling and Ainsley Ellison's son works there and he's bound to know about Conti. They have one of the biggest private art collections in the Midwest."

"Are you talking about Skyler?" I asked, not quite remembering the name of the tall, ponytailed, green-shoe-wearing man.

"No idea," Barb said. "But the Ellisons are big names in the art world. They have a couple of Cade's early works."

Ellison. That was it. "Lots of money, then?"

"Buckets of it. From oil, I think. Or was it natural gas? Although, come to think of it, it's been a while since I've heard anything about them. They're, oh, at least twenty years older than us. Maybe thirty. They could have passed. I'm sure you could look them up online, if you want to know more."

Maybe, but probably not. "Thanks, I just—Hey! No, not you, Barb. The cat."

Because Eddie had jumped from his seat to the kitchen island, where he knew he wasn't supposed to be, and was sauntering across the length of it. I reached forward to give him a gentle shove. He evaded me by the simple technique of jumping. He landed on top of the mail pile, where he looked over his shoulder and saw that I was still reaching for him.

"Mrr!" he said, and made an annoyed leap to the floor, scattering mail every which way.

I sighed and said to Barb, "And now he's managed to make a mess."

She laughed. "He seems to have a gift for that, doesn't he?"

After we'd vowed to get together for lunch soon, we hung up and I crouched down to clean up after Eddie. "Why was it," I asked of him, because he was now back on Rafe's stool, "that you suddenly needed to walk across the island? I mean, honestly, what was the point if all you were going to do was go right back to . . . huh."

I was looking at an advertisement flyer in my hand, one of those big full-color postcards from a real estate agent that extolled what a good time it was to buy lakefront property. "Huh," I said again, looking at the photos of a few choice houses for sale. "Pug and Sylvia didn't have any children. I wonder who would inherit the cottage if they were both gone."

Was it possible that Pug was killed for the sake of the property? Could Sylvia also be in danger?

"Mrr!"

"It's a possibility," I told him.

Eddie gave one more loud "Mrr!" then jumped to the floor and ran through the dining room and living room and up the stairs.

I ignored my cat, murmuring, "It's a definite possibility."

Now I just had to figure out how real the possibility actually was.

For the next few hours, I intermittently tried to think of a way to find out who would inherit Pug and Sylvia's place that didn't involve contacting a newly widowed woman. None of the ideas I came up with would work. My best idea was to go out to talk to John Pinnock again and see if he happened to know. My worst idea was to call each attorney in town, ask if the Mattocks were clients, and if so, ask if their most recent will was handy and could they please review quickly and let me know who was supposed to get the cottage?

But John Pinnock wasn't likely to know and probably wouldn't tell me even if he did. And though the attorney idea would, of course, never work because of that confidential thing, Pug and Sylvia's attorney was probably downstate, not local, and therefore in the needle-in-a-haystack category. There were no ideas between the two, so I mentally pushed everything to simmer in the back of my head, hoping for a subconscious miracle.

In midafternoon, Rafe came up the basement stairs and into the living room, whistling.

"Is that a song of satisfaction?" I asked, looking up from my laptop, where I was paying the latest round of utility bills. I was on the couch, a blanket draped over my legs and Eddie on my shins. The blood flow in my feet was starting to be questionable, but I could still wiggle my toes, so all must be well.

Rafe gave me a smacking kiss on my forehead. "Sure is. Made up the tune myself, what do you think?"

I hadn't actually been paying that much attention but automatically said, "Best ever. And you're the best fiancé ever."

"Good to know."

"And since you're the Best Ever," I said, "maybe you can answer something for me." It was a forlorn hope, but I'd been surprised more than once with the scattered knowledge Rafe had bouncing around in his head. "Do you happen to know who inherits the Mattocks' cottage if they both die?"

"Is something wrong with Pug's wife?" Rafe asked, sitting on the raised fireplace hearth. This was a good location, because if he'd sat anywhere else, I would have scolded him since he was covered with bits of drywall from head to toe. As it was, I'd probably be picking up crumbly bits of white for days, but that was the price I was willing to pay for not having to help with the installation.

I shook my head. "Not as far as I know. Just wondering, that's all."

Rafe popped the top of the beer he'd brought into the living room and took a swig. "Let me guess. You're wondering if the inheritance could be a motive for murder."

"They don't have any children," I said, trying not to sound defensive, "and the property is valuable. If whoever is next in line for the family cottage is having financial troubles, if Pug and Sylvia were both dead, they could sell it and walk away with"—I tried to remember what property on Trout Lake was selling for and realized I didn't have a clue—"enough money to solve their problems."

"Makes sense." Rafe took another drink. "But I don't know who comes next in the Mattock line of succession. And I can't think of anyone who would know."

"You are no help," I muttered.

Rafe grinned. "Ah, you'll come up with a reason to call Sylvia and find out." He stood. "I'm headed upstairs. Let me know what you find out, okay?"

The shower had been running for a few minutes when I came up with a workable idea. Since Sylvia and I had exchanged numbers at the funeral home, all I had to do was reach for my phone and call.

"It's Minnie. I just wondered how you were doing."

"How nice to hear from you," Sylvia said. "I'm doing . . . as well as could be expected, I suppose." She sighed. "Like they say, one day at a time."

I yearned to comfort her but knew there was nothing I could say or do that would help in any substantive way. "I'll keep an eye out for the date of the memorial service. The bookmobile staff will be there in full force."

"Including Eddie?"

I heard a smile in her voice. "He's right here. Let me ask him. Hey." I wiggled my toes to dislodge him the slightest bit. "Do you want to go to Pug Mattock's memorial service?"

"Mrr," he said softly.

Sylvia laughed. "I heard him! He said yes, didn't he?"

What I was pretty sure he'd said was, Quit moving, you're messing up my sleep, but whatever. "He'll be the best-dressed cat at the service."

"You always make me laugh, Minnie," she said, and I could hear the smile in her voice. "I hope you have someone who makes you laugh."

"Eddie does," I said promptly. "It's why we keep him." And then, so I didn't completely lose track of the reason I'd called, I said, "So I met a neighbor of yours. John Pinnock."

"That man," she said, disgust obvious.

"Yes, I wasn't impressed, either." I hesitated, then ventured into fictionalized reality. "Is it true? That since Pug is gone, the cottage goes out of the family?"

"John said that?" she asked, her voice rising.

"Well, not exactly, but—"

"That man!" she said again. "Do you know what he did last summer? Fired up his chainsaw at five thirty every Saturday morning all through July! If it were possible to make a living being annoying, he'd be rolling in cash. Of course the cottage stays in the family. We've set it all up in a trust. Charlie will get it, Pug's oldest nephew."

"Charlie . . ." I prompted.

"Seller," she said. "Charlie Seller. But what a silly thing for John to say. There's not a chance the cottage will ever leave the family!"

"Maybe I heard him wrong." I did a bit more conversational dancing around, and ended the call with another promise to bring a cat to a memorial service. But at least I knew the next step in my plan—find out everything I could about Charlie Seller.

"Charlie who?" Ryan asked.

"Seller," I said.

The two of us were sitting on the floor of, for want of a better phrase, Ryan's cabin. He'd spread a blanket over the smooth surface of the hard-packed dirt and we were eating Cookie Tom's baked goods and drinking his coffee. I'd also brought along some apples, a bag of baby carrots, and a couple of sub sandwiches I'd picked up from Fat Boys Pizza the day before.

We were inside because yesterday's sunny warmth had vanished under a front of low clouds and it had started to rain just as I reached the cabin. I'd been a bit concerned that the space would feel too crowded with two people inside, especially when only one of them was as efficiently sized as myself, but with our backs against two of the four log walls, our feet didn't even touch.

"Sorry, don't know him," Ryan said. "Minnie,

these doughnuts are awesome. My mom just sends me healthy stuff."

I wadded up my napkin, because that way maybe I'd refrain from having another doughnut. "Charlie Seller is Pug's nephew and next in line to inherit the cottage."

Ryan studied what was left in the doughnut box and reached for a custard-filled Long John. "You think he might have killed Pug? For the sake of a cottage?" He sounded as unconvinced as Rafe had.

"I'm saying it's a possibility, is all." A teensy bit of annoyance had crept into my tone, so I reminded myself of Ryan's pastry choice. Anyone who picked a custard Long John could be forgiven a few small errors. "There are other possibilities."

"For what?" Ryan asked. "Because I'm still trying to figure out the tie between Pug's murder and a guy stealing my wallet to help him rob a bank."

I'd already explained this to him. But since it was raining and I had no desire to traipse through sodden underbrush, I decided there was no harm in reviewing. "Between the crimes themselves, nothing. But what we're trying to salvage is your reputation. The general public is assuming that since you're accused of the downstate theft and that guard's death that you must have murdered Pug."

He didn't say anything, so I went on.

"Unanswered accusations stick like the gooiest glue ever, and what do you think a prospective employer will find during an Internet search for Ryan Anderson?" He twitched a bit at that. I nodded, saying, "Finding who killed Pug will prove you didn't, and it might work in your favor for demonstrating innocence for the downstate stuff."

"Okay, I guess I can buy that." Ryan nodded. "Back to the possibilities. Who do you have?"

I held up my right hand, fingers splayed. "Five possible suspects. In no particular order, the first is Charlie Seller. Second is Ian Breece. We're figuring he's the one John Pinnock saw at Pug's cottage, so he's on the list."

"No way," Ryan said, his voice going a little loud. "No way could Ian kill anyone."

"Probably not," I agreed mildly, "but no stone unturned, right? And I have another suspect you're not going to like. Keegan Kolb. No, don't say anything. I know she's your upstairs neighbor and cute as a button, but it seems odd that someone you don't know all that well could be so vehement you're innocent."

Ryan made objection after objection about Keegan being on the list, but I countered all his arguments with the same response. "We have to consider everyone." Finally, he ran out of steam and I went on with the fourth suspect. "John Pinnock. By all accounts he is a perpetually cranky man. He couldn't stand the idea of Pug and Sylvia being up here year-round and maybe he just snapped."

I looked at my fingers. "Next is . . . oh, right. If we're going to count Conti knowledge as one of the elements of being a suspect, Skyler Ellison from the art gallery should be included."

"Keegan couldn't have done it." Ryan's voice cracked slightly. "She's too . . . too good. She would never . . . I mean, she just wouldn't."

I looked at him. "Sounds like you have a thing for Keegan."

"What?" Even in the dim light, it was obvious that his face was turning a fun shade of red. "No. I mean . . . not really. I mean . . . you know?"

His embarrassment was adorable, and I felt a surge of . . . something. Not maternal instinct, because I wasn't anywhere close to old enough to be Ryan's mother—but something like that. Was there a word for a sisterly version of this? I settled on "familial" as the closest comparison. Ryan was part of my family. My bookmobile family. And I was going to do whatever I could to help him.

I stayed in the cabin while the rain poured down, talking about this and that. I did my best to keep the conversation away from sports, because that never boded well for Minnie, but there was only so much I could do, especially since the baseball season had recently started and there was a die-hard Detroit Tigers baseball fan in the cabin.

Ryan was deep in a very one-sided discussion of pitching staff when the rain stopped and the sun broke through the clouds.

"Oooh, look at that," I said, jumping to my feet. "The sun's out. I really need to get moving. Sorry to leave you, Ryan, but I need to work on digging up information about Charlie Seller. And John Pinnock. And all the other suspects. The sooner I do that, the sooner you can get back to your regular life."

Ryan nodded. "Sure, I get it. And thanks for the books."

He patted the pile that I'd brought him; a heap of selections from the Friends of the Library book sale room. Five dollars for a full bag of books, and not a little plastic bag, either, but a nice big brown paper bag from Chilson's grocery store, complete with handles.

"Should keep you going for a couple of days," I said, smiling, as he stood. "Maybe next time I'll bring Rafe, if that's okay." Though we'd never been on hugging terms, I pulled Ryan into a huge one. "It'll get better," I said as I stepped back.

"Hope so," he said, and opened the door.

I went outside, and quickly turned around to face Ryan, gesturing at the sky. "Look!" There was a massive rainbow. A double, solid from left to right, and growing more and more brilliant. "It's a sign!" Mostly a sign of the specific physical circumstances that created a rainbow, but still.

When I reached the far edge of the clearing, I glanced back. Ryan was still standing in the doorway, staring at the rainbow, his expression full of hope and longing.

"I'm going to figure this out," I said quietly to myself. "Soon."

Back home, I changed out of my wet pants, and Rafe and I talked about lunch options. Making something was a possibility, since that morning we'd planned to start the thawing process of a pound of hamburger, but neither of us had remembered to get the hamburger out of the freezer.

"It's good to patronize local establishments," Rafe said as we walked into Shomin's Deli.

"Supporting the community is just who we are." I gave him my order and went to choose a seat. Halfway to one of the empty booths, I spied Chelsea Stille, sitting alone, her wavy brown hair falling forward as she scrolled through her cell phone. I hadn't talked to her since the breakup with Ash, so I took a short detour toward her table.

She looked up and smiled. "Minnie. How are you?"

I looked down at her and once again thought how well matched she and Ash were, not just in personality, but also physically. Ash was the best-looking man I'd ever dated, and Chelsea had to be the prettiest woman I'd ever met face-to-face. "Good," I said. "But the bigger question is how are you? I heard that you and Ash broke up. Please tell me that's unfounded rumor."

This time, her smile was so weak her mouth barely curved. "That one's the truth."

"I'm so sorry." I waited a beat. Then another one. Chelsea didn't say anything, and it felt as if she might not ever speak again. Finally, I said, "I know I was Ash's friend first, but whatever happened, I'm sure it was his fault. Completely and totally. Front to back and top to bottom."

She toyed with the crumpled-up ball of white that had been her paper napkin. "Thanks, Minnie. I appreciate it. But this was nobody's fault. Really, it wasn't."

That didn't sound right. It had to be Ash's fault. Chelsea was too nice a person. Ash was, too, but he had the handicap of being a man. Clearly she didn't want to talk about it, so I wouldn't push. "See you later," I said, raising my voice a bit at the end to make it sort of a question, and she nodded.

I slid into a booth, pulled out my phone, and started scrolling through my contact list. Since I hardly ever deleted people, surely I still had . . . and, yes, there she was. Lindsey Wolverson, Ash's über-successful, elegant, and extremely nice mother.

Minnie: *Minnie Hamilton, here. Just saw Chelsea. She looks miserable and won't talk about Ash.*

Lindsey (after a short pause): *Nice to hear from you! Ash is also miserable, but he won't talk about it, either.*

Minnie: *Any idea what happened?*

Lindsey: *None whatsoever.*

Minnie: *Makes me sad.*

Lindsey: *You're not alone. They're so good together. Well, "were" so good together, I suppose.*

Minnie: *I'll keep poking gently at them both. If I figure out what happened, I'll let you know.*

Lindsey: *Likewise.*

I turned off my phone and glanced over at Chelsea, who was ripping her napkin into small shreds. There had to be a way to fix what went wrong between her and Ash. There just had to be.

Rafe, it turned out, would have nothing to do with helping to figure out the breakup's cause. "Not a chance," he said, when I asked him to ask Ash. "If you want to know, you ask him."

"I did. He wouldn't tell me."

"Well, there you go."

By then we were halfway through our tall-stack sandwiches. I looked at him over the top of my ham, turkey, and provolone with avocado on sourdough. "There I go what?"

"If you've already asked him and got nothing back, why do you think I'd get a different response?"

I sighed. Sometimes he could be ridiculous. "Because you're a guy. Guy-guy conversations are different from girl-guy. He might tell you something he wouldn't tell me, and if you tell me, maybe between us we can figure out what to do."

He eyed me. "What if there's nothing that will fix this? Which is pretty likely."

"Then we have to accept that fact. But what if there's some silly misunderstanding? What if we can help?"

"Mmm," he said, sounding a bit like Eddie. "Fine. I'll ask. Once."

"Thank you." I gave him a brilliant smile. "You're the best fiancé I've ever had."

He looked up from the packet of horseradish he was squishing onto his roast beef sandwich. Two packets had already gone in, but apparently that wasn't enough. "I like that I've been picked from a pool of one for that honor."

"If you want, I can get you a medal." I amused myself by thinking about the possibilities. On a ribbon or a pinned version? Ribbon. Definitely a ribbon. And shiny. You could order pretty much anything off the Internet, but I bet the local print shop would do something fun for me, especially if I told them who it was for.

I was more than halfway through a mental design of the award when Rafe nodded at something behind me.

"See who just came in? No, don't look," he said, maddeningly, because how could I see who'd come in if I didn't turn around? "It's Ian Breece. No mistaking that hair."

Without pausing to think, not about what I was going to say or the possible consequences or how I was going to quell Rafe's irritation, I stood and went to the counter, where Ian was ordering two club sandwiches to go.

"Ian, right?" I asked, smiling up at him. "Minnie Hamilton. We talked the other day about a party for Kristen." Which had ended on a sour note, but maybe Ian's memory was like mine.

"How are you doing?" he asked in his big, booming voice.

When Rafe and I had discussed Ian as a possible murder suspect, Rafe had repeatedly said there was no way Ian could have killed anyone, because he was such a good guy. Later, I'd asked for proof on which that claim was based, but the best he'd come up with was, during the annual Chilson summer softball tournament, that Ian always volunteered to bring the meat for the pig roast, which I didn't see as definitive proof of innocence.

"Good, thanks. How about you?"

"Fine." He handed his credit card to the cashier. "Has Kristen had her baby?"

"Not yet. Say," I said, because he'd been handed his bag of food and was turning away. "I'm sorry about the other day. On the phone. I didn't mean to upset you, talking about Pug Mattock."

He briefly stood still, then turned back to me. "What you were saying. That a neighbor had seen me," he said, speaking quietly. "I, um . . . well . . . you, um, caught me off guard, is all. Being a murder, it just . . ." He pulled in a deep breath and blew it out. "Anyway, I felt bad, later, that I'd lied. Because

I did stop at the Mattocks' place. But I didn't have anything to do with his death."

I shut my mouth, which had started to hang open, then said, "That's good. I mean, I'm glad. But just out of curiosity, what were you doing there?"

"Oh. Well." He rearranged his hold on his bag of food. "We were just talking about . . . he was interested in buying . . . in buying some shares from the farm. Maybe setting up a delivery stop down their road."

He nodded good-bye, and when the door had shut behind him, I returned to the booth and my half-eaten sandwich. Rafe's was gone and he'd started eating my potato chips. "Get Ian to admit to murder and mayhem?" he asked.

"No," I said, pulling my chips out of his reach. "But he did admit to being out at Pug's cottage."

Rafe blinked. "So he lied earlier?"

"Yep." I summarized the conversation. "Only I don't think he was telling the truth about being out there to set up a delivery stop." I went over the conversation in my head. "What felt like the truth was Pug was interested in buying something."

"What would it be if not a farm share?"

Something went *click!* in my head. "Let's go," I said, standing. "We need to go to the Round Table."

"What? I just ate. And you're not done."

I pulled on my coat. "Bring it if you want. I need to talk to Cookie." The twenty seconds it took him to wrap my sandwich and scarf down the remaining chips were the longest seconds ever.

"Come on," I said, grabbing his hand and towing him outside, keeping my head down and so avoiding eye contact and subsequent conversations with whoever might be in the restaurant. A short walk later, we barged in the door of the Round Table. "Is Cookie back there?" I asked the young woman at the cash register, nodding at the kitchen.

"Sure, but you can't—" She stopped. "Oh, hi, Mr. Niswander."

"Hey, Hannah. How are you? Still taking classes at the community college?"

I released Rafe's hand. Chatting with former students was one of his favorite things, and today it served as an excellent distraction. I pushed on the kitchen's metal-covered door and poked my head inside. "Cookie? Can I ask you a quick question?"

He glanced up, then went back to flipping burgers on what must have been a searing-hot grill. "As long as I can keep working, sure."

"Remember a week or two ago, you said Pug Mattock was in here, talking with a guy about buying a sculpture?"

"Sure. What about it?" He peeled cheese slices off the top of a tall stack and laid them atop the burgers.

"The other guy. Was it Ian Breece?"

"Could be." Cookie shrugged. "Don't know the guy."

"What color hair did he have?"

Cookie reached for the cheese again and added a second round of dairy product to the burgers. "Red," he said. "Really, really red. And he had one of those big voices. Like he didn't have an inside voice, you know?"

I thanked him and left him to his work. Ian had been trying to sell a Conti sculpture to Pug? In what world did it make sense that Ian and Felicia owned an expensive modern sculpture? Unless . . . I stopped short, then hurried toward Rafe.

Because there was somewhere else we needed to go.

Right away.

Chapter 11

Rafe stood next to me on the front porch of Herb Valera's cottage. Or, to be more specific, the cottage that had been in the Valera family since its construction. I'd never had reason to set foot inside, but bookmobile workers tended to learn where their regular patrons lived.

I'd dragged Rafe out here because I needed him to bolster my courage. And we'd had to do it straightaway, because if I'd stopped to think it through, I would have ignored my deep-down instincts and convinced myself it was silly and wholly unnecessary.

The Valera cottage was an old-style Up North place, with its exterior of logs and window screens that bulged out toward the bottom where small children and dogs had pushed against them for decades. The porch floor could have used a new coat of dark green paint two summers ago, and the screen door showed generations of wear from hands at various heights opening and closing it.

"This guy is a judge?" Rafe asked.

I heard his dubious tone. "Retired. This is a family place," I explained. "Takes everyone agreeing to make any changes."

"Dumbest thing we've ever done," said the silver-haired Mr. Valera, who'd suddenly appeared at the open door. "Of course, it was my father and his siblings, not us, who started this ridiculous method, but you'd have thought we'd have the sense to come up with a new plan in the thirty years we've been in charge. Ah, well. Perhaps our offspring will find a way."

He spoke with a smile, which softened his words significantly, and I got the sneaking suspicion that he actually enjoyed the family wrangling required for every decision. And perhaps, witnessing it as a child between the elders in his family, it had directed him into law and a judgeship.

"To what do I owe the pleasure, Miss Minnie? Can I assume this is your intended?"

The men shook hands, and I said, "Sorry to drop in unannounced, but we were wondering about your Conti sculpture."

One of his eyebrows went up ever so slightly. "Oh?"

"It's just . . . I mean . . ." I sighed. "It's kind of a long story."

Mr. Valera glanced at Rafe, then back at me. "You do realize that I'm retired and have all the time in the world. Come on in."

In short order, Rafe and I were in a living room whose walls were crowded with artwork, sitting next to a fieldstone fireplace, side by side on an upholstered rattan love seat. Mr. Valera was across from us in a Morris chair, its green leather cracked with age and wear. We'd accepted his offer of sodas, and my glass of root beer was almost gone by the time I stopped talking.

Mr. Valera, his elbows on the wide wooden chair arms, tented his fingers and looked at the air just above my head. "To summarize," he said, "you believe that Ian Breece was selling a Conti sculpture to Pug Mattock. Mattock was shot and killed. The whereabouts of the Conti is unknown."

I nodded and he went on.

"This brings up numerous questions," Mr. Valera mused. "Where is that Conti? Did Mr. Breece own one? Was it a scam? Or did Mr. Breece steal ours?"

"And that's why we're here. Have you found out if your sister sent it away to get cleaned?"

He shook his head. "Unfortunately, no. Marguerite has improved, but the stroke's impacts were severe. She will likely never recover completely."

Except for the ticking of a distant clock, the room was quiet.

So many things could go wrong with the human body. So many of them could now be cured, but there were still a host of conditions and diseases that might flatten any of us at any time. I reached for Rafe's hand and grabbed on tight.

"Well." Mr. Valera slapped the arms of his chair and stood. "Tell you what. I was about to leave for the nursing home to see Marguerite. You two come along. Some days are better than others. Perhaps the stimulation of new visitors will help and we'll learn once and for all what happened to that wretched sculpture."

After Rafe and I exchanged a glance and a mutual head-nodding shrug, we got back into his truck and followed Mr. Valera's big old Buick to Chilson and the Lake View Medical Care Facility.

I'd expected Marguerite to be a female version of Mr. Valera. Siblings and all that. But any family resemblance I might have seen was eclipsed by Marguerite's lustrous black hair, combed smooth and pulled into a loose, thick braid that draped over one of her shoulders.

"Gorgeous," I said quietly, trying to tamp down my hair envy.

Her eyes, which had been closed, fluttered open as Mr. Valera pulled up a chair next to her bed. Well, more one eye than the other, technically. The stroke had done its cruel damage to her left side, and everything from eyes to toes wasn't working anywhere near normal.

"Afternoon, oldest sister." Mr. Valera kissed her forehead and took her good hand. "I brought youngsters for you." As he made the introductions, Marguerite fastened her gaze on Rafe. "Ah," Mr. Valera said. "You still have an eye for the handsome ones, don't you?" He chuckled, and Rafe—a man I'd thought unembarrassable—went pinkish.

"Nice to meet you," Rafe said. I said the same thing, but Marguerite didn't give me a single glance.

"She's not herself," Mr. Valera murmured. "Truly, she's not. It's the stroke."

My eyes stung with tears that he felt the need to apologize. "No worries," I whispered.

"Darling sister." He tugged gently on her braid. "The daffodil bulbs you planted last year on the south side of the cottage are in full bloom. They look as glorious as you said they would. Once again, you were right and I was wrong. Why do I ever question you?"

These were words practically guaranteed to get a response, but he might as well not have spoken as far as Marguerite's actions were concerned. Apparently this wasn't going to be one of her good days.

Then I had a flash of brilliance. I elbowed Rafe. "Ask her," I said. "About the you-know-what."

"Me?" Rafe went a deeper shade of pink. "But—"

"She's right." Mr. Valera kept his focus on his sister. "Go ahead and ask."

Rafe cleared his throat. Inched a bit closer to the bed. Cleared his throat again. "Um, Marguerite? We were just wondering about your family's statue. The one by Vittorio Conti. No one can find it. Did you send it out to be cleaned?"

She blinked once. Blinked again. Her lips started to move and we all leaned in, waiting for, hoping for, yearning for her to speak.

Then she did. Only it wasn't the breathy whisper we'd anticipated, not the cracked voice of age and disease. When she said her one word it was strong and sure.

"No."

And a tear trickled down her cheek.

"I am not jumping to conclusions." It was the umpteenth time I'd said so and I was going to keep on saying so until Ash Wolverson acknowledged the innate truth of my statement.

"Minnie . . ." Ash sighed. Looked at Rafe. "Hey. Buddy," he said. "Help me out here."

Rafe laughed. "Side with you against my fiancée?

How stupid do you think I am? No, don't answer that."

Ash made a grunting noise. "You could at least toss some questions at her theory. You must have some, right?"

"Sure." Rafe slid the bottle of ketchup across to his friend. The three of us were eating in our dining room, looking for all the world like actual adults. Ash had dropped by to give us a half-full bucket of drywall mud that he wasn't going to use and we'd told him to stay and eat. Rafe had fired up the grill for the first time since October and I'd opened a bag of chips, which went along just dandy with the hamburgers and the grilled red peppers.

Rafe picked up his burger, loaded with lettuce, tomato, cheese, and bacon, with two hands and raised one index finger. "Question number one. Was Marguerite's hair natural or dyed? She was, what, eighty years old. Can't be natural, right?"

"Mr. Valera said it is." I added another pickle to my burger. "I asked him when you stopped at that jigsaw puzzle. Runs through the female line in their family."

"Yeah? Huh." Rafe took a bite. Chewed and swallowed. "Okay, question number two. How big is that stolen sculpture?"

Mr. Valera had told me that, too, as we'd waited for Rafe to find "just one piece" to fit into the hallway puzzle. "Heavy, but not huge." I held out my hands to illustrate. "It's made of some metal. About eighteen inches high and a foot around, set on a black granite base. He's going to look through photo albums for a picture."

What he'd actually said was, "I suppose I have to

report it as stolen to keep everyone happy." He'd made a face, then brightened. "Maybe I can wait and see if someone else notices. Last thing I want is to get the frightful thing back." But then he'd remembered how much his sisters—particularly Marguerite—loved the object and grumbled that he'd talk to the sheriff's office first thing on Monday.

"Question number three." Rafe rotated his burger to keep the slippery bits from falling onto his plate. "Nope. Don't have a number three," he said, and took a massive bite.

"See?" I demanded of the deputy at the table. "He doesn't have any real questions, because it just makes sense. The person who killed Pug is the same person who stole the Valeras' sculpture."

"Makes sense?" Ash repeated. "Is that what you'd tell Hal?"

I rolled my eyes. Why did he think I was telling him all this on a Sunday evening instead of stopping in at the sheriff's office on Monday morning? Of course it was so I could talk to him and not Hal.

"What I'd tell Detective Inwood," I said patiently, "is that while correlation is obviously not causation, the commonality between the theft of the Valeras' property and Pug's murder is the sculptures of Vittorio Conti. Therefore, it only makes sense that the thief is the one who killed Pug."

"Even if you're right," Ash said, "and I'm not saying you are, but if you are, please tell me how a burglary maybe months ago helps us find Pug's killer."

At that particular moment, I'd taken a large bite of food and so was able to take a nice long amount of time chewing and swallowing and thinking. After a sip of water to help wash everything down, then another sip, I was able to say, "The nexus of everything is the Conti sculptures. There can't be many people around here who know their value and there can't be many who know that the Valeras have one. All you have to do is figure out who knew both of those things."

Ash gave me a sour look. "Sure. That's all. Any bright ideas on how to do that? Again, given the assumption you're right about this."

"Lots. First, look at Ian Breece. Then talk to Mr. Valera. Talk to his other family members. Talk to their neighbors. I'm sure there are art blogs out there that talk about sculptures," I said, ideas now spinning out of me. "Spend some time reading the posts. Find the experts on Conti sculptures and talk to them. Find a Conti sculpture and go take a look; that might help you think of something else." I waved the remnants of my burger at him. "These are good ideas. You should be taking notes."

"They're not bad," he said. "But Hal's the one working on Pug Mattock's murder. I'm still stuck with the job of finding Ryan Anderson."

It took all of my power and strength to not look at Rafe. "Any leads on that?" I asked as casually as I could. For a brief moment, I desperately wanted to tell Ash about the cabin. To tell him the whole thing was a case of mistaken identity. That Ryan was innocent of everything except trespassing.

"You know I can't talk about it," Ash said. "But if I could, I'd say the fact that we still can't find him makes him look more and more guilty."

My remorse for keeping information from Ash vanished. When this all shook out, our friendship might suffer, but so be it. No way was I going to give Ryan up to a sheriff's office that had already figuratively tossed him in jail and thrown away the key.

I was upstairs, changing from dinner's attire of fleece pants and hoodie into jeans and sweater for Sunday night dessert with Kristen, when my phone dinged with an incoming text.

Kristen: *Sorry, but Cooper is messing with me big time tonight. Don't feel up to any dessert, let alone crème brûlée.*

Me (after taking a minute to remember that Cooper was the baby's new nickname): *No worries. You take care of yourself, Mom.*

Kristen: *I am going to be the world's worst mother. I can tell.*

Minnie: *Little late for that, isn't it?*

Kristen: *You always know how to cheer me up.*

Minnie: *Part of my charm. But seriously, can I do anything for you? Rub your feet? Feed you bonbons?*

Kristen: *Maybe tomorrow. Right now I just want to lie down. See you later.*

That was very unlike Kristen. I spent a few minutes worrying, then texted Scruffy, who replied that Kristen was fine, truly, and yes, he'd let me know if I could do anything.

I tried to shake off my concern. This, of course, didn't work for beans, so I put my sweatpants back on and wandered downstairs to tell Rafe what was going on. He hugged me. "It'll be fine," he said.

"The Blonde has the strength of ten and the stubbornness of ten thousand. No way will anything bad happen to her or her offspring."

He gave me a squeezing hug and kissed the top of my head. "And since you're not going to have a fancy Kristen dessert, you probably need a replacement. Ice cream? Hot chocolate? How about popcorn?"

Soon we were settled on the couch, eating nicely buttered popcorn and watching multiple episodes of *Broadchurch*, with Eddie somehow flopped across all four human legs, putting twenty toes to sleep. It was a cozy way to spend an evening, and I envisioned many such nights in future winters, snow hurling itself against the windowpanes with the three of us safe inside.

I gave a sigh of contentment and snuggled in close to my beloved.

Half an hour later, however, stray thoughts started to zing back and forth inside my brain. They started with poor Ryan, wondering what he was doing on this chilly spring night, hoping that he had enough battery power in his lantern to read the books I'd brought.

The next stray thought went to Kristen, but Rafe's reminder that she was a force of nature consoled me and I moved on to planning how to gather information about each person on the suspect list.

I might have uncovered myself from cat, blanket, and fiancé to get a pen and paper, but Eddie was purring, so that was clearly out. Instead, I worked on the list mentally, tallying up the knowledge in tidy declarative sentences.

Charlie Seller was Pug's nephew.

Ian Breece was an organic farmer.

Skyler Ellison was an employee at the art gallery.

Keegan Kolb was an upstairs neighbor of Ryan's.

John Pinnock was a bad-tempered neighbor of the Mattocks.

I perused the list. The two most lacking in information were Charlie Seller and Keegan Kolb. But who was the most likely candidate? "I'd be okay if John Pinnock did it," I murmured.

"What's that?" Rafe glanced over at me, but I shook my head.

"Nothing. Sorry." I went back to considering my list, using my fingers.

Index finger was Pinnock. It probably wasn't fair that I was pushing him into the number one slot, just because he was cranky. Was I profiling? Hmm. Probably. But since I wasn't law enforcement, I wasn't going to be overly concerned about my sad tendency toward bias. What did I need to find out about Pinnock? If he knew anything about Conti sculptures.

Middle finger was Skyler Ellison. He knew about the sculptures, but what I needed to learn was if he knew the Valeras had one. And if he knew anything about Ian Breece selling a Conti to Pug.

Ring finger was Ian Breece. I had a witness in Cookie that Ian had been trying to sell Pug a Conti, but did Ian know the Valeras owned a Conti? That was what I needed to find out. Had Pug bought the Valeras' stolen sculpture? And how many Contis were likely to be running around in northwest lower Michigan, anyway?

I shook my head and moved on. Pinky finger was

Keegan Kolb. She was in the Pinnock category: find out what she knew about Conti sculptures.

And Charlie Seller, the final suspect, was my thumb. He had the most question marks, because I knew absolutely nothing about him, and I needed to find out everything I could.

For all of them, the first thing I'd try would be social media, but while I'd had some success with that in the past, it wasn't what you might call reliable, and besides, I didn't envision John Pinnock as a computer kind of guy. You never knew, of course, but I just didn't see it.

I let my mind wander, trying to come up with methods of information gathering and not getting much of anywhere. Maybe this was the wrong way to go about it. Maybe instead I should be trying to find out if any of them had alibis for the time of Pug's murder. But . . . how?

Sighing, I rearranged my feet, trying to regain some circulation without disturbing the feline presence.

Trying to find a murderer was complicated. No wonder the police used a team of people to do it. And no wonder the sheriff was always concerned about the budget. I could see a murder investigation requiring hours and hours of overtime.

Thinking about overtime costs made me think about the library's budget, which in turn made me think about my personal budget, which brought me smack up to something I'd wanted to talk to Rafe about for months, but which he kept pushing off.

I waited for a break in the television action and pushed the remote's pause button. "Remember last fall, when I moved in? You said to talk to you about paying for my share of the house when my student loans were paid off."

He plucked the remote from my hand. "It's within a month of your last payment. Doesn't count."

Ignoring him, I said, "I need to be paying half. Two-thirds if we count Eddie."

We looked at the length of purring fur on our legs.

"He's part of your dowry," Rafe said. "Added value."

I frowned. What value was that, exactly? No, never mind. I needed to stick to the topic. "Okay, then half. We need to—"

"Hang on." Rafe's phone was on the end table, set to vibrate, and it had suddenly started bouncing around like a jumping bean. He picked it up and said, "It's Tank. If he's calling, it's probably important."

I waved him off, and he got up and went into the kitchen. Before I turned the TV's volume back up, I caught a few random words, all of which were baseball oriented.

"Important, he said," I told Eddie. "I think he was using Tank's call as an excuse to get out of talking about money. What do you think?"

Eddie, for once, didn't say a word.

"Siding with your fellow male?" I asked, trying not to be miffed.

He slid himself onto my lap and closed his eyes. "Mrr."

Rafe managed to deflect all monetary discussions the rest of the night. The next morning he'd got himself up, showered, dressed, fed, and caffeinated before I'd done much more than yawn and open bleary eyes, wondering why on earth I'd stayed up so late. During his important baseball conversation with Tank, I'd continued to be encumbered by cozy blanket and purring cat, so I couldn't get up for a book, and I didn't want to keep watching *Broadchurch* without Rafe. I'd switched to *Arrow* and hadn't managed to tear myself away until way past bedtime.

"It was fun," I said to Eddie, "but I could have watched it tonight. Tomorrow. Whenever I want. So why did I stay up so late?"

Eddie gave me a classic cat look, the one that said, "I have the answer to that. Not going to tell you, though, because you're human and I can't break the cat code," and went back to sleep.

Then again, he could have been saying, "Hey," and gone back to sleep.

"One of those," I said, kissing the top of his head. "Guess I'll never know for sure."

"Are you out of bed?" Rafe called up the stairs.

I immediately slid out from under the covers and stood. Of course I was. Why wouldn't I be? "Yes," I called back.

"Okay. I'm off. See you tonight." And he was gone.

"Well, what do you think about that?" I asked Eddie, who apparently wasn't thinking about it at all, because his response was a quiet snore. Which, to me, meant only one thing: that I needed to go out for breakfast.

Accordingly, not much more than half an hour later, I was sliding my knees under a Round Table booth, turning over the slightly chipped white coffee mug, and waiting patiently for Sabrina.

"I'm hearing the French toast is really good today," Sabrina said as she poured out the brain-wakening fluid.

"From whom? Cookie, because he's trying to get rid of the bread before it goes bad?"

She glared at me. "Do you know what French people call French toast? Stale toast. It's supposed to be that way."

"No kidding." The things she knew. "Sign me up. Especially if you sprinkle on some walnuts and about half a banana of banana slices."

"Fancy-pants Minnie-style French toast." She made a notation on her order pad. "Any meat with that? One sausage link it is. Anyone else coming, or can I put this order in?"

"Flying solo," I said, and just as she disappeared through the kitchen door, I realized that life would be better with some hazelnut creamer to go with my coffee, but there wasn't any on my table. I got up, perused the nearby tables, and finally found a couple next to the table where Bill D'Arcy was working.

Bill, who was Sabrina's husband, spent his days working in a booth at the back corner of the restaurant, hunched over his laptop, doing mysterious things with stocks and bonds and making a small fortune.

"Huh," I said to myself. I pulled out my phone. Working. A workplace. Figuring out where the suspects worked would be an excellent place to start on finding out more information. Okay, we already knew about Ian and Skyler, but what about John Pinnock? Was he retired or still working? And what about Keegan? And the so far completely un-known Charlie Seller?

I started with John Pinnock, and by the time my food arrived, I'd come to the conclusion that the man had zero social media presence. Though I'd suspected as much, it was still disappointing, which somehow made me even more okay with having him be the killer.

By the time I'd eaten most of my breakfast, I decided that I needed to know more about Charlie Seller before I could track him down on social me-dia, mainly because of his first name. Did he go by Charlie, or was that just what his family called him? Did he go by Chuck? Charles? Or something else entirely?

After taking a final bite of (stale) French toast and a fortifying swig of coffee, I started the social media hunt for the final suspect.

I'd saved Keegan until last, figuring that as a fe-male millennial, odds were good that she'd be easy to find. And my instincts had been correct, because she popped right to the top.

According to the information she'd added to Facebook, Keegan had grown up in Gaylord, grad-uated from Michigan Technological University, and was working as a project engineer at S & S, Inc., a cybersecurity company here in Chilson.

"S and S," I said. Wasn't that . . . ? I sat back, trying to remember the name of the place where Mia had started working in January. Mia was a computer programming whiz and the wife of Josh, the library's IT guy. "Duh," I said out loud, and typed Mia's name into the Facebook search. Sure enough, Keegan and Mia worked at the same place.

Which was just down the street.

My phone's clock said I had almost an hour before I needed to be at the library, so I finished the last bite of French (stale) toast, paid my bill, and hurried off. As I walked the last block, I tried out various ideas for starting a Keegan conversation in my head but came to the obvious-in-retrospect conclusion that the harder part might be maneuvering myself face-to-face with her. After all, did I really expect her to be walking into her office at the same time I happened to be walking past? A better plan was called for, only—

"Minnie? Is that you?"

I smiled at the young woman who'd just climbed out of a battered SUV. "Hey, Keegan. I was hoping I'd see you."

"Is something the matter?" Her face took on a pinched look. "Have you heard anything about Ryan?"

Her concern gnawed at my guilt, but if Ryan wanted her to know where he was, he'd tell her himself. And, I suddenly thought, maybe her anxiety was due to her own guilt.

"I talked to the sheriff's office yesterday," I said, "and it didn't sound as if they had any idea where he is."

"Super." Her shoulders lost some of their tension. "That's great. I mean, not that he's still missing, but if the cops can't find him, they can't put him in jail for something he didn't do, right?"

I sort of nodded, then had a flash of sheer genius. "I hope they don't start trying to pin other crimes on him, just because they can't find him."

"Other crimes? What do you mean?"

"I heard that a piece of artwork was stolen from a cottage."

"A painting, you mean?" she asked. "I've heard that Cade has a summer place here. You know the guy who paints those landscapes you see on every other greeting card?"

"No, a sculpture. Expensive. By a guy who sounded Italian."

"Conti?" she asked, her eyes narrowing to small slits. "Vittorio Conti?"

I stared. "That's the guy. How do—"

Her phone blared with a loud foghorn noise. "My boss," she said, pulling out her phone. "Sorry, Minnie, but I have to go. Talk to you later, okay? Hey, boss," she said. "I'm just walking in, but I uploaded that code half an hour ago."

I watched her go, thinking and wondering. The suspicious part of me had a theory that her concern for Ryan might be an act. Maybe, since she was obviously well aware of Conti sculptures, she'd been the one to steal the Valeras' piece. And whether or not Pug had bought his Conti from a thief, maybe Keegan had killed Pug to steal it and was now trying to implicate Ryan for both crimes.

But in all honesty, most of me was hoping that she was innocent of any of that. I liked her. I flat out didn't want her to be the killer.

Then again, what I wanted didn't matter a hill of beans. The important thing was to find the truth.

No matter what.

Chapter 12

By the next morning, I'd convinced myself that Keegan was what she seemed to be: a young woman in the early stages of her career with a wide variety of interests, one of which happened to be art and other of which happened to be Ryan Anderson.

"That's my opinion, anyway," I said. "What do you think?"

"Sorry?"

I blinked. Somehow, I'd managed to forget that I was in the bookmobile not only with Eddie, but also with Hunter, who was driving. Since Eddie hadn't responded, I shrugged and said, "How much have I told you about Ryan, Pug, and the Contis?"

Hunter glanced over at me. "That sounded like a new music group. Or maybe a bunch of attorneys."

After saying it out loud again a couple of times, I agreed. "But the question remains. I'm not sure I've told you much about what's going on. Are you interested in what I've learned?"

He was.

"Even if I might be talking for a long time?"

There was a short pause. Then he said, "I only met Pug that once, but I liked him. I liked him a lot. Anything that has to do with finding his killer, I want to know about. I want to know it all."

Once again I was so very pleased that this fine young man had decided to become a part of the bookmobile. "Okay, then," I said, and started talking.

I didn't tell him everything, of course. Certainly I didn't tell him about the cabin in the woods. And I didn't tell him my own personal instincts about the innocence—or guilt—of the five suspects, because I wanted to hear his conclusions. Maybe he would see a hole that had been invisible. Maybe a fresh viewpoint would give me something that would help me push Mr. Detective Hal Inwood toward an avenue of investigation that didn't involve Ryan.

So I talked and talked, and by the time I was finishing, Hunter was tidily parking the bookmobile at our newest bookmobile stop: the parking lot of a popular restaurant that only served lunch and dinner and so was completely empty at nine in the morning. The owner and core staff would show up soon, but they parked behind the building. We wouldn't be in anyone's way unless we had vehicular problems, which absolutely wasn't going to happen.

Hunter rotated the driver's seat and turned on the laptop computer on the small desk facing the seat while I set up the computer at the rear of the bus. ". . . and that's about it," I said.

"Mrr!"

"Sorry, Eddie," Hunter said. "You may be last, but you're definitely not least." He reached over and unlatched the wire door. Eddie jumped to the console, bounded to the driver's seat, rotated, then ran back over the console and into his carrier.

"Anyway," I said, "what do you think? Lots of speculation about lots of people without any real proof of anything, I know. I'm trying to find out more, though."

Hunter didn't say anything for a moment. "Do you really want to know what I think?"

"Sure. I wouldn't ask otherwise."

"Seems like the biggest problem is there's no proof that Ryan's innocent."

In a nutshell. I nodded.

"But," Hunter added, "I think Ryan is really lucky to have you helping him."

Eddie bumped his head against Hunter's shin. "Mrr!"

Hunter grinned. "And you, too, of course, Mr. Ed. If anyone can figure out who did it, you two can."

"Did what?"

Eddie, Hunter, and I turned to see Mrs. Dugan, a seventy-six-year-old loyal bookmobile patron, climbing the bookmobile steps.

"Morning," I said. "We're just talking about"—I floundered for a response, because Mrs. Dugan was the chatty type and I didn't want any new rumors running around, but gave up and told her the truth—"Pug Mattock's murder. Did you know him?" I didn't expect her to; the Mattocks were es- sentially summer people and Mrs. Dugan was a lo- cal, but you never knew.

She shook her head, her tight white curls moving in perfect unison. "What is the world coming to? So many people are up here now, I hardly know any of them, it seems. John was saying just the other day that the widow should stay downstate, that her moving up here all by herself was a horrible idea. He said he told that to her face and she was downright rude to him, can you believe it?"

I could, actually. But then something went *click*. "John? Are you talking about John Pinnock?"

"Well, yes," she said, puzzled. "Who else would I be talking about? His place is next to the Mattock cottage. His family has been there over a hundred years. It's a shame how so many old families can't afford to stay in homes that have been theirs for generations. I've written letters to the editor about it many a time, but nothing seems to happen."

She carried on with her diatribe against the world—one that I certainly understood—but only part of me was listening, because most of me was thinking hard.

John Pinnock was encouraging Sylvia to stay downstate. Was that the next step in his campaign to keep his October-through-April solitude? Had the first step been killing Pug? And how did the Conti theft intertwine with any of this?

That evening, Rafe went to a meeting with his northern Michigan counterparts—the definition of "meeting" in this instance a loose one, because the group was getting together at Vivio's, a restaurant in Indian River well known for its extensive pizza menu.

"Hey," Rafe said indignantly when I called him

on it. "There's an agenda. We talk about stuff. Real stuff."

"Of course you do," I said soothingly. "And I'll be sure to tell your parents so if they ask."

He laughed, promised to keep his beer intake low, and gave me a kiss that left me breathless. I spent an hour doing household chores I should have done weeks ago, half an hour paying bills, then figured I'd done enough for the night and flopped on the couch to watch *Gilmore Girls* with Eddie stretched out on my legs, his chin on my knees and the tip of his tail gently whapping the soles of my slippers.

Rafe got home early enough for us to do a smidgen of wedding planning. Neither one of us was overly excited about spending thousands of dollars on a big formal event. My parents had said they'd be happy to pay for a large share of whatever we wanted, but when Rafe and I told them we were planning something informal and (relatively) inexpensive, the sighs of relief were audible.

But now we had to figure out what that something was.

"We figured the third Saturday in September, right?" Rafe asked.

Maybe? I knew that was a date we'd discussed, but we'd talked about a lot of dates and now they were all mixed up in my head. "I thought you knew."

Simultaneously, we reached for our phones, and, after a short period of tapping, we simultaneously said, "Third Saturday in September," and grinned at each other.

Rafe held up his fist for a bump. "Okay, what do we do first?"

"No idea. And if you say I'm supposed to know because I'm the girl and girls just know that stuff, the wedding might be off forever. I'd ask Kristen, but I don't want to bother her right now. Pending baby and all that."

"Maybe she'd like the distraction."

"She probably would, but you know Kristen. She'd get all into it and then wear herself out when she should be resting."

He nodded. "Yeah, you're right." There was a short pause. "There must be websites out there to tell us what we should be doing. We're, what, five months away, so there can't be much to do right now."

I smiled at him fondly. So smart, yet so very silly. Even I knew enough to know that we were way behind. But we did have some things in hand. Kristen would, come what may, do our catering for cost and deal with the cake. A good friend of Rafe's had already volunteered to take photos, and after seeing his outstanding professional portfolio, I'd happily agreed.

"We need to figure out where we're going to have it," I said.

"Here?" He looked around, including the living room, front entry, dining room, and, judging by the way he stretched his neck, kitchen. "Should be warm enough in September to use the deck and backyard."

My fondness went a bit stiff. "If we were having a small wedding, that would be great, but—" I took a deep breath and felt myself calming down. "But," I said easily, "what we should do first is come up with a guest list. That way we'll know the kind of numbers we're looking at."

Because he wasn't stupid, no matter how much he sometimes pretended to be, Rafe agreed, and we spent the rest of the evening typing names into a spreadsheet.

The next morning, as I walked to the library, I mentally added a few more names to the list. My first librarian boss would love to have an excuse to come Up North and see my library, and my college roommate and her husband had been talking about coming up for years.

I started a pot of coffee and watched the brown liquid trickle down, shying away from the feeling that the proposed guest list was becoming far too long for our as-yet-undetermined budget.

"Leave it for later," I told myself. I filled my Association of Bookmobile and Outreach Services mug as close to the top as I dared, and headed to my office for a half hour of research. Abiding by the library's newly revised employee policy regarding personal use of library computers, I used my phone to access the public Wi-Fi and started trolling social media for possible suspect alibis.

This was a limited effort, since John Pinnock had no visible electronic presence, and I still didn't know enough about Charlie Seller to be sure I'd actually found him, but I did learn two things: that there were a lot of cat pictures on Facebook and I had no idea what I was doing.

I put my phone on my desk and spun it around.

Pug had been found by his mail carrier just over three weeks ago, and they'd estimated he'd been killed the night before he'd been found. So, he'd been killed on a Monday night. The first Monday in April.

Hmm.

Were there any community meetings that night? City council, county board of commissioners, township boards, planning commissions, anything? Meeting minutes sometimes named the members of the public who attended . . . but even if a suspect had attended a meeting, he (or she) could still have driven to Pug's cottage afterward.

And then there was Ryan.

What Hunter had said on the bookmobile was still pinging around in my brain. Best-ever solution would be to prove Ryan's innocence. But how could I do that, other than asking all my suspects if they'd killed Pug, and there wasn't much point in doing that. The guilty one would just lie, and I wasn't confident that I could detect an accomplished liar. Even bad liars had an excellent chance of getting away with their lies with me, especially if they had a good story about—

"A story," I breathed.

At the cabin, Ryan had mentioned that the first week he'd been there, he'd heard distant emergency sirens all one night, and had hardly slept, wondering if they were coming after him. That obviously hadn't been the case, but if something big had happened, surely the newspaper would have written a story about it.

I turned to my computer, logged onto the website of the *Chilson Gazette*, and sure enough, there it was, an article about an odd glitch in the security systems of almost a dozen homes out near Breece Farms.

For me, that was proof enough. If Ryan had

heard sirens throughout the night, that meant he was at the cabin the whole time. That he hadn't left with a gun in his hand, with the intent of stealing a sculpture, ready to kill anyone who got in his way. That he hadn't left at all.

He was innocent.

"He didn't kill Pug," I told Ash.

The attention of my deputy friend was primarily on making sure the dressing on his Fat Boys sub sandwich didn't goop out onto his desk. "Good to know," he said, then took a fast bite before the goo dripped down. After some chewing and swallowing, he added, "But why are you telling me? Hal's the detective on this case."

I shouldn't have said anything at all, because explaining the specifics of why I thought Ryan was innocent would require me saying that I knew where he was. And, in spite of the guilt I was suffering for withholding information from law enforcement, I was not going to share that particular piece of news.

At least not yet.

"You're right," I said to Ash. "And I will tell Hal, just as soon as he gets back from lunch."

"Have fun with that." Ash took another messy bite of what looked like the Italian sub with double dressing. "Hal's not . . . well, let's just say his investigation isn't going where he thought it would."

So the seasoned, skilled, and experienced Hal Inwood wasn't making any progress in finding Pug's killer. Interesting. Would that make him more receptive to hearing what I'd learned, or less?

I smiled on the inside and started looking forward to the pending conversation. But I wasn't here just to talk about the murder investigation.

Since timing was everything, I waited until Ash had taken another big bite of sandwich so I could talk without interruption. "Saw Chelsea the other day. Rafe and I ran into her at Shomin's. She said the breakup wasn't anyone's fault. I said that couldn't be true, it had to be your fault. She's the best thing that ever happened to you. I want to know what you did so we can fix this."

Ash's face, handsome even behind the sandwich and the chewing, looked bleak. When I'd finished, he swallowed and looked past me. "We want different things," he said. "It wasn't going to work out in the long run, so we called it quits before either of us got hurt."

I studied him and thought very loudly that that ship had already sailed. "Talk to me, Ash. What do you want that's so different from Chelsea? I mean, I know your main goal in life is to simultaneously watch every major sport on the planet, but surely that's something you can work out."

He didn't give even a hint of a smile. "Leave it alone, Minnie. There's nothing you can do. Nothing anyone can do."

I felt my face set into stubborn lines, into the expression my mother always told me would stick someday if I wasn't careful. "There's always something that can be done. Maybe you're just not seeing it. Maybe what you need is another point of view, and how can I help with that if you don't talk?"

We sat and stared at each other. Me, trying to

look how I felt: imploring, sort of patient, and helpful. Ash, looking like a particularly silent rock. I didn't move. Didn't speak. Barely breathed. Ash shifted. Shifted again. And, just as his mouth started to open, there was a knock on the doorjamb.

"Ms. Hamilton?" Detective Hal Inwood asked. "You wanted to see me?"

I gave Ash one last look. "Talk to you later," I said in a tone laden with meaning, and trailed Hal into the interview room.

Not one to waste any time, the detective was already seated and paging through a small notebook, pen in hand. As I sat, he continued paging, head down. "To what do I owe the pleasure?" he asked dryly.

So it was going to be one of those days.

"How's Tabitha?" I asked. "How is her sister's snowboarding injury coming along? What was it, a wrist?"

"Recovering from surgery as expected. Tabitha expects to be home next week," Hal said, then added almost under his breath, "If she remembers how to get here, that is."

Someone who hadn't witnessed numerous interchanges between wife and husband might get the impression that their marriage was in jeopardy, but last year I'd watched—and listened to—enough Tabitha-and-Hal discussions to recognize that this was just the way they rolled.

"Good to hear," I said. "Please tell her I said hello. And now," I went on, sensing his rising restlessness, "to make best use of your time and mine, I'm going to talk until half past and you're not going to say a word." I pointed at the wall clock, which read 12:25. Hal nodded—wonder of wonders—and I launched into a prepared speech.

Well, mostly prepared. I told him about the theft of the Conti statue from the Valeras' cottage and about how Pug had been seen purchasing a Conti. I told him about John Pinnock and Skyler Ellison, about Ian Breece, Charlie Seller, and Keegan Kolb, squinting at Hal's list to make sure he spelled everyone's name correctly, then gave him what solid information I had about each. "All I know about Charlie Seller is that he's Pug's nephew," I said. "No idea where he lives."

"Grand Rapids," Hal murmured, still writing. "He goes by Charles."

I beamed, pleased to have those nuggets of information. My beam dimmed, though, because Hal flipped his notepad to the shut position, slid it into his shirt pocket, and gestured at the clock with his chin. "Twelve thirty-one. Your time is up, and so is mine. Thank you for your thoughts. I'll consider them as I would consider all tips regarding an investigation. Now, unless you have any information regarding the whereabouts of Ryan Anderson, I need to—"

He'd started to stand but came to an abrupt halt halfway. "Ms. Hamilton. Do you know Mr. Anderson's current location?"

"Me?" I blinked. "Why would I know something like that?"

Hal gave me a hard look. "If you are withholding information pertinent to a murder investigation, it could well be considered illegal."

"I have no idea where Ryan is," I said, enunciating

each consonant and each syllable clearly. And I didn't. It was a beautiful spring day, and there was no way he'd be in the cabin. He'd be out in the woods somewhere.

The detective stood to his full height and looked down on me. I looked up at him, completely unintimidated, except for the teensy part of me that was laden with guilt.

"Have a good day, Ms. Hamilton," he said.

I watched him go and blew out a long breath. Now, more than ever, I needed to find out who killed Pug Mattock.

For Ryan's sake—and my own.

Chapter 13

I picked up my own Fat Boys sandwich, vegetable style, and hurried back to the library, scooting inside through the side entrance and managing to make it to my office before the sandwich lost all its warmth. Sure, I could have warmed it up in the microwave, but that meant more sogginess and less toastiness.

Toastiness? I pondered as I pulled extra napkins out of a desk drawer. Probably not a word, but why not? Sogginess was . . . wasn't it?

I tapped at my keyboard with my pinkies, the only fingers both free and not greasy, and soon learned that while Merriam-Webster considered "sogginess" a word, it did not recognize "toastiness." However, "toastiness" did come up in a wiki-type dictionary, so maybe Merriam and her cohorts would eventually make the acknowledgment.

Sitting back, sandwich in hand, I felt an odd sense of comfort. The world changed around us, sometimes at a breakneck speed and sometimes so slow that only rocks understood the long-term impacts. Language, though, moved with us.

"What are you smiling about?" My boss was in the hallway, poking his head in my office. "Got a good joke to share?"

"I've already told you the canoe joke, so no. I was thinking about how language shifts over time, how we adapt it to fit our needs."

"And that made you smile?" Graydon laughed. "You were destined to be a librarian. Or a teacher."

Since librarians often served as ad hoc teachers, I figured I had the best of all professional worlds. Not everyone would agree, of course, but that was okay. Somebody had to do all the other jobs that needed doing.

Graydon sketched a wave and headed up the stairs to his office, and I continued using my pinky fingers on my phone to work on a more targeted Internet hunt for Charlie Seller, now known as Charles. With the right name and an approximate location, maybe I could—

"Well, there you go," I murmured.

Charles Seller lived and worked in Kentwood, a town directly south of Grand Rapids, Michigan. He was an orthodontist and, if Yelp reviews were any indication, had a popular and thriving practice.

I sat back and finished my sandwich while I thought about it all. It didn't take long, and I came up with one big question and a number of possible answers.

The Big Question: Why on earth would an orthodontist with a successful business murder anyone?

Minnie's possibility number one: He wouldn't.

Minnie's possibility number two: He'd coveted the cottage since he was a child and couldn't stand the idea of Pug and his wife living there year-round and doing who knew what to it.

Minnie's possibility number three: To get the cottage, as he needed the money, because (a) he'd overextended when buying his fancy office, (b) he was not actually as financially successful as he seemed, (c) he was greedy, (d) he was being black-mailed for cash, or (e) something else I hadn't thought about.

"Anything else?" I asked. Since I was at the library, and not at home or on the bookmobile, Eddie didn't answer. At least not that I could hear. Without feline assistance, I had to rely on my own brain, so I went back to Facebook, first to Charles Seller's business page, then to his personal page, and started looking deeper. At what people had posted. At who had posted. Maybe from all of that I'd glean some bit of information that—

"Would you looky there," I said. Because my nugget was in the middle of a thread Charles had started about the Seven Slot Grille, a restaurant in Reed City. Right there, Melinda Hedges had typed a short message: *Hey, cuz. Bob and I ate there last winter. Loved it!*

I did a bit of social media confirmation, and learned that, yes, the Melinda posting to Charles Sellers's Facebook page was indeed the same Melinda who was a regular library patron and some-time bookmobile patron. Melinda and her husband were in their early thirties and ran a small and thriving accounting business. During income tax season, she didn't have time to read a word, but the filing deadline had been almost a week ago, so maybe she'd have time to talk.

Before I could think too much about my actions, I opened the library's database, looked up the contact phone number for Melinda, and dialed. By the time she answered, I'd come up with a plan, which only proved that I could do well under pressure.

"Hey, Melinda. It's Minnie Hamilton from the library."

"And the bookmobile," she said, laughing. "How's Eddie doing?"

"Fine." At least as far as I knew. While he was almost certainly lounging somewhere cozy and comfortable, there was also a chance he was on top of the kitchen counter, clawing at the paper towels, yanking out paw-sized chunks to strew about the floor.

"Got a question for you," I said. "We're setting up the library's summer lecture schedule"—I quickly used my computer mouse to open the pertinent spreadsheet to make it true—"and I remembered that you had some programming suggestions, but I can't recall any details. Do you remember?"

"Sure. I think an introduction to stargazing would be great. And wouldn't it be fascinating to learn about education systems in other countries?" She spun out a number of other ideas, all of which I added to the list.

"Great," I said, meaning it, but also very much meaning the next thing I said. "Do you have any ideas about who might be willing to teach some of those? For free, ideally?"

"Oh. Well. Um, you know, I never thought about that."

It was a rare person who did. "That's okay. It's always good to get some fresh ideas, no matter what. And you never know who's going to end up in northern Michigan, especially in summer."

"Truth," Melinda said. "There's an Airbnb place down the street from us, and the wife of one family who came last year is a puppeteer for some big children's television show."

"Can you find out if she's coming back?" I asked. "And if she'd like to give a library program?"

"Will do."

The conversation was wrapping up, so I jumped in with my last question. "Someone told me you're related to Pug Mattock. I was so sorry to hear about his death."

"Distant cousin," she said, "but thanks. Sylvia and Pug are more like an aunt and uncle to me. When we were kids, we spent a lot of time at the Mattock cottage. All those summers is why I ended up moving here."

"What do you think is going to happen to the cottage?" I asked. "Is Sylvia going to keep it going? I know Pug wanted to move up here full time."

"No idea." Melinda sighed. "I hope she does. Probably too early to say. But I hope so. Last thing I want is for Charlie to get his hands on that place so soon."

"Charlie?" I asked tentatively.

"Well, we're supposed to call him Charles now, but it's hard to remember. Charlie is Pug's nephew and is next in line to inherit the cottage. But last summer I overheard him talking to his wife. The first thing he'll do is redo the kitchen. And then the bathroom. And then he'll remodel the screen porch into a glassed-in three-season porch. Right now it's all original, every square inch of it."

"That's, um, bad?"

"It would change the cottage forever," she said vehemently. "It's fine the way it is. Perfectly fine. Why change something for the sake of change?"

I made soothing noises, though I was thinking that an original bathroom might need an upgrade, and there was no way an old kitchen functioned the way people lived now.

"Charlie's nothing but a bully," she went on, "and bullies sure seem to get their own way. I mean, take that car of his. I know his wife wanted something for the whole family, but no, he goes and buys that bright yellow thing. Barely a back seat at all. Does that make any sense?"

A stray piece of memory surfaced. "Yellow?" That day Rafe and I were out biking, we'd seen a yellow car parked in Pug's driveway.

"Yeah," she said. "Some kind of Mercedes. Cost more than my first house did."

I eventually edged her back to library programming and extracted a promise that she would contact the Airbnb owners about the puppeteer. But when I hung up, I was thinking about Charlie Seller, trying not to jump to conclusions and failing spectacularly. Why was Charlie at the family cottage just days after Pug's death? Was the need to control the family cottage a strong enough desire to be a motive for murder?

Surely not. But . . . maybe. There was always a maybe.

The rest of the afternoon passed in normal and quiet library ways. Well, except for the hour I spent at the reference desk. And even that was almost relatively quiet except for the moment when I'd helped a white-haired lady track down a copy of a book she'd loved as a child and had never been able to find.

"But . . . this is it," she said, her voice trembling as she turned the pages of Elizabeth Goudge's *The Little White Horse*. "This is the book my grandmother gave me, right after the war."

It had taken some careful questioning, but eventually her original description of a blue book with either a horse or a dog on the cover had resulted in enough information about the book itself for me to take her to the right shelf.

The woman, a summer visitor, threw her arms around me and hugged me hard. "My neighbor said you'd help me find my book, and she was right. Thank you, thank you, thank you."

With more than a little embarrassment, I patted her arm awkwardly, said it was all part of the service offered by the Chilson District Library, and made my escape.

"What was that all about?" Kelsey asked. She was at the main desk, checking in a massive pile of returned children's picture books. "It looked as though she wanted to take you home and adopt you."

"Just another satisfied patron," I said, trying to flatten my ruffled hair, which was always a losing battle. Speaking of losing battles, there was one last effort I wanted to make. "Have you heard anything about what happened between Ash and Chelsea? Neither one is saying a word. You'd think they signed confidentiality agreements."

She shook her head. "And here I thought they were going to be the next ones getting married, right after you and Rafe. So sad."

The whole thing was puzzling. They'd fit together like peanut butter and jelly. Laughed at the same things. Cared about the same things. Did the same things, as long as you discounted Ash's bowling and Chelsea's hobby of flea market flipping. How could it have gone so wrong? And they'd both looked so sad, apart.

"One more," I said to myself. I'd give the Ash and Chelsea Reconciliation one last try, because their relationship had been so solid it was worth the effort, and then I'd leave them alone. After all, if Rafe had given up on me where would I be? Sad and lonely or with the wrong guy. Where would anyone be without a healthy dose of stick-to-itivness? And where would Ryan be if I didn't prove his innocence by helping to find Pug's killer?

But first, I had to talk to Chelsea. After thinking a bit, I pulled out my phone and started texting.

Minnie: *I need to get a present for Kristen and Scruffy's baby—you have more nieces and nephews than anyone I know. Want to help? I'm free right after work if you are.*

Chelsea: *Love spending other people's money! Let's start at Older Than Dirt.*

And so, a few hours later, we were standing side by side, arms crossed, looking at the three things

Pam Fazio had selected as suitable for the occasion. "What do you think?" Pam asked. "And they're all within your price range."

Only, I suspected, because I was being given the secret Friends and Family discount, but Pam would never admit to that. Choice number one was a rocking horse, number two was an adorable little upholstered chair, and number three was a toddler-sized white wicker rocking chair. I was shying away from the rocking horse because the D. H. Lawrence short story had scared me silly in junior high, but I was trying not to let that influence my decision.

"What do you think?" I asked Chelsea. "I already gave her normal baby stuff at a shower last month, but I want to give them something that lasts. Something that could be eventually passed down to grandkids."

"They're all great," Chelsea said. "But I'd be afraid a little kid would spill stuff on that upholstered chair, even though you said the fabric is stain-resistant."

Pam nodded and nudged the chair aside. "Down to rocking horse or rocking chair. And don't feel pressured to buy either one, okay? My tender feelings won't be hurt if you buy Kristen's baby present from someone else."

I grinned. "Can I quote you on that? Never mind. I think the wicker rocking chair. They can keep it here in Chilson to use during the summers."

"Works for me," Pam said cheerfully. "Now, what do you want me to do with it?"

"Can it stay here until the baby is born?" I asked. "Afterward, I'll take it over to the house."

Pam nodded. "I'll put a Sold tag on it and put it

in the back. And I'll get a tag right now before I forget." She bustled off and Chelsea and I admired my purchase.

"This is a really cool thing to give," Chelsea said. "You're a good friend."

"Works both ways," I said. "She's done so much for me over the years. There's no way I could ever repay her."

She smiled. "Kind of what friendship is all about, isn't it?"

"Kind of what relationships are all about, too," I said gently. "Chelsea, I'm going to ask one more time and then I promise I'll stop. What went wrong between you and Ash?"

For a moment she didn't say anything. Then, finally, she sighed. "Nothing. I love him so much it hurts. But I know who I am and what I am, and it wasn't going to work. Not in the long term."

Who and what she was? All sorts of possibilities flashed through my head. She was already married. She had a congenital and inheritable disease. Or she was secretly an undercover federal agent. Or maybe she was in witness protection because she'd seen a mob assassination. "Um . . ."

Sighing again, she said, "Ash will never leave Chilson. Or at least this part of Michigan. And I've never stayed in one place for more than five years since I was eighteen. I just get itchy to move on. I like it here, I like it a lot, but I'm already wishing away November through April, waiting for warm weather and sunshine. What kind of marriage would we have if I was unhappy for six months out of twelve?"

Her voice cracked at the end and she rubbed her eyes with the heels of her hands. "And now I'm crying again. Minnie, I'm sorry, but I need to go, okay? Sorry."

I was almost crying myself as I watched her hurry through the store and outside. Poor Chelsea. Poor Ash.

But . . . at least now I knew what was wrong.

And I was going to find some way to fix it.

I banged on the back door of the Three Seasons kitchen and barged in without waiting for anyone to answer. The restaurant was officially open, but it was April and the number of cars in the parking lot was a teensy fraction of what it would be in a few weeks. In June, I wouldn't have dreamed of walking in just before the dinner rush as I would have been lambasted by Kristen's wrath or run over by a speeding waiter. Or both.

"It's just me," I called out.

"Hey, Minnie." Harvey, Kristen's longtime sous-chef, nodded at me. This was slightly worrying, because to do so he'd taken his attention away from the knife he was using to fast-chop a stack of green onions, but he didn't seem concerned, so I tried not to be. "If you're looking for Her Highness, she's in her office."

"Any chance that she's sitting down and putting her feet up?" I asked.

Misty Overbaugh, Kristen's head chef, who was almost as tall as I was, gave me a look over the top of a huge pot. "That's a joke, right?"

That hadn't been my intent, but it probably

should have been, because even before I reached Kristen's office, I could hear thumping and fluttering noises that didn't sound anything like someone sitting in a chair, resting.

I stood in the doorway and surveyed the scene. The thumping was the sound of filing cabinet drawers being slammed shut. Kristen was in the act of flinging more papers up into the air and letting them flutter down, adding to the glorious mess already on the floor.

Idly, I wondered who was going to clean it all. Certainly not Kristen herself, who hadn't seen her feet in weeks. Bending over to pick things up off the floor was a physical impossibility for her.

"This is you taking it easy?" I asked.

Kristen whipped her head around, flinging her long blond braid over one shoulder as she did so, and glared at me. "You weren't supposed to see this. I told Misty and Harvey to keep you out."

"Looks like you're going to have to fire them again."

"Already fired them three times today," she said.

"Is that a new record?" I asked.

She grinned. "Not even close. Best ever was two summers ago. Remember? Ninety degrees out and the air-conditioning broke. I think I fired everyone ten times that day. Except for me, and that was twelve."

I laughed and was reminded once again how it was that the temperamental, no-holds-barred, tongue-lashing-inclined Kristen had a staff that came back to Three Seasons year after year, like migratory birds. She was hard on them, but harder on herself, and freely admitted when she was wrong. It all just worked.

"Are you purging your files because the IRS is coming after you?"

Kristen snorted. "I hire accountants to keep me out of that kind of trouble. No, I was looking for an idea I know I wrote down for stuffed whitefish. It's filed here. Somewhere." She said the last word in a grim sort of way, and I knew she wasn't going to rest until she found what she was looking for.

"Can I help?"

"Do you know the difference between a good recipe idea and a stupid one?"

My eyebrows went up. "Of course not."

"Didn't want to assume," she said, turning her attention back to the open file drawer. "So, thanks, but no. I pay people to clean up after me. You don't need to . . . oh, hey. I remember this."

I peered over her shoulder. She was holding a plain white paper napkin with her handwriting scribbled all over. Chocolate shavings, cream cheese frosting, powdered sugar, maple syrup. Though I was pretty sure that didn't have anything to do with whitefish, you never knew with Kristen. "Anything I'd like?" I asked.

"Hmm? Oh, probably. It's a red velvet beignet I was working on. Never did get the maple flavor right." She waddled over to her desk, sat heavily, reached for a pad of paper and a pen, started writing, and was mentally gone from the current time and space.

"Okay, then," I said. "I'll see you when the baby graduates kindergarten."

She said what might have been "Sounds good," but also might have been something in French, so I left her to it and headed home.

When I got there, Rafe and Eddie were in the kitchen, starting supper. More specifically, Rafe was heating water in a big pot on the cooktop and Eddie was sitting on a stool at the kitchen island, watching Rafe's every move.

"Is he helping or criticizing?" I asked, sitting next to my cat and patting his head.

Rafe looked over his shoulder. "Give you two guesses, and the first one doesn't count."

"Mrr!"

I laughed and told Rafe about Kristen's interpretation of light work. "And then she accused me of not knowing the difference between a good recipe idea and a bad one. Can you believe it?"

"Yes," my beloved said. "Also not sure you'd recognize a real recipe from a fake one."

If he hadn't been so completely correct, I might have been annoyed. But then something rearranged in my brain. "Say," I said slowly, "you know how we think the Conti statues have something to do with Pug's death? I just thought of a way to draw the killer out of hiding."

Rafe dropped a huge handful of spaghetti into the pot of water. "Yeah, what's that?"

"What if we come up with a Conti ourselves? A fake one, I mean. See if that tempts somebody."

"Mrr." Eddie butted my arm with the top of his head.

"Sorry," I said. "Didn't mean to stop petting you."

"I don't know, Minnie," Rafe said, stirring the spaghetti. "That pottery class wasn't exactly a success, was it? And your brother told me about the coffee mug you made for your dad."

My chin went up. "It was a pencil holder. And I was only six. Besides, I'm not saying to actually make a sculpture. Just try to, I don't know, maybe sell one."

"Mrr!"

Clearly I wasn't petting Eddie the right way. Cats were sooo critical. "All Detective Inwood wants to do is find Ryan and arrest him," I said. "He hardly paid any attention to the suspect possibilities I told him about this morning. Let's see if we can think up a solid plan."

Rafe put down the pasta fork and looked at me. "Okay. But if we can't figure out a safe way to do this, you give up the idea, right?"

"Promise," I said.

But we'd find a way. I wouldn't rest until we did.

Chapter 14

Thursday morning I stood in the library parking lot, hugging myself tight against a gusting northwest wind that was chilling me to the bone, and watched Hunter zip through the preflight checklist from top to bottom.

"Shipshape, Captain," he said, standing tall and giving me a crisp salute.

I saluted back. "Carry on, First Mate. You know the schedule."

"Yes, ma'am, Captain. You can trust me, Captain, ma'am." He saluted again and opened the door.

"Hang on." Julia, who was standing next to me, frowned. "How can the newbie be first mate?"

"You're first lieutenant," I said.

She squinted at me. "I thought first mates were next in line after the captain."

Like I knew anything about naval ranks. "On the bookmobile, it's the first lieutenant. Unless we're in England, and then you're the first 'leftenant.'"

Julia brightened. "I always wanted to do a Gilbert and Sullivan show, but it never worked out because I can't carry a tune in a bucket. Hunter, do you know any of the lyrics to *H.M.S. Pinafore*?"

"Um, maybe."

I was sure he didn't, but I was equally sure that Julia, with the help of her cell phone and YouTube, would get him on board—on board? hah!—by the end of the day.

"Mrr."

"Yes, Mr. Edmeister," Julia said, "you can sing any part you'd like. Maybe you could do multiple parts? How do you feel about being cast as both Captain Corcoran and the First Lord of the Admiralty?"

"Mrr!"

"Now you've done it," I said. "He's going to want to be an admiral the rest of his life."

Julia picked up the cat carrier. "Say good-bye to your mom, Eddie. Tell her we promise to take good care of you."

"Absolutely," Hunter said. "If anything happens, we'll call right away. If he even sneezes, we'll let you know."

"Well, maybe not sneezes." Julia looked doubtful. "Sometimes he does that a lot."

I laughed and reached into the carrier to give Eddie a chin scratch. "Hope all of you have a fun day. I'll be here when you get back to help you unload."

It was all smiles and waves as they drove off, but the second they were out of my sight, I found breathing a little hard. What had I been thinking? How could I let the bookmobile go out without me?

How could I let Eddie be out there without me? How could—

My very personal version of fearmongering was interrupted by the ringing of my cell phone.

Julia. I thumbed the Accept button immediately. "What's wrong?"

"Nothing," she said. "And the odds of there being anything wrong this entire day that you've released Eddie to our custody"—I heard a faint "Mrr" from the background—"are infinitesimal. Now go forth and do your librarian thing so you can come out and play on the bookmobile next week."

She was right. I knew she was right. Even still, it was hard to think that the bookmobile would be fine without me. And then I realized something not so terribly profound. It was *better* if the bookmobile could go on without Ms. Minnie. Way better. What if I wasn't paying enough attention when crossing the street and got whacked by a truck? Or needed a leave of absence to take care of my mom or dad, post-surgery? I should be pleased that there were qualified and trusted people to take over the bookmobile's operations.

"Okay," I said. "I will. Bye, Eddie Freddie. Be as good a boy as you can."

"Say good-bye to your mom, Eddie."

Since he was a cat, the last thing my fuzzy friend was going to do was respond on cue, so I wasn't surprised when I heard a very fake "Mrr" from Hunter.

"Lame," I said, laughing, ended the call, and headed to my office, thinking about the coming day. There were two big things on my to-do list: (1) attending the monthly Friends of the Library meeting, and (2) attending the monthly Friends meeting while keeping a smile on my face throughout.

The second task was far harder than the first, because this year the Friends president was, once again, Denise Slade. For years I'd tried very hard to like the woman. There were lots of reasons to do so; she was smart, was dedicated to the library in general and the Friends in particular, and could always be relied upon to lend a hand any time volunteers were needed.

But there was something about Denise that set my teeth on edge. Polite and professional was my current mantra when dealing with her. We didn't have to be best buddies, or even friends, after all.

"Polite," I told myself later that morning as I climbed the stairs. The book sale room the Friends ran was on the second floor, and holding the meetings was a simple matter of setting up a couple of folding rectangular tables and rearranging a few chairs. "Professional," I murmured, walking into the room.

"Talking to yourself again?" Denise laughed. Loudly. "Isn't that the first sign of insanity?" she asked as she pushed the last chair into place.

I smiled. Politely. "How are you this morning?"

Denise, a stocky woman with short and tidy brown hair, rolled her eyes. "It's April in northern Michigan. Too warm for ice fishing, too cold for boating. How do you think I am?"

I'd had no idea Denise fished. I sort of remembered that her late husband had been interested in fishing and hunting, but that was about it. "Well, time will take care of that problem," I said calmly. And politely.

"You know what other problem time will take care of?" she asked. "Your director."

"Graydon?"

She put her fists on her hips. "Who else would I be talking about? If you have another director hiding around here, I'd love to know about it, because this guy has to go."

"But the Friends are getting along with Graydon just fine." At the last meeting, they'd been all sunshine and kittens.

Denise sighed heavily. "What do they know?"

I suddenly remembered that she'd been out of town during the last meeting of the Friends. "Is something wrong?"

"Wrong?" She rolled her eyes. "The only thing that's right is I just talked to everyone on the library board, and they were happy to listen, believe you me. Now I'll tell you what's wrong with Graydon, and you can agree or not, but it doesn't matter, because I know what I know."

She launched into a detailed list of slights and complaints, starting with Graydon's recommendation to change insurance companies, moving on to the way he'd quoted a native of Ohio in the last library newsletter, and continuing with the fact that he got his hair cut in a neighboring county.

I listened, but as her list went on and on, the insides of my stomach started to clench. Everything on her list was ridiculous, of course, but Denise was a forceful personality, and her opinion mattered to more than one board member.

"There is no way," she said, "that his contract will be renewed. Not if I have anything to do with it. The way I see things—and my vision is better than twenty-twenty—the board should get rid of him." She nodded sharply. "Soon."

The rest of the day, I did my best to push Denise's threats from my mind. Mostly, I succeeded, and that afternoon I stood in the back parking lot, trying to find a location that was in the sun and out of the wind. This was impossible, because it was a parking lot and there was no such thing as out of the wind, but searching for a sheltered spot had to be the reason I kept walking from one side of the lot to the other, because it couldn't be that I was nervous about an Eddie-laden bookmobile being out there in the wild without me, right? No, it couldn't be, not at all. No way was I nervous that I hadn't had a single text from Julia since they left the last bookmobile stop. They were fine and—

"There they are!" I sang out to absolutely no one, waving madly, and smiled wide when Julia waved back.

Hunter parked in the exact spot where they'd been that morning, and turned off the engine. With great restraint, I stayed where I was and didn't run around the vehicle, checking for dings, scratches, or scuffs. Everyone was back, safe and sound, and that was the only thing that really mattered.

I opened the door and Julia descended the stairs carrying a crate of books. Hunter was right behind her, carrying two crates, one atop the other. "Everything is already checked back into the system," Julia said.

"Nice," I said, climbing up into the bookmobile. That meant the only tasks left were to reshelve the materials. Some went into the bookmobile's rotating stock; others went into the main library's stock. We'd kept the two groups separate to track differences in reading habits, and though doing so was extra work, the resulting data was fascinating. Our bookmobile readers tended to check out more biographies than the brick-and-mortar library patrons, and the brick-and-mortar people tended to check out more do-it-yourself books. And the seasonal variations—

"Mrr."

"Hey, buddy." I leaned over the console and unlatched the strap that kept Eddie's carrier in place. "How was your first full bookmobile day without me?"

"Mrr!"

"Don't believe a word of it," Julia said. "Say, did you know that Hunter can carry three crates of books?"

"I did not, but that's good to know. Of course, we don't want to injure him."

"Of course not." She grinned and I made a mental note to talk to Hunter about appropriate carrying techniques and making sure he knew his limitations.

I picked up the cat carrier and Julia did the tidying-up chores. "It was a good day," she said. "And it was nice to see Sylvia Mattock out and about. I was wondering if she'd be staying north with Pug gone."

"Has she decided that already?" I asked, surprised. "It's only been, what, a little over three weeks since . . . since it happened." I carried Eddie down the stairs as levelly as possible and, outside, waited for Julia to exit.

"Oh, I don't know that she's decided long term, but she's taking a leave of absence from work to think things through."

That sounded like a good idea, especially since the weather was getting nicer by the day.

"But," Julia said, shutting the door, "you should have heard her complaining about her neighbor. Sounded almost Shakespearean. You know, vile worms, kindless villains, smiling rogues, and ill-roasted eggs."

I ignored her blatant hint for Guess the Play, a game I would never, ever win. "Hang on. What neighbor? And what did he do?"

"John somebody."

"Pinnock?"

She shrugged. "Don't remember. What I do remember is that he's cranking his stereo at three in the morning, playing marches by John Philip Sousa loud enough to make Sylvia threaten to call the sheriff's office."

"Has she?" I asked.

"Not yet, but one more time and she will." Julia laughed. "Sousa marches in the middle of the night. Bet law enforcement has never been called out for that one. Weird, isn't it?"

Yes, but no. My guess was that John Pinnock was still trying, through what my dad would call sheer cussedness, to convince Sylvia to abandon any plan to move north full time.

"What do you think, Eddie?" I asked a few minutes later as I put his carrier into my car and belted him in. "What would be worse at three in the morning, rousing marches or that heavy metal music Rafe likes so much?"

"Mrr," Eddie said, flopping against the side of the carrier.

"Yeah, you're right. Anything played loud at that time would be bad, wouldn't it? Genre isn't the point; it's the decibels. And I have a favor to ask. Are you okay with a quick stop for some investigation on the way home? It won't take long, I promise. Eddie?"

A light snore told me that a short stop wouldn't bother him in the least because Hunter and Julia had kept him awake all day.

Smiling, I drove to Gallery 45.3 and blew Eddie a kiss as I parked. I told my sleeping cat that I'd be back in a jiffy and went inside, blinking at the stark white of the walls and ceiling. The sky had darkened with cloud cover and the white seemed whiter than it had before.

"Hello, can I help . . . Oh, hey. Minnie, right?"

It was Skyler, who was again wearing a black turtleneck, black pants, and bright green shoes. I wondered if it was a uniform but hoped it wasn't. "Yes, hi."

"You were asking about Conti sculptures. Did you decide to buy one for that wedding present?" He smoothed his beard. "If you'd like, I can ask around for you. Finding a Conti would be such a pleasure that I'd cut my finder's fee by twenty-five percent."

"Thanks, but what I was really wondering was how easy it might be to fake a Conti."

"Fake?" He reared back and his face turned red. "You want to buy a forgery?"

"No, no, of course not," I said. "It's just that . . . a friend of mine heard about a Conti and the price was so low he thought it might be a forgery."

"It's all about the provenance," Skyler said. "If you're going to buy a true work of art, you need to have proper provenance. Otherwise you're wasting your money."

"Is there a market for Conti forgeries?"

He gave me a long look. "There are forgeries of any artist who has produced works that have high monetary value."

That made sense. I wasn't sure it got me any closer to a plan to tempt the murder suspects with a Conti, but at least my knowledge base was a little broader, and that had to be worth something.

"Thanks," I said. Then I nodded at a wall calendar I'd noticed hanging next to the register. It looked like a scheduling tool, with names written in each day. "My first real job, we did this same kind of thing for scheduling." I inched closer. "Kind of takes me back."

My mother was the only person I'd ever met who used a wall calendar for scheduling purposes, but my name had been on it for doctor and dentist appointments, so I was at least partially truthful.

I pointed. "Looks like you had a couple of days off there." His name had been written in blue ink across the top of four consecutive early April days, Saturday through Tuesday. Pug had been killed that Monday night. "Hope you were somewhere warm, having fun," I said, smiling.

"Yes, I'd scheduled time off to attend an art opening at my favorite Chicago gallery. It was a group show, five artists of contemporary modern street art."

Before he could tell me too much about it, I thanked him for his time and headed out.

So Skyler had an alibi. One suspect down. Four to go.

I drove the rest of the way home well below the speed limit. Partly because I always tended to drive cautiously when Eddie was in the car—he was fine on the bookmobile unless we hit a massive pothole, but he really didn't like it when the car took a corner and let me know in a vociferous manner that I was doing it all wrong—and partly because I was thinking about how to set up a Venus flytrap for the Conti thief.

"You know what that is, right?" I asked. "It's a plant with these leaves shaped like, well, a trap. But the insides of the leaves have these hairs. Bugs fly in, trigger the hairs, and *snap!*"

I heard a noise from the passenger's seat and looked just in time to catch the end of his yawn. "So nice that you're paying so much attention to me. I'm trying to teach you something, and this is the thanks . . . oh, no . . ."

"Mrr?"

I sighed. "No, it's not you. Not this time." My moan had been one of sadness, not irritation, because there, walking down the sidewalk, was Deputy Ash Wolverson. He had his hands in his pockets and was moving at a snail's pace, head down and shoulders slumped. This, from a guy who regularly told me to sit up straight or I'd lose what little bone density I had.

Then I sighed again, because there, on the other side of the street, was Chelsea. Her posture and attitude mirrored Ash's and it didn't take much detecting to conclude that they'd seen each other.

"Someone has to do something," I murmured, watching Chelsea wipe her face with her fingertips.

"Mrr!"

"Well, yes, I know that someone has to be me, but I can't come up with any ideas to fix things. There's no fairy dust to sprinkle on Chelsea that will ease the pain of winters that last forever." I glanced up at the low gray clouds that didn't show so much as a hint of blue and averted my eyes. "And there's no magic wand to wave and suddenly make Ash eager to leave his career, family, and all the friends he's ever known."

"Mrr," Eddie said.

"Thanks for the vote of confidence. Let me know if you have any ideas, okay?"

By this time we were at the house and I was opening the back door. Rafe looked up from the bags of groceries on the kitchen island. "You need ideas?" he asked. "I have lots, especially if you're looking for suggestions on how to unstick bubble gum from the underside of desks."

"Chewing gum is still a thing?" I set Eddie's carrier down gently and opened the door. Instead of zipping out, like a normal cat, he flopped on his side and looked up at me, opening his mouth in a silent "Mrr."

"You are so weird," I told him. "What I need ideas for," I said, straightening and moving to give Rafe a hug, "is how to resolve the Ash and Chelsea conundrum."

Rafe squeezed me and kissed my forehead. "Big college word."

"Well, it's a big problem." I related what I'd

learned, and, after a moment, he folded me into his arms for a long and comforting embrace.

"Sometimes," he said, "there isn't any way to fix things. Sometimes the best thing to do is walk away."

I knew that, of course I knew that, but that didn't mean I had to like it. Or, in this particular case, even accept it. At least not yet. "There has to be a way," I said, and even to my ears I sounded like a stubborn toddler.

Rafe laughed and kissed me again. "If there is, you'll figure it out. But promise me one thing? Keep me out of it."

"Some friend you are," I said, breaking out of the warmth of his arms.

"On the contrary." He grinned. "I'm trying to keep the friends I have, and the best way to do that is stay out of their love lives."

He had a good point, and in most cases I wholeheartedly agreed with him. But this was different, although I kept trying, and failing, to come up with reasons why the entire time I packed up a box for Ryan and drove out to the seasonal road near Breece Farms, and all through the hike back to the cabin.

The last time I'd been there, I'd told Ryan to expect me back on Thursday evening so I didn't frighten or startle him. Even still, as I neared the cabin, the door was flung open and he ran pell-mell out into the woods.

I sighed. Nothing made a person look as guilty as rapid flight. "It's Minnie!" I yelled. "I come bearing gifts of great joy!"

He slowed, then jogged toward me. "Hey," he said, not out of breath at all. Ah, youth. "Sorry about that. It's just now that it's getting warmer, more people are out here. Way more than I thought there'd be."

"Mushrooms," I said, nodding. "This is a good spot for morels. Saw a couple on my way in."

"Oh, man." Ryan sagged. "Never thought about that."

Hunting for morel mushrooms—the easiest of all mushrooms to identify—was a strong northern Michigan tradition, and the locations of prime morel finds were handed down from generation to generation. Lots of restaurateurs, including Kristen, paid a hefty amount per pound for the spring delicacy, and so did vendors at farmers markets.

Ryan glanced around, and I wasn't sure if he was looking for a new place to hide or if he was checking for mushroomers. "My mom might have found a place for me to stay for a while," he said. "But it won't be ready for a couple of weeks."

"You won't need it," I said confidently. Or at least with all the assurance I could summon. "We're close to finding the killer."

"Really?" His eyes opened wide and the hope on his face almost destroyed me.

"We're almost there," I said, trying to sound confident. "Just be patient a little longer, okay?"

After a long second, he nodded. "Okay. I can hang on for a while. But, Minnie, please don't take too long. I'm not sure how much longer I can do this." He smiled, but it wasn't a very good one.

"It'll work out," I said.

But both of us knew it might not.

* * *

With Skyler out as a suspect due to his solid alibi, I turned my attention to the others on my list. Charlie Seller, the nephew. Ian Breece, the farmer. Keegan Kolb, Ryan's upstairs neighbor. John Pinnock, the Mattocks' cranky neighbor.

"What do you think?" I asked.

It was the next evening, and Rafe and Eddie and I were in the backyard, enjoying the warmth brought to us by a kindly southwest breeze that had pushed the cloud cover away. Up above us now was a deeply blue sky that conjured memories of jumping into a lake off the end of a dock, summer art fairs, and dripping ice cream cones.

"I think lots of things," Rafe said. The humans were sitting in Adirondack chairs we'd moved to the sunny corner of the yard, and the feline part of the trio was flopped at our feet, belly up to the last of the day's sunshine. Rafe was edging his left foot forward to the part of Eddie that was closest—his tail—with a clear intent to annoy.

"You realize that isn't going to end well, right?" I asked, watching.

Rafe gave me a "What?" look, but didn't stop his attack. Sure enough, the moment he trapped the tip of Eddie's tail with his foot, Eddie instantaneously curled himself into a defensive ball. His paws clutched at Rafe's running shoe and his pointed teeth sank into the layers of nylon.

"Ow!"

Rafe jerked his foot back and Eddie sprang to his feet and galloped to the safety of the back deck railing, where he sat up tall with perfect posture, his tail lashing back and forth and back and forth.

"Rotten cat," Rafe muttered, peering at his shoe's new puncture marks.

"Seems to me you got what you deserved."

"Well, sure, but that doesn't mean I have to like it."

I rolled my eyes. "Yet in five minutes, he'll be back, up on your lap and purring."

"We have an understanding," Rafe said contentedly. "Right, Mr. Ed?"

"Mrr."

Human or feline, men were men. "Back to the thinking thing. What I meant was, what do you think about the suspect list?"

"Right. We're down to four, what with Skyler's alibi and assuming you've given up the ridiculousness of including Jenica Thomas on the list."

I had, but . . . "You know," I said slowly. "She met up with Pug right before he was killed. It's a long shot, but it's possible he told her something that didn't mean anything to her or Hal Inwood, but might to us."

"Let's go find out." Rafe heaved himself out of the low-slung chair and offered me his hand. "It's Friday night, which means that in forty-five minutes, Jenica will be at Moose Jaw Junction for the fish fry. You know, that place at Larks Lake? We need to eat, so let's take advantage of this happy coincidence and go on a little road trip."

I let him pull me to my feet. "How is it you happen to know her eating habits?"

"Genius," he said, tapping his chest. "Can't believe you forgot."

Just under an hour later, after we'd encouraged Eddie into the house and driven into the heart of

Emmet County, we parked on the roadside strip of gravel that was the parking lot, and went inside, hand in hand.

Moose Jaw Junction had gone by various names over the decades, and the interior had likely seen a few revisions, but I was willing to bet its classic Up North feel hadn't changed since the day it opened. These days, there was pine paneling on the bottom half of the walls and green paint above, and the long bar did indeed have a moose jaw hung above. It was the kind of place that sponsored softball teams and welcomed snowmobilers, and the friendly atmosphere was almost palpable.

"Niswander!" a male voice called out. "You here to play pool or to eat?"

Rafe held my hand up high and kept walking. "Eating. Catch you later, Charlie."

"Who was that?" I asked, looking around for a familiar face and seeing none.

"No idea," he said easily. "Used to play pool here a lot, though. And there's Jenica. With two spots open next to her. What do you think?"

He was nodding at the long bar. A woman about my age, with short dark hair that looked as if it always did what it was told, sat at the far end, turned slightly so that she half faced the door.

The one time I'd met the conservation officer, it had been outside in early December, and she'd been dressed so appropriately in cold weather gear that getting an impression of her physical attributes beyond the fact that she was taller than me—such a surprise!—had been impossible.

As Rafe and I slid into the tall chairs to her left, I noted her trim figure, and if the muscles she was using to raise her pint were any indication, she was also fit and strong, something I appreciated in law enforcement officers.

"Hello, Rafe," she said, then looked at me. "We've met."

I blinked. It had been once. Almost four years ago. "Yes," I said. "At the Jurco River dam."

"Yes." She nodded. "I recall. You were interested in the accuracy of the recordings, but I don't believe I learned your name."

"Minnie Hamilton," I said, holding out my hand across the front of Rafe. "Nice to meet you."

"She's my fiancée." Rafe slung his arm around my shoulders. "We're getting married in September."

"Congratulations." Jenica nodded at us. "Although the more correct response is felicitations."

"Well, thanks, either way." I smiled. "Or should it be both ways?"

Jenica seemed to be seriously considering the question, so I was happy when the bartender came over. We told her no menus were needed as we'd be having the fish fry, and she nodded and asked Jenica if she wanted a refill on her cola. She did not, and the bartender nodded and said our orders would be up in about ten minutes.

"Mine took twelve," Jenica said, forking off a piece of fried fish and dipping it in tartar sauce.

Rafe and I exchanged a glance. Now was as good a time as any. "You probably don't know," I said, "but I work at the library. I drive the bookmobile."

Jenica didn't say anything, so I plunged on.

"Anyway, one of my favorite patrons is Pug Mattock. Or, he *was*, because he was killed a couple of weeks ago."

Still, Jenica didn't say a word.

Getting a bit desperate, I started to babble. "He was on the bookmobile a few days before he died, and he said he was going to meet you, to report some poaching he'd seen. Turkeys, I think it was. Anyway, I was wondering if when you'd talked to him, if he'd said something or if you'd seen something that might help figure out who killed him and—"

"There was nothing." Jenica stood, pulled a wallet from her coat pocket, and tossed cash down on the bar. "It's time for me to go."

Then, without another word, she fled.

Chapter 15

W as that weird?" I asked, looking through the restaurant's window as Jenica got into her small SUV and backed out onto the road.

Rafe, who'd been taking a first drink of his beer, set the mug down and said, "For most people, yes. Not so much for Jenica."

"It sure seemed to me that she didn't like the questions I was asking, so she ran away."

"That's because you don't know that Jenica is a die-hard hockey fan. Tonight is the last game in the conference playoffs and there's no way she's going to miss the national anthem, let alone the puck drop."

So it was sports weirdness. Just as mysterious to me, but common enough. "Well," I said, "let's move on to the next suspect on the list. Charlie Seller." I sat up. "Say, you said hello to a Charlie on our way in. Is there any chance that's—"

Rafe shook his head. "How long have you known me? When I can't remember someone's name, I always call them Charlie. Works for all genders."

"You really are a genius," I said admiringly. "No, I guess I never noticed that particular habit of yours. I suppose it's too late for me to pick up on it?"

"Way. Get your own trick." He toasted me with his mug. "But tell you what. I might have a way to get some info about that real Charlie. What are you doing tomorrow morning?"

And so, the next morning, I found myself at the Round Table, sitting next to Rafe and across from Connor, a college friend of his from back in his undergraduate days at Northern Michigan University. We'd been provided coffee and ordered our breakfasts, and I was sitting back, listening to the two of them talk about events I'd never heard about and people I'd never met.

After they'd laughed loud and long about an incident involving duct tape, plastic wrap, and a doorway, Connor wiped his eyes and looked at me. "Sorry, Minnie. You're probably already tired of these stories."

"Turns out I rarely hear any stories that make him look bad," I said, smiling. "So some of these are new to me."

Connor leaned forward. "Well, then, you definitely need to hear about the time—"

"Speaking of time," Rafe interrupted. "Don't you have a lot to do today?"

He certainly did. I'd learned the night before that Connor and his wife had just purchased a lakefront cottage not too far away. A fixer-upper, apparently, which was why he'd contacted Rafe and asked for advice. Connor was north this weekend to work on the cottage and try to get it livable before summer.

"That's right." Connor snapped his fingers. "I'm here to work. Ten minutes with you, Niswander, and I forget all about my responsibilities."

Rafe nodded. "Glad I could help. But Minnie and I do have ulterior motives."

"Figured." Connor grinned. "Knew you wouldn't buy my breakfast for old times' sake."

"Not a chance. We're looking for info on a fellow orthodontist."

Because I'd also learned the night before, on the drive back from the Moose Jaw, that Rafe's friend had started as a biology major, become interested in dentistry, and eventually enrolled at University of Detroit Mercy to get the education and training needed to become an orthodontist.

Connor added more sugar to his coffee. "Yeah, I know," he said, catching my half smile. "Sugar is bad for your teeth, coffee stains, blah blah blah. Do as I say, not as I do, kids. What kind of info do you want?"

"Anything you're comfortable telling us," I said. "We don't want you to break any confidences"—a complete lie, because if he knew something about Charlie that led to Pug's killer, I didn't care what doctor-patient confidentiality rules he broke, but I couldn't say that out loud—"but anything you can tell us about Charlie Seller would be helpful. You probably know him as Charles."

"Seller?" Connor looked off into the distance. "Yeah, I know him."

"Is he a friend?" Rafe asked.

Connor shook his head. "We've met at conferences, is all. My practice is too far away from his to be a competitor."

"What's he like?" I asked. "We're asking because . . . because he's the nephew of a friend of mine, and she's recently widowed, no children of her own. I just want to make sure a family member will be looking after her." All true, but not all of the truth.

"One of my business partners," Connor said slowly, "is a good friend of his."

Rafe and I exchanged a look. "But . . . ?" I asked.

"It's just rumor, okay? But what I heard was Charles wanted to be the president of the state orthodontist association. It usually goes to orthodontists close to retirement. We have an executive director who does all the real work; this is mostly a figurehead thing."

I nodded. So did Rafe.

"Anyway, the story I heard was that Charles wined and dined enough of the members to get the votes. Winner was announced at the end of the conference, and the guy everyone had originally thought was going to be president looked like he'd taken a bite of the sourest apple ever. Charles smiled and said better luck next year, but the guy died that fall. Heart attack."

"How sad," I murmured. It was just like Melinda had said: Charlie Seller tended to get his own way. And now we'd learned that if his way didn't come easily, there was precedent that he'd use sheer brute force. Not the violent kind, but force nonetheless.

Charlie was definitely staying on the suspect list.

I'd scheduled myself to work from ten to two, so after I finished eating, I said good-bye to Connor and kissed Rafe.

"Have fun," I said to them both.

"Fun?" Rafe gave me a shocked look. "This is going to be work, not fun."

I was not fooled. "Connor, didn't you say the most important thing to get done before your Fourth of July family reunion was to replace the kitchen cabinets?"

"Um, that's right," he said.

"You're doing demolition today, correct? Which always takes longer than expected, so you're going to get started right away, right?"

Rafe and Connor exchanged a glance. "She's on to us," Connor said. "My wife will be thrilled."

My fiancé beamed. "Told you I was going to marry a smart one. Do I know how to pick 'em, or what?"

Even Connor, a man I'd known for less than an hour, knew that hadn't gone over well. "Ah, Rafe, buddy, you might want to restate that comment."

Buddy Rafe squinted up at me. "Over the top, wasn't it? Sorry. Got a little carried away. Connor here is a bad influence. Always has been."

I smiled at him sweetly. "Blaming someone else is making it worse. Just remember what they say about paybacks. See you tonight, okay? Nice meeting you, Connor."

Outside, the fresh April air whooshed in my face as I walked up to the library. "Refreshing," I murmured, as I leaned against it. "Invigorating. Exhilarating. Revitalizing. Fortifying, even."

"Are you channeling a thesaurus?"

I looked up—because my head had been down against the wind—and saw the board president standing in front of the library's front door.

"Oh, hey, Trent. No, I was just trying to think of words to describe the wind and . . . actually, I guess I kind of was being a thesaurus." I laughed and took out my key to unlock the door. "What are you doing here on a Saturday morning?"

"Actually, I was hoping to talk to you. In private. Do you have a few minutes?"

Having your boss's boss ask for a secret meeting was not a good way to start the morning. "Sure." I opened the door, let us both in, and locked it behind us, because the library technically didn't open for another hour. "Coffee?"

He nodded, and we made our amiable way to the kitchen. Even on a Saturday morning, and even in jeans and a plain zip fleece sweatshirt, Trent looked polished and professional. He looked exactly like what he was, a retired professional out to do good and give back to the community, even if Chilson wasn't the community where he'd spent most of his adult life.

Trent was a downstater, and an attorney to boot, but I was learning to overlook all that. He was a decent guy and I needed to get over my knee-jerk reaction of thinking that extremely good-looking men, especially ones above a certain age, were condescending jerks who couldn't accept a good idea unless it came from them. Or someone who looked a lot like them.

I pulled out a filter and started measuring out coffee. "Cream is in the fridge," I said over my shoulder. "Mugs are over there and sugar is on the counter."

After a short second, the refrigerator door opened, and I felt an odd sense of satisfaction. While it was possible he'd assumed I would fix his coffee for him, he'd also quickly adapted to the very clear circumstance that I wasn't about to. Yes, Trent was a decent human being, and if I ever got the opportunity, I'd thank both his mother and his wife.

We watched the coffee drip down in a stream that always seemed too slow, and eventually we were rewarded with a full pot. Trent took the handle, filled my mug, and then his own.

"Cheers," he said, toasting me, and we both breathed in the magical, life-giving scent and gave identical *mmms* of pleasure.

My eyebrows went up. "Didn't know you were a coffee freak."

"Only since law school." He smiled, and what had up until then been purely a professional relationship between board president and hired hand became something a little bit more.

"So you said you wanted to talk to me?" I asked, leading the way to my office. He settled in the guest chair and I sat in my desk chair. "Is something wrong?" But I couldn't imagine what. Chain of command dictated that he talk to Graydon first, and Graydon would talk to me.

Trent sipped his coffee. "I believe you know that Graydon's first performance review is coming up. Late, because so many board members went south last winter. Our bylaws allow us to have a certain amount of virtual attendance, but none of us wanted to do Graydon's review remotely."

Was that good or was that bad? Did it even matter? I clutched my mug tightly, because Trent hadn't asked a question, and I was going to keep my mouth shut until he did.

"It's come to my attention," Trent said, "that the Friends of the Library are not complete fans of Graydon."

"That's because—" I bit off my words. So much for staying quiet.

"Because?" he asked, leaning forward.

How to say this without sounding snippy and snarky? "The president of the Friends," I said carefully, "has a tendency to assume that the decisions of others are personal when they are, in fact, not personal at all."

Trent waited. And waited. When another glacial age came and went and I didn't say anything more, he finally nodded. "Thank you, Minnie. The board will, naturally, have to consider the comments of the Friends during Graydon's review."

"Oh. Um, sure. I understand. It's just . . ." I struggled for the right thing to say. "Can you please make sure the board is listening to what all the Friends think? Not just one person?"

"We have to trust that the president speaks for the entire group," Trent said.

Even if it's Denise? For a second I was afraid I'd blurted that out loud, but there was no reaction from Trent, so I assumed that I'd managed to keep the thought inside.

Trent finished his coffee, thanked me for my time, and left, carrying his mug with him.

"What was that all about?" Holly stood in my doorway, frowning in Trent's direction. "What's he doing here on a Saturday morning? Don't tell me he's checking up on us."

"He left something in the conference room," I said, making it sound like a question, then quickly hunted for a new subject. "Say, did I tell you what Eddie did to the toilet paper in the downstairs bathroom?"

Holly laughed. "This I can't wait to hear."

She plopped down in the chair Trent had vacated. I told her the story of the shredding, and most of me was paying attention to what I was saying, but a small part of me—small but mighty—was worried about Graydon and his future at the library. I had to do something to help. But what?

I worked long past the time I'd scheduled myself to work, no doubt earning another black mark from some omniscient record-keeping librarian, the same one that metaphorically whacked my knuckles with a ruler whenever I thought my duties at the library or on the bookmobile were so important that no one else could do them.

"The library will not fall apart without me," I said as I stood up from my desk. At least not between Saturday afternoon and Monday morning. In truth, I knew the library would hum along merrily without me even if an alien spacecraft sucked me up and took me away. Well, maybe not merrily, because surely someone would care that I was suddenly gone. But everyone was replaceable, a thought that was simultaneously comforting and horrifying. Comforting, to know that the library and bookmobile would go on. Horrifying, to know that someday no one who worked in the library would recognize my name.

To shake off the existential fears that had suddenly descended, I decided to walk home by a slightly different route, and by the time I'd gone half a block, I began to feel better, because even if the library eventually forgot about me, there was no way it would forget about Eddie.

And just like that, I was cheerful again. I made a mental note to tell Eddie all about it when I got home and sauntered down the street, swinging my arms and practically whistling. It was spring, the air wasn't freezing cold, the sun was mostly out, and I had a good shot at a sideways type of immortality.

"Is that you, Minnie?" a voice called.

I turned and saw Bianca Sims in a nearby parking lot, shutting the door of a shiny black SUV. The intelligent and energetic Bianca was one of the most successful real estate agents in the area. She and Mitchell Koyne, a former slacker who'd lived in his sister's attic for years but was now managing a downtown toy store with great competence, had married not long ago. To everyone's surprise, the marriage seemed strong and solid, which just proved that you never knew about people.

"Hey, Bianca," I said. "Haven't seen you in ages."

She grinned. "You didn't hear? I kidnapped Mitchell a few weeks ago. Dragged him down to Florida. We just got back the other day."

"Mitchell? In Florida?" I closed my eyes, trying to summon the image. Failed completely and opened my eyes to see Bianca, still grinning.

"Hard to wrap your mind around, isn't it?" She laughed. "He'd never been outside the state, let alone all the way down there. He was kicking and screaming the whole trip, but after a few days, he looked around and realized it wasn't so bad."

"Good to hear," I said faintly, closing off my

mind forever to the image of the very tall and quite wide Mitchell anywhere close to a beach.

"You headed to the farmers market?" Bianca nodded at city hall, where there was a slow but steady stream of people both walking in empty-handed and walking out laden with bags of all shapes and sizes.

Though I'd heard that an indoor farmers market in the lobby of city hall had started this last November, running through April, somehow I'd always managed to miss every one. "Well . . ."

"This is the last Saturday," Bianca said. "Won't be much here, but there will be something. Always nice to have something fresh, isn't it?"

A fresh-baked pizza delivered to our front door sounded really nice to me, but Bianca, sensing my hesitation, went into full-on sales mode. "Minnie, I know you're not big on cooking, and there's nothing wrong with that, but aren't you curious about what our area growers have to offer?"

Because sometimes it's just easier to go along—and besides, once inside, it would be easier for me to escape—I let Bianca tow me along. Three steps in the front door, I was glad she'd been so convincing.

"Wow, I had no idea," I said, scanning the variety of vendors. Maple syrup, morel mushrooms, and honey. Fresh pasta, root vegetables, fresh fish, and I was pretty sure I smelled fresh cinnamon rolls. "This is fantastic!"

"Told you." Bianca elbowed me. "I'm off to see if any of the hoop-house folks have spring lettuce. Talk to you later!"

Since I didn't want to miss anything, I planned out a careful route through the spread of tables, shelving units, and booths. Once I had a path mentally mapped out, I turned right.

"Hi, Minnie."

I looked up from a display of more hummus flavors than I'd ever imagined existed. "Hey, Sylvia. It's good to see you." And it was. "Coming along with reading *Wolf Hall*?"

"Not as far as I'd like," she said, smiling. "I have good intentions, but . . ." She shrugged, her happy face sliding away. "Some days are harder than others, that's all." She half smiled. "I miss Pug. I really, really miss him."

I touched her sleeve but didn't say anything. Nothing I could say would help.

"Anyway." She shook her head. "All this isn't getting the jam made, as my grandmother would say. I had a list of things I wanted, but I left it at home on the kitchen counter."

I laughed. "So glad I'm not the only one who does that."

"You are definitely not," Sylvia said firmly. "I'm trying to blame it on sleep deprivation, though. That man, I tell you!"

"What man?" I asked, then clued in. "Your neighbor? John Pinnock?"

"For my sins." She harrumphed. "Now he's up before dawn, running a leaf blower just outside my bedroom window. A very loud, gas-powered leaf blower. He must have purchased it for the high decibel level."

Huh. So John Pinnock was continuing his annoy-Sylvia-into-leaving campaign. "Have you called the sheriff's office, or talked to the township? Maybe there's a noise ordinance."

Grimacing, she said, "I keep thinking he'll get tired of it and give up. But if not . . ." She gave a half smile. "I'm developing a plan."

I deeply wanted to know details but figured I'd be better off not knowing. Plausible deniability and all that. She asked for recommendations for new or upcoming releases, and we talked books for a few minutes, then parted amicably.

A few minutes later, when I was standing inside the fabric walls of a booth selling jams, jellies, and salsa, I heard a quiet male voice say, "Did you hear about the Breece Farm?"

My ears practically swiveled. *Please,* I thought desperately, *please don't let me hear about a discovery of Ryan's cabin. Please . . .*

"No," said another voice. "But I haven't seen Ian or Felicia in weeks."

"Remember their new well?" asked First Voice. "It went bad last fall, right? They had to spend thousands to get a new one drilled, to get down to the good aquifer."

"Sure," said Second Voice. "I remember. What was it, eight hundred feet down?"

"More than. Well, now their second well went out. You know, the one they use to irrigate the hoop houses and water the stock?"

"Oh, man," said Second Voice. "They were scraping to find the money last fall. Now what are they going to do? If they can't irrigate the hoop houses, they'll lose their spring and early summer product."

Both voices moved off. I peeked around the end of the booth and saw the backs of two thirtyish men in brown canvas jackets and jeans as they walked away.

I felt a pang of empathy for Ian and Felicia Breece. Two expensive projects when you didn't have the money for one was going to hurt their finances badly. How were they going to raise the money?

But I was avoiding the real question, so I took a deep breath and faced it.

Was one of the money-raising methods stealing a Conti statue? And, when that proved lucrative, stealing it a second time? Only getting caught in the action and committing murder?

Chapter 16

Back home, I wandered from room to room, dusting a little, tidying a little, and thinking a lot.

"John Pinnock," I told Eddie, who was sometimes following me so he could criticize everything I did and who was sometimes curled up in a big Eddie ball wherever the sun was hitting something upon which he could flop himself. "Still a suspect. And he's driving Sylvia nuts, so doesn't that mean he's really vested in keeping anyone from living next to him year-round?"

Eddie, at that point lounging on the wood floor just inside a parallelogram of sun, yawned.

"Not helpful," I said through my own subsequent and inevitable yawn. "And there's Charlie Seller. He wants the cottage for himself and he likes to get what he wants. Ian . . ." I sighed. "It really doesn't look good for Ian and—and what are you doing?"

Less than two seconds previously, Eddie had

been flopped flat on the floor. Now he was scampering around the living room, bouncing frenetically from couch to chair to ottoman to end table.

"Watch it, will you?"

Since Eddie was a cat, my question was essentially rhetorical. Yes, he'd watch it, because he was fleet of foot and very concerned about his image. But would he be careful not to damage anything? Not so much.

"You're troubling me," I told him, as he continued his pinball-like actions. "Don't wear yourself out, okay? You're not as young as you used to be."

He stopped and glared at me. "Mrr!"

"Sorry, but it's true. None of us are. Aging is a fact of life."

"Mrr!" he said, and bolted into the dining room, a room that doubled as our library.

"You are so weird," I muttered, following just to see what he was up to. Of course he got up on the dining table when we weren't home, but it would be nice if he stayed off it when a human was in the same room.

I got there just in time to see my fuzzy friend crawl on top of a low bookshelf. "Seriously?" I asked. "You honestly think you're going to fit behind those books?"

Though I'd expected a "Mrr" in response, what I got was the sight of Eddie's hind legs flailing in the air as his front half tried to slide behind a shelf full of oversized books. Atlases and nature photography, mostly, with a smattering of art and architecture.

Eddie made a noise that wasn't quite a "mrr" and disappeared from view.

"Hope you don't think I'm going to get you out," I said. "You got yourself in, you can get yourself— Hey! Quit that!"

Because my cat was squirming around behind the books and pushing them onto the floor, where they made quiet thudding noises as they hit the area rug.

"Did you really have to?" I asked, crouching down to pick up Ansel Adams's *Yosemite and the Range of Light* (Rafe's), the *Oxford Atlas of the World* (a Christmas present to us from Rafe's parents), and *The Art of Robert Bateman* (mine). "And by that I mean crawling back there at all, let alone . . . Okay, that's enough already."

"Mrr!" Eddie squirmed out through the gap he'd created, used my shoulder as a launching pad, and thundered up the stairs.

"Cats," I muttered, and picked up Eddie's final selection, which was *The Architecture Pop Up Book* by Anton Radevsky, which I'd purchased on a whim at the local used bookstore. Since I hadn't looked through it in a while, I sat on the floor and opened it, admiring the Parthenon and wondering if I'd ever see the Acropolis complex in person. Because it wasn't just the Parthenon; it was the theater of Dionysus, and the temples, and the statues . . . which were sculptures.

It suddenly seemed like there were sculptures everywhere, but I supposed it was a frame-of-reference thing. Like thinking about buying a certain pair of boots; suddenly you saw people everywhere wearing them.

So if there were even more sculptures . . . if there were more Contis . . .

My brain did one of those *snap* things, and surged back to the idea that Rafe and I had started to work on, but never completed. A fake Conti. Did it make sense to create a fake Conti as a lure for the killer? Or—new idea!—how about a borrowed one? Maybe we could use the promise of a Conti and not create a fake one at all, but if we could borrow one, wouldn't that be even better?

I pulled out my phone, found Keegan Kolb's number, and started texting.

"Mrr!"

I watched Eddie as he galloped past me and into the kitchen. "No idea what you're trying to tell me, pal," I said. "Maybe you should work on your communication skills."

"Mrr!"

Minnie: *Hey, Keegan. Minnie Hamilton. Remember the other day, I mentioned a Conti sculpture?*

Keegan (after a pause): *You said it was stolen—did someone find it? Those things can be super expensive.*

Minnie: *That's what I was wondering. It sounded like you knew a lot about Vittorio Conti, so I was hoping if you ever came across one for sale, that you'll let me know. It might help track down who stole the one from that cottage, and keep Ryan's name out of it.*

Keegan: *LOL only things I know about Conti came from an art appreciation class I had to take in college—Prof LOVED all things Conti. Didn't get it myself, but I'm a software engineer.*

Minnie: *Okay, thanks.*

Keegan: *Any closer to clearing Ryan?*

Minnie (after a pause): *Some. Will let you know when I know more.*

I started to thumb off the phone but saw the three dots of an incoming text. I waited, but they faded away to invisibility. Whatever Keegan had been going to say, she'd changed her mind.

"Mrr." Eddie bumped my elbow with his head.

I pulled him onto my lap and snugged him tight. "Yeah, I know. We need to find Pug's killer."

Too many people had already been hurt. We needed to get Ryan in from the cold before something else happened.

On Sunday, after attending church with Rafe's parents and a quick meal of tacos, courtesy of reheated frozen taco meat, tomatoes and olives from the grocery store, and some of the lettuce I'd bought at the farmers market the day before, Rafe and I waved good-bye to a snoring Eddie and drove north to Ryan's cabin.

"Wonder what the cabin was called before Ryan moved in," I said as Rafe parked the car. After squinting at the sky, I reached into the pocket on the back of the passenger's seat and took out the umbrella. Better to have and not need than need and not have, I always figured. Or at least that's what I figured when I remembered to pack something that I might not need.

"You want a real answer or a fun answer?" Rafe took my hand as we started down the narrow road and swung it high, back and forth. "Never mind, I know you want the fun version. How about—"

We both stopped abruptly. Two men were emerging

out of the woods, coming from the direction of the cabin.

Rafe gripped my hand tight. I edged closer to him, the two of us projecting one solid front. Not an even front, because one side of us was much bigger than the other, but solid nonetheless. And it wasn't that the men were threatening in any way, but . . . still.

"Afternoon," Rafe said casually.

The two were now close enough for me to see their faces. I didn't recognize either one, and from Rafe's relatively formal greeting, I was sure he didn't know them, either.

"Hey," said the guy on the left. The other nodded. They were both fortyish, dressed in jeans, light hiking boots, and smooth nylon jackets with wraparound sunglasses on their heads. They also each carried a bag partially filled with small and lumpy things. Morel hunters, for sure, who had a distinct downstate flavor.

"Looks like a decent haul," Rafe said, nodding at the bags. "Keeping or selling?"

The guys exchanged a glance. "There's not much out there," said Left Guy. "Weather hasn't been warm enough."

Though they appeared pleasant enough, I felt a swell of hostility. I hefted the plastic bag of groceries I'd packed for Ryan. "We're looking for a place to have a picnic. Know of a good spot?"

Instantly, the hostile aura subsided to mere wariness. "No," Right Guy said. "Sorry."

"Thanks anyway," I said cheerfully.

"That's right." Rafe slung an arm around my shoulders. "We're just hoping for a quiet place to

eat and, you know, do whatever might come next."
I glanced up in time to see him give a huge wink.

"Sorry, pal," Left Guy said, smirking. "We saw
probably half a dozen people out here in the last
couple of hours. And there's more." He nodded behind us, and we turned to see a family of four hiking our way. Mom, Dad, one child about ten,
another maybe thirteen.

The Guys left, and we exchanged greetings with
the family, who Rafe knew from the school and I
sort of knew from the library. We wished them
good luck with their mushroom hunting and they
headed into the woods, in the direction opposite
Ryan's cabin.

I watched them go. Troubling thoughts tumbled
around in my head. "If there are this many people
out here now . . ."

Just then, a whispered voice came from behind a
scrubby clump of cedars. "Are they gone?"

Rafe and I turned and saw Ryan. I looked left
and right. "All clear," I said. "But it might not be in
five minutes."

"Yeah, I know." Ryan laughed, but it wasn't a
very good laugh. More like the worst ever. "Turns
out I'm trying to hide in the county's prime morel
mushroom hunting grounds. Who knew?"

I glanced at Rafe, Mr. Lifelong Resident Except
for College. He shrugged. "Morels aren't my thing."

"We'll find you a new spot," I said, although I
had no clue how to go about doing so. "Most of the
mushroom traffic is probably weekend, right? Get
through the rest of today and you'll be fine, because
we'll have a new place for you by Friday. Or
maybe . . ." I paused, then forged ahead. "Or maybe

we'll have found Pug's killer by then. We're getting closer."

"Yeah?"

The question itself was hopeful, but his slack body language suggested otherwise.

"We're eliminating suspects," I said confidently. "Skyler Ellison was out of town. And Keegan only knew about Conti because of a required course in college."

His brow furrowed. "Why would—"

"Never mind," I cut in. "What it means is we're sure Keegan is in the clear. That leaves three, and if we eliminate one a day, we'll figure out the killer before Thursday."

It all sounded weak, even to my own ears, and I didn't dare look at Rafe because I knew his disbelief would be obvious. The only option was to keep Ryan's attention on me by going on as if I knew what I was talking about.

"So," I said easily, "we're down to three. Let's review, okay?" I ticked them off on my fingers and talked about Charlie Seller, Ian Breece, and John Pinnock. "We have ideas for looking into all of them," I said. "But if you think of any—"

"Someone's coming," Rafe said, tilting his head in the direction of the road. "Here." He handed Ryan the bag of groceries and did the shoulder-clasp thing. "Hang in there, bud, okay?"

"Sure. Thanks, you two. I owe you a lot." He nodded and melted away into the woods without a sound.

"He's getting good at disappearing," I said, hoping he didn't get too good at it. Because I was suddenly afraid that Thursday he'd be gone, headed for a lifetime of running and hiding.

"We'll find the killer," I said a little louder. "We promise."

But the only response was the sound of the wind.

That evening I wandered into the Three Seasons kitchen with one main objective. Well, two, if you counted trying to convince Kristen to quit working until after the baby was born, but I'd pretty much given up on that.

"I mean," I asked the room in general, "why waste my energy?"

Harvey, who was sorting tiny squares of something green into good piles (squares the same size and therefore worthy of plating) and bad piles (uneven squares and thus suitable only for cooking) flicked me a quick look and went back to the task at hand. "You got to pace yourself," he said.

"Absolutely." Misty, at one of the cooktops, nodded in my direction as she picked up a sauté pan and gave its contents a flip. "Life's a marathon, not a sprint. Go all out now and you won't have anything left for the end."

"Good advice," I said. "Any chance Kristen has hung up her chef's hat for the day? Gone home, even?"

Two sets of eyes rolled simultaneously.

It had been a vain hope. I sighed, dodged a tray-wielding waiter, and headed back to Kristen's office, where the woman herself was standing in front of the room's tiny window, peering outside.

Since the window's view was of the back corner of the parking lot, this seemed odd. I walked in and stood next to her. All I saw was what I'd expected to see: a slice of empty parking lot because this part of the lot only filled up in summer. Though Kristen, at almost a foot taller than me, had a different vantage point, there really wasn't anything else to see.

"Um, what are we doing?" I asked.

"Thinking."

She didn't say anything else for about a year, so I eventually asked, "About what?"

For a long moment, she stayed silent. Then: "Do you realize I'm about to give birth?"

I glanced at her bulging midsection. "I'd gotten that impression."

"Like any second now?"

Anxiety flared. "What? Did your water break? Are you having contractions? You called Scruffy, right? How far away—"

"Not that kind of 'any second.'" She laid her hands on her belly. "Soon, but not that soon."

I took a breath and let the adrenaline rush fade. "Oh. Good."

Kristen turned. "Help me sit, will you? Sometimes the chair wants to roll out from underneath me."

I blocked the chair's wheels with my feet to keep it from moving and held one of her hands while she put the other flat on her desk as she lowered herself down.

"Easier to keep standing," she muttered, "but then my feet swell. I am so ready to have . . . to be unpregnant you wouldn't believe it."

Though I was pretty sure "unpregnant" wasn't a word, I also wasn't about to argue with a woman eight months and three weeks into pregnancy. "So what were you thinking about?" I went around the desk and sat in the guest chair.

"That this might be our last Sunday dessert for a long time."

Since I'd already come to that same conclusion, I nodded. "It'll be different, after the baby," I said, stating the obvious. "And maybe we won't do Sunday desserts ever again. But we'll do something else."

"Yeah." She sighed. "I'm just tired, I guess."

Kristen admitting to fatigue? Truly, wonders never ceased. "It'll be okay," I said softly.

"Hope so." She sighed and shook her head. "All these hormones. Driving me crazy. Harvey will be in with dessert in a minute; can you distract me until then?"

I didn't want to trouble her with the Ryan-Pug-Conti issues, so I went in another direction. "Did I tell you about Ash and Chelsea? I finally figured out what was behind their breakup."

Kristen leaned forward and put her chin on her hands as I talked. Her eyes started drooping before I got even halfway through the explanation, and when they shut completely, I stopped talking, pulled out my phone, and texted Scruffy. "You're going home," I said.

"Wait, what?" Her eyes flew open. "No, no, I was just resting and—" She sighed. "You're right. I'm exhausted. It's hard for me to get enough sleep. Lots of kicking going on down there, you know?"

I did not, but the fatigue she was now letting me see, on the face of one who had the stamina of ten, told the story. By the time I got her up and headed down the hall, Scruffy was there to take over the ushering duties. I helped with the seat belt and waved good-bye as they drove off, but it looked like she was already asleep.

"Hope she's okay," I said. Misty, who'd come out with me, patted my shoulder.

"She's fine. Scruffy will make sure of it."

My concern eased a bit, because she was right. The ultracompetent Scruffy would indeed do everything humanly possible, and then some, to make sure his wife and child were happy and healthy.

Chef Misty went back inside and I started walking home, back across downtown. The mix of scattered clouds we'd had earlier in the day had solidified into a low, thick mass. If we were lucky, the cloud cover would only hang on through the night and blow off in the morning. If we were unlucky, it would hang around for days.

I pulled my phone out of my pocket to check the hour-by-hour picture forecast on the weather app but decided against it. Sometimes a detailed forecast was a lose-lose situation. If the pictures were nothing but clouds as far as the forecast went, that would be depressing. Better to be happy to see any sunshine at all.

Then I smiled, because that was such an Aunt Frances thing to think. Maybe I was going to grow up to be like her after all, something that had been on my wish list for years.

Cheered, I moved into a fast walk, as there was nothing like a bit of exercise to clear the mind and make you feel alive. Not a lot of exercise, of course, because I didn't want to get all hot and sweaty and then need to take another shower, but a marginally increased heart rate did a body good.

I decided to take a longer route than normal, turning left and skirting downtown by a couple of blocks. Back here were a handful of retail stores, a resale shop, and a place that sold incense and crystals, but it was mostly residential. Some homes were tidy and well cared for; others were in dire need of new roofs and fresh paint.

It was a neighborhood of transition. The stores rarely hung on for more than a year, and the houses were mostly rentals, leased mostly to people who worked in the hospitality industry, but weekly rentals for vacationers were starting to become popular and there were concerns about the future of area housing. If all these houses went to expensive weekly rentals, where would the people who worked in our restaurants and hotels live? They'd have to move farther out and drive in, like Keegan, and then—

My fast walk slowed. Was that . . . ? Why, yes, it was. Across the street, Skyler Ellison, still in black jeans and bright green shoes, had just parked an old battered sedan in the driveway of an equally battered house. He shut the driver's door and it bounced back open.

I heard a mutter and he slammed it hard. It stayed shut that time, and he went around to the car's trunk. He used a key to open it, leaned down to get an armload of groceries, and shut the trunk's lid with his elbow. It, too, rebounded on him, and this time the mutter was louder and more distinct.

He tromped up a set of rickety-looking stairs, set the groceries down, unlocked the door, used a hip to shove it open, and went inside, shutting the door behind him.

I resumed my walk at a much slower pace, looking back every so often but not seeing any sign of Skyler.

So. Skyler drove a decrepit car and lived in an upper apartment of questionable quality. But he'd grown up with parents who had oodles of money, and since his parents' money was from gas or oil, they must have been recession-proof.

Why, then, was he driving a car that looked older than I was and living in some of the cheapest housing in Chilson?

Chapter 17

The next morning, under Eddie's curious and critical gaze, I rooted a large canvas bag out of the front closet and filled it with an object I'd wrapped in a thick blanket. "It's not for me," I said. "Okay, normally it's for me, but I'm lending it to someone else. All part of the plan."

"Mrr?"

"It'll work," I said. At least I hoped it would. Rafe hadn't been so sure, but he had said it couldn't hurt and had given his blessing on his way out the door an hour earlier.

"I have to try something," I told Eddie, and that he must have agreed with, because he head-butted my shin and purred. "Thanks. It's always good to have the Eddie stamp of approval," which was not sarcasm, but the absolute truth.

After giving him a long pet, I sent him an air-kiss and walked out the front door, walking in through the front door of the sheriff's office ten minutes later.

Chelsea slid the sliding glass window to one side. "Good morning, Minnie. Who are you looking for today?"

"You," I said. "I'm lending you something. You can't keep it, because long term I might crumple up into a sad and whining ball, but I'm lending it to you and I don't want it back for at least a week." I put the bag on the counter and pushed it her way. "Two would be better."

"Mysterious Minnie," she said, smiling a little. "Can I guess what it is?"

"Sure," I said. "Five bucks says you won't be even close."

"Hmm. If you're so sure about that, maybe I won't bother guessing at all." She took the bag and peered in. "You're lending me a blanket?"

"Temporary protective wrapping. It's around something breakable."

"Mysteriouser and mysteriouser." Carefully, she took the object out of the bag and set it on the counter below. I inched closer and stood on my tiptoes to watch the unwrapping process. "Okay," she said, hunting through the layers of fleece blanket, "there's a cord and a plug, so it's something that uses electricity . . . and I can feel it's plastic . . . and there's a switch and it's . . ."

She freed it from the blanket. "It's a . . . light?"

I grinned. "Yes, indeed. A very special kind of light. One that fends off seasonal affective disorder. You know, SAD? I get it, especially after the time change in the fall, so I always eat breakfast with this little gem shining its light on me."

"Uh, thanks?"

My grin continued unabated. "You're not convinced. I get that, I really do. But try it. Half an hour a day. Seems silly, I know, but . . . please, just try it for a week."

"For a week?" Chelsea looked at it dubiously. "You mean, every day?"

"What do you have to lose?"

"I suppose it can't hurt," she said.

"There you go." I beamed. "And if you want to keep it for two weeks, we can work out a custody arrangement."

She laughed, and it sounded almost like a real live laugh, not one of those fake ones. "Okay, I'll try it. But only because I can tell you're not going to take no for an answer."

"My aunt gave me this for Christmas the first winter I moved north," I said. "I put it in my closet and made excuses for not using it. She finally snuck into my bedroom one morning when I was in the shower and turned it on at breakfast. It was . . ." I smiled, remembering. "Never mind. I don't want to oversell. But like you said, it can't hurt. And if it helps?" I lifted one shoulder.

"All right." She reswaddled the light in the blanket. "You've convinced me. I'll try it."

"Good." I turned to go, then came back. "Say, any news on finding who killed Pug Mattock? Or who stole the Valeras' family sculpture?"

"You need to talk to Detective Inwood about that, Minnie. I'm just the office manager."

I gave her a fierce look. "Do not say 'just' the office manager. Do not say 'only' the office manager. You are worth your weight in gold and if these guys don't know it, they need to learn it fast."

"Oh, I know."

I glanced up at the new voice. "Sheriff Richardson," I said, nodding. "Good to see you."

"Morning, Sheriff, ma'am," Chelsea said, her shoulders suddenly squared.

"Always a pleasure to see you, Ms. Hamilton." Sheriff Kit Richardson leaned against the now-open doorway. "How's Eddie?"

The sheriff was trim and taut and exuded confident competence. In her mid-fifties, she had been sheriff for more than ten years and hadn't had a challenger since the first election. To most people, she was intimidating. But I'd seen her early one morning, dressed in an old bathrobe and fuzzy slippers, hair mussed, while cuddling my purring cat.

"Eddie's fine," I said. "Stop by sometime, I'm sure he'd like to see you."

A small smile curved her lips briefly. "Maybe I'll do that. I heard you asking about Pug Mattock. And the missing Conti."

"You're familiar with Vittorio Conti?"

A grin flashed past so fast I wasn't sure if I'd actually seen it. "I am now," she said. "And here's a fun fact for you."

I blinked. The sheriff was giving me insider information? "How fun is it?" I asked cautiously, not wanting to look a gift horse in the mouth, but also not wanting to look any more stupid than I actually was.

"Too subjective for me to answer." The sheriff pushed herself off the doorframe. "So here's the fact. I believe you know Ian Breece? I'm told he owns a Conti sculpture. Has done for years."

And, before my brain could form the words, "Wait, what?" she gave me a nod and was gone.

* * *

My brain occupied itself for the first half of my walk to the library with trying to figure out how Sheriff Richardson had learned that Ian Breece owned a Conti. Did sheriffs have secret resources for modern art knowledge? Probably not, but you never knew. Or had Ash actually taken me seriously when I'd talked about the Contis and Ian Breece, and he'd talked to Ian, learned that he owned a Conti, and told the sheriff?

As if.

By my commute's midway point I'd reconciled myself to never knowing for sure how the sheriff had come by that knowledge and, instead, shifted to figuring out how to make the most of that new information.

The first conclusion was that Ian, when meeting with Pug at the Round Table, had been trying to sell his own sculpture, not one stolen from the Valeras. This made sense, in light of the Breeces' unfortunate financial troubles.

But that didn't mean the deal hadn't taken a bad turn. Maybe Ian had just pretended to sell the sculpture; had instead taken Pug's money and killed him, thus keeping the sculpture and trying to sell it again to make the money all over again. And again. Or Ian might have sold the sculpture to Pug, returned later to steal it back. Or—

"Doesn't matter," I said out loud, startling the small black squirrel who had started scooting across the sidewalk. "Sorry," I called to it, feeling a little silly for apologizing to a squirrel, but also feeling it was the right thing to do.

"Still doesn't matter," I said more quietly. Because

it didn't. As long as there was any kind of motive for Ian to kill Pug, he needed to stay on the suspect list.

During the rest of my walk, I thought about the list's names. Alphabetically, because I was a librarian, but by first name, because I was Minnie.

Charlie Seller, the nephew.

Ian Breece, the farmer with the Conti.

John Pinnock, the cranky neighbor.

I re-sorted the names in order of least to most likely. First on the list, the least likely, was Charlie, with John Pinnock at the most likely end.

The next task was obvious: I needed to learn more about Charlie and Ian. "In that order," I said to myself as I walked into the library. Because alphabetical by first name was as good a way as any to create a task list.

"Order is good," Kelsey said, nodding hello from behind the front counter. "But too much order puts you into a straitjacket. Doesn't allow anything except prescribed ideas. No creativity. No thrill, no excitement, no life!" She saluted me with her coffee mug.

All of this could only mean one thing. "You made the coffee, didn't you?" I asked.

"Got here early to finish processing that box of new books that came in yesterday. Almost done with my second cup."

That was obvious. Luckily, Kelsey's caffeinated cheer was more infectious than annoying, so we chatted amiably about the new books as we wandered back to my office, where I left my coat and backpack and picked up my own coffee mug.

In the kitchen, I used the microwave to heat half

a mug of the dilution water, filled the rest with Kelsey coffee and added a hefty dollop of creamer. "Say," I asked. "Do you happen to know a Charlie Seller? Charles, he goes by now. He's Pug Mattock's nephew."

Unfortunately, she did not, and she'd never heard of John Pinnock.

"You're no help," I said.

"Not today." She smiled. "Try again tomorrow. You never know what I'll learn between now and then."

That was a good point, and I told her so. Didn't help me at all, but it did make me think about Melinda Hedges, cousin to Charlie and neighbor to a short-term rental. The first thing I did when returned to my office was to send Melinda an e-mail, asking her to call when she had a minute.

Ten minutes later, my phone rang.

"It's Melinda. Got your e-mail and figured I should talk to you right now."

I laughed. "You sound a little breathless. Don't tell me you ran to your phone to call me."

"Sort of. You're calling about that puppeteer, right? Well, I just found out that she'll be here in the middle of July. And," she said triumphantly, "I have her e-mail address. I'll send it on to you right now. Hang on . . . there!"

I glanced at my computer and saw my unread e-mail count go up by one. "That's great. Thanks so much."

"No problem. I was taking the garbage out just now and saw my neighbor. Easy to ask; the hard part was remembering to ask in the first place." She laughed. "My mom says that's going to get worse as

I get older, which doesn't bode well, because I'm already memory challenged."

"Huh. Your mom's name isn't Sally is it? Because my mom says the same thing."

Melinda laughed again. "Lynn. But maybe we're distant cousins."

And that was the opportunity I'd been hoping to have. "Speaking of cousins, how's Sylvia doing? I saw her the other day and she seemed okay, but it's hard to tell."

"Good days and bad days. I know she's not sleeping well." Melinda sighed. "I wish the police would find whoever killed Pug. It's hard on her to have so many questions. And it's scary, because we still don't know *why* Pug was killed."

"How much other family support does she have up here?" I asked. "Didn't you say there's a nephew? Charles, was it?"

"Charles to some, Charlie to us," she said. "I know I'm snotty about him, because he's way too busy with his career and his beautiful wife and the sporting events of his young perfect children to come up here to give his aunt Sylvia a hug."

I heard a "but" coming.

"But . . ." She took a deep breath. "Remember when we talked the other day? I was saying that Charlie and his wife wanted to make all these changes to the cottage?"

"Sure. Kitchen. Bathroom. Glass porch."

"That's it. I thought he was making plans for when he got the cottage. Only it turns out he was also talking about the plans Pug and Sylvia have for the place. They were all on the same page. Going to split the cost, even."

Melinda went on, and I mostly listened, but I also mentally rearranged my suspect list, because Charlie Seller had no reason to kill Pug.

The list was down to two names.

Talking about Charlie Seller and his aunt Sylvia and his uncle Pug made me think about my aunt Frances, so I stopped at her house on my way home. She and Otto were in the kitchen, cooking together in a way that made me think of choreographed dance moves.

I sat in the nook, sipping the glass of red wine Otto had handed me, and watched them step around each other. It was the same kind of thing that happened in the Three Seasons kitchen, but for some reason I expected it there. Not here, in the cozy comfort of the space Otto had renovated for his new bride as a wedding present, just a year ago.

And now, the two of them moved around each other with grace and beauty, never clashing or bumping into each other. But there was the occasional touch of a hand to a back, or a slide of one shoulder against another, gentle caresses that spoke of love without saying a word.

Aunt Frances caught my smile and misinterpreted it completely. "Something funny?"

I shook my head. "No, just admiring the way you two work together. Rafe and I don't. Not in the kitchen." A sudden fear struck me. "Do you think that's a sign of a problematic marriage?"

My loving aunt snorted. "It's a sign of you not liking to cook."

Well, there was that. I grinned, feeling better already. She really was the best aunt ever.

"Is Katie coming up this summer?" Aunt Frances asked.

My oldest niece, Katie "don't call me Katrina because I'm not a freaking hurricane," had been sent north from her home in Florida by my brother and sister-in-law to spend the summer. I'd looked forward to it immensely, eager to forge an aunt-niece relationship that would last the rest of our lives. We'd had a rocky start in the classic adolescent style, but all had ended well. Eventually.

"Not sure," I said. "Mitchell at the toy store and Rianne Howe from Benton's both say they'd love to have her back, but now that she's a high school graduate, there are opportunities for her at home."

"And miss a chance for another Up North summer?" Otto's eyebrows went sky-high. "What's wrong with that young woman?"

I had a feeling it was a boy, and one her parents actually liked, but I shrugged. "We'll see what happens. If she doesn't come north this year, I'm already working on Ben."

My only nephew was two years younger than his older sister and two years older than Sally, my mom's namesake and the youngest Hamilton. If it didn't work out to get Ben north, I could always start setting the stage for Sally.

"Not sure I ever asked," Otto said. "How did you enjoy the pottery class?"

Since my thoughts had been far elsewhere, I was startled into showing my actual thoughts and feelings about the experience.

Otto, who had been watching me closely, laughed out loud. "Never mind. I get the idea."

In defense of artistic endeavors everywhere, I

said, "It wasn't the pottery itself. Or the location, the instructor, or"—I took a deep breath and made myself face the brutal truth—"or even the other people taking the class. It was what I brought, the baggage I carried in with me, that turned it into a poor experience."

My aunt looked up from the bowl of batter she was stirring and smiled. "How wise and mature of you."

"Won't last," I said. "I'm sure of it." To demonstrate the short-term length of my maturity and wisdom, I crossed my eyes and stuck out my tongue.

Aunt Frances shook her head and went back to stirring. Otto smiled and said, "Speaking of mature things, guess what your aunt has decided to do about her retirement plans?"

Fear clutched at me, sending an icy-cold shiver down the back of my neck. What next? Please don't let her want to form a quilting circle. Sewing was so far outside my wheelhouse it would be on another boat altogether. Same with needlepoint, knitting, crocheting, or anything with needlelike and cloth-like objects. They were all wonderfully satisfying, beautiful, and rewarding pursuits for billions of people, but the thought of sitting down with a pair of needles and a pile of yarn made me break out in a sweat.

"Whatever it is," I said, as bravely as I could, "I'll be right there with you."

My aunt eyed me. "You look a little pale. What is it you think I want to do? Cross-stitch? Well, maybe someday, but don't worry. I know how you feel about all things sewing. Dragging you to a quilting bee wouldn't be fun for anyone."

I took a long sip of wine. "Good to know. What's your new plan, then?"

"To not have any plans at all." Aunt Frances smiled at my blank expression. "Yes, I know I was intent on finding things to occupy my time, and afraid I wouldn't have any human contact all day other than this one." She gave Otto a light hip check as he passed behind her. "But you know what? I was doing what I'm always telling you not to. I was worrying too much. It'll work out."

"It will?"

"Things tend to, if you stop poking at them with sticks. Far better to let things develop at their own pace. Forcing things rarely gets good results."

I nodded slowly, recognizing wisdom when I heard it.

And then I tried to apply it to the problem of Ryan and Pug's killer. Was I trying to poke that with sticks? Because it certainly seemed as if I was getting poor results. Maybe what I needed to do was let things develop at their own pace.

But . . . if I did that, what was going to happen to Ryan?

Chapter 18

I woke the following morning with a brain fuzzy from lack of sleep. All night long I'd alternated between lying awake trying to think of the best next steps for finding Pug's killer and having dreams ranging from silly to downright disturbing.

The silliest had been when Eddie, wearing my favorite pajamas and eating crème brûlée, had used my cell phone to call Katie and ask her to bring Disney World tickets when she came up for the summer. The creepiest had been when I'd been walking through a forest, enjoying the sounds of a breeze in the trees and the twittering of birds, when all the noise suddenly stopped. I'd turned in a circle trying to figure out what had happened, trying to see, and then I did see. Looming over me was a dark shadow, human in form, its arms raised high, holding something dark and large and heavy and—

Happily, I'd woken up at that point, sweating and breathing hard. But out of the murky mist and into the light of day, one big question emerged.

"How did I know it was heavy?" I now asked.

Eddie looked pointedly at my cereal bowl. "Mrr," he said.

"You know perfectly well that you don't get the leftover milk until it's, you know, actually left over." I ate another bite of toasted oats to firmly demonstrate that I was still eating. "But as I was saying, back in that dream, I was trying to get away from the shadow because he was about to thump me with something heavy. How did I know anything about its weight?" I thought it all through again. "Plus, why am I saying it was a male? Is that the default gender when you're attacked, even in a dream? Odds are for it, but it's not as if women don't do bad things."

"Mrr."

I looked down at him. He was sitting on the floor, tail curled around his feet, eyes focused intently on mine. With our gazes locked, I ate a bite of cereal. Ate another one. Then, finally, I scooped out the last few round pieces and put my empty bowl on the floor.

Eddie gave the bowl a long, hard look. Then he gave me a long, hard stare and stalked away, his tail one tall flag of protest.

"Now what did I do?" I asked. But, of course, he didn't answer.

Muttering about cats in general and ones named Eddie in particular, I opened the cupboard door that held the cat carrier. "Don't go far," I called. "It's a bookmobile day, remember?"

"Mrr!" Eddie galloped back to the kitchen. "Mrr!"

"You are so weird." I put my bowl and spoon in

the dishwasher and opened the carrier's door. Eddie pranced in and flopped down on the pink blanket made by a nice lady who'd stayed at the boardinghouse in the days of my aunt's ownership. It was getting tattered, but I knew Eddie would have a fit if I swapped it for new, so it stayed.

We drove up to the library's back parking lot, where Julia was already waiting, leaning against the door of her car, ankles and arms crossed, fingers tapping against her upper arms. "Uh-oh," I said to Eddie as we parked next to Julia. "Something's going on." And judging from the look on her face, it wasn't a good something.

I unfastened our seat belts and started to open the car door when Julia grabbed the handle and flung it open.

"Did you hear?" she demanded.

Her hands were now on her hips and her face was set in stark lines, but this didn't have the feel of Julia playing one of her theatrical roles. This had the feel of the real Julia, all the way down to the bone. And since the real Julia was one of the calmest and most centered people I'd ever met, seeing her upset was troubling. "What's the matter?" I asked.

With her chin, she gestured toward the library. "Didn't you see?"

I got out of the car and looked. Then frowned. "The library doesn't open for almost two hours. What's with all the cars?"

"Don't you recognize them? No, wait, you barely know what you drive, let alone anyone else." She pointed. "The Mercedes is Trent's car. That SUV? Linda's. And the old pickup is Otto's."

My frown deepened. "The library board is meeting this morning? I didn't know anything was scheduled."

"Special meeting," she said. "To discuss a personnel matter. I saw the meeting notice online. It was just posted yesterday."

My stomach went all tight and knotty. "They're talking about Graydon." I was sure of it. "They'll end up having the meeting as a closed session."

Julia nodded.

We looked at each other, then back at the library.

"Well," I said, "there's nothing we can do about it. And whatever they decide, we'll find out sooner or later."

The morning, as always on the bookmobile, went quickly, and soon after lunch we were back at the library, as Hunter was driving the last few hours of the day.

"Have fun," I said, waving the three of them off, feeling like a mom saying good-bye to a child going off to kindergarten. I walked into the library, and the door had barely shut behind me when Holly and Josh pounced and dragged me into my office.

"Do you know what happened this morning?" Holly asked.

"Did Graydon tell you anything?" Josh demanded. "Did they fire him? Mia's place is hiring and if we end up with another director anything like Stephen, I'm out of here."

Slowly, I sat in my chair. I needed to reassure everyone that things would work out, no matter what. But how could I do that when I had no idea what was going on?

"I know the board met this morning to discuss a personnel matter," I said. "That's all I know."

"That's all anyone knows," Holly said. "You need to find out for us, Minnie. Everyone's . . . we're all terrified they're firing him. Denise has been out for his blood for weeks, and you know that she's good friends with half the people on the board."

I nodded. That had been my fear, too. "I'll go up and talk to him," I said. "But that doesn't mean he'll tell me anything." Or that if he did, I'd be able to share it with the rest of the staff. He might only tell me in confidence and I couldn't break my word on something like that.

Josh, who rarely asked for anything, glowered at me. "But you'll try. Right?"

Of course I would. I got up and went to the door. "On my way."

When I got upstairs and poked my head in his office, Graydon was talking on the phone, his voice low and his face serious. He saw me, paused, put his index finger up, indicating that he'd be done in a minute, and turned away, still talking quietly.

Not wanting to intrude, I went back downstairs, assuming that he'd give me a call when he was done.

But he never did.

Over the weekend, I'd managed to persuade Rafe that, if I came up with a plan to reunite Ash and Chelsea that (1) wouldn't be anything that would show up on the front page of the paper and cause one or both of us to lose our jobs, and (2) didn't involve too much effort on his part, he'd join me in carrying out the plan.

I'd decided on a two-pronged strategy. We'd talk to Ash first, then Chelsea, same night in two different locations. Ash was easier, because he'd been on the same bowling league for years, and it should be easy enough to pull him aside between games. Chelsea was a little harder to figure out, because we didn't know her nearly as well, but I finally came up with a plan that didn't involve Rafe at all, which pleased him so much that he started whistling as we walked to the bowling alley.

Over our clasped hands, I squinted up at him. "That's from a musical, isn't it?"

He whistled a few more notes. "I can't wait to tell Julia that you didn't recognize 'Oh, What a Beautiful Mornin',' from *Oklahoma!*"

I refrained from saying it might have been his whistling skill that was the problem, not my powers of song recognition, but as neither one was all that outstanding, instead I asked, "Do you know any other song from that show?"

It turned out that he did, and in show order, from the opening scene to the rousing closing eponymous "Oklahoma!" itself.

"You never cease to amaze me," I said. "Why do you know all those songs?"

"Got cast in the show my senior year of high school." He shrugged. "Wanted to be the bad guy, but they stuck me as the male lead. Ladies first." This last was because we were at the bowling alley and he reached out to hold the door for me.

I gave him a look as I went in, wondering how it was I'd never learned that he'd done musical theater, and making a mental note to hunt up his high school yearbook and look for pictures. Not that I doubted him, of course. More that I wanted to see a young Rafe dressed in a cowboy outfit.

"Something funny?" Ash asked.

He was sitting on a bench close to the front door, switching from street shoes to bowling shoes. "Almost always," I said as Ash and Rafe did the fist-bump thing.

"What are you two doing here?" Bowling shoes tied, Ash stood and picked up his worn running shoes. "Subbing for someone?"

I could feel Rafe looking my way. He'd made it clear that he would take only a supportive role in this, so it was up to me. "Um," I said. "Do you have a minute?"

Ash glanced at the bowling lanes. "The first league is running a little over, so yeah. What's up?"

"Um, it's . . ." All capacity for words suddenly fled. There was nothing in my head except for that little voice telling me how stupid I was for interfering in a relationship between two reasonable and intelligent adults. "It's just . . ."

And then Rafe's hands were on my shoulders. "Do you love Chelsea?" he asked bluntly.

"Look, guys," Ash said, "I know you want to help, but—"

"Do you love her?" I asked, reaching up to feel the warmth and strength in Rafe's hands. "Because that's what matters."

He looked away. "Yeah," he finally said. "I do. Nothing seems to fit anymore. Everything's flat, you know? Nothing makes sense. But . . ." He shook his head. "Love isn't always enough."

"Of course it isn't." I felt my jaw set. "But what if there was a way to get things to work out? You say you both want different things, but what if there's a way for both of you to get what you need?"

Ash's eyebrows went up. "How do you compromise between one person wanting to stay in one place and the other not wanting that at all?"

I took a breath. This was the tricky part. "Maybe," I said gently, "that's not the real issue. Maybe it's not so much about a reluctance to put down deep roots. Maybe it's more about not being willing to move outside comfort zones."

He frowned. "What are you talking about?"

"Sleep on it, okay?" Because sometimes the best solutions tiptoed in quietly, catlike. Then again, sometimes you ended up with nightmares involving heavy objects, but with any luck Ash's experience would be more productive.

Ash gave us a tight nod. "Got to go," he said, and headed off to his league.

"Think it'll work?" I asked.

Rafe, still holding my shoulders, kissed the top of my head. "It's almost time for your meeting with Chelsea."

He was right, I needed to get going, and, accordingly, a few minutes later I was sitting with Chelsea at Hoppe's Brewing, enjoying the soft pretzel bites and almost enjoying a small mug of cider.

After checking with her on the use of the happy light—"You know, I really think it's helping"—I started a conversation very similar to the earlier one with Ash, and this time I was prepared. "I have a personal question for you, if that's okay. Do you still love Ash?"

"So very much," she said quietly. "He's my sun

and my moon. My earth and sky. But . . ." Her voice trailed off.

"I know. Love isn't always enough. And it sure seems that you both want different things. But what if there's another way?"

She shook her head. "How do you get to a compromise when one person wants to see what the world has to offer and the other isn't interested in that at all?"

Back to the tricky part. "Maybe," I said, "that's not the real issue. Maybe it's not so much a determination to stay. Maybe it's more a reluctance to break out of lifetime habits."

Chelsea's face took on a thoughtful look. "Huh," she said. "I hadn't thought about it that way."

I nodded and took another bite of pretzel. My work here was done, and I suddenly realized that maybe what I needed to help Ryan was to think about the suspects in a different way.

Only . . . how?

"Think a different way," I murmured. "Different, different, different."

"Mrr!"

I looked down at Eddie. It was the next morning. Rafe had left for school half an hour earlier. I'd eaten breakfast with him, then showered and dressed. Technically, I didn't have to arrive at the library for another hour and a half, but I usually arrived early to get a head start on the day. This morning, however, I was wandering around the house, doing some mild tidying and trying to think out loud. Eddie was sometimes wandering with me, other times ignoring me completely. This time his comment was loud enough to get my attention.

"You're right," I said, sighing. "Saying the word over and over isn't helping. So how do I think differently about something I've been thinking about for weeks? How do—um, what are you doing?"

Eddie was walking up the stairs, but on the outside, between the edge of the stair tread and the vertical balusters. I wouldn't have thought he would fit, but there he was, ascending the staircase without an apparent thought to the increasing drop to the floor if he mis-stepped.

I watched and moved close, concerned for his safety, but when he reached the halfway point, he slid between two of the balusters to reach the stairs proper, and trotted up and out of sight.

I'd have to ask Rafe, but as far as I knew, he'd never done this before. He'd sat on a stair edge, but not walked up the outside. "Why?" I asked. "What got into your little kitty mind?"

No answer. Of course.

"Well, that was different," I muttered, then blinked. Maybe to get my brain thinking in another direction, what I needed was to *do* something different. Obvious, in retrospect. "Better late than never," I said, more cheerful now that I had a direction.

"Mrr!"

"Thank you!" I called up the stairs. "Although it would be even more helpful if you gave me an idea about what, exactly, to do differently. In the next hour, preferably." It was Wednesday already, and mushroomers would be crawling all over the woods soon. "Won't help Ryan if I walk up the outside of the stairs, and—"

I stopped. Outside stairs. Skyler lived in that upper apartment with outside stairs. Which meant there was a downstairs apartment, just like Ryan lived downstairs and Keegan lived up above. Skyler had an alibi, so he'd been crossed off the suspect list. But there was something that made me think there was more to his story. The wealthy parents? The deep knowledge of Conti? The bright green shoes? None of those things by themselves were an indicator of anything, but there was a tiny piece of me that, in spite of the alibi, continued to wonder. Maybe, just maybe, I could talk to a neighbor and learn enough to put my questions to rest.

And so, after a late lunchtime, I left the library and walked to Skyler's apartment, first passing the art gallery and peering in the windows to make sure he was there. He was talking to a sleek white-haired couple, all three giving the appearance of settling in for a nice long chat about art.

Perfect. I upped my speed and arrived at the house a few minutes later. The wood door of the downstairs apartment was painted a color somewhere between green and brown, the paint peeling to reveal a grimy white beneath.

My knocks didn't summon anyone, either the first, second, or third time I tried.

Well, rats.

Sighing, I retreated toward the sidewalk, thinking about how to schedule another visit.

"You looking for Bob?"

I jumped. Next door, a sixtyish man in a patched canvas coat was pointing the handle of a leaf rake at the house I'd just left.

"Because he's gone on a long haul," Rake Man said. "Taking hardwood lumber to West Texas, I think it was. Won't be back for three days."

"Oh. That's . . . too bad." I thought quickly. "But maybe you can help me. I'm really looking for information about the man who lives upstairs. The place I work is very particular about who they hire"—true enough—"and I was hoping to learn more about Skyler's background."

Rake Man laughed. "The Ellison kid? He's trying for a real job? Who would have guessed. What kind of place do you work? Oh, you can't say, I get it." He winked. "Ellison. What a name, eh? Makes you think of money. From what I've been able to figure, he grew up with cash coming out his ears. But then he got the art bug. Told his parents he wanted to be an artist. They said, sure, do what you want, but you don't get any of our money unless you give up the art thing and go to business school like an Ellison should."

I blinked at the torrent of information. "Skyler walked away from his family?"

Shrugging, Rake Man said, "All I can say for sure is he's lived here about two years, and I've never seen him have any visitors or go anywhere overnight. What does that tell you?"

Mostly that Skyler's neighbor was paying a little too much attention to the comings and goings of other people.

"Thanks for your help," I said.

"No problem. Not sure I'd hire the guy, but hey, maybe he'll be fine for wherever it is you work."

I thanked him again and started back to the library, thinking about Skyler and his family and how hard it must have been to break off from everyone and everything you've ever known, to be estranged from the people who raised you. How hard, how impossible, it must be to create anything resembling a family support system.

"Minnie Hamilton."

I stopped short. I'd been thinking so hard I'd almost run into Conservation Officer Jenica Thomas, standing in the middle of the sidewalk. "Oh," I said. "Hi. How are you?"

"Healthy, thank you." She nodded. "I saw you and wanted to answer your question about Mr. Mattock. The other night, at the fish fry, I wasn't free to respond, but now I am."

"Oh," I said again. "Okay."

"Mr. Mattock had provided me with information about a hunter taking turkeys out of season. Poaching. He'd wanted to help me trap the hunter, and that's why I was at his cottage that day. We were discussing ideas. The hunter has just been apprehended and been given multiple citations, so I now feel free to mention this to you."

"Thanks for letting me know," I said, meaning it.

"You're welcome." Jenica nodded. "I wasn't comfortable answering your question the other night due to personal time constraints and the fact that it was an ongoing investigation, but I also wasn't comfortable not responding. The best solution was to respond as soon as I could."

I thanked her again, watched her drive away in her dark green truck, and continued back to the library, thinking about traps.

A trap with a Conti as a lure hadn't been necessary to eliminate Charlie or Keegan from the suspect list, but maybe setting a trap would help figure out who *had* been the one to kill Pug.

That's what I told Rafe, anyway, over the dinner that I'd laboriously ordered, picked up from the Chinese restaurant, and put onto plates. He used the wood chopsticks that came with the food; I used a fork out of the kitchen drawer. There were times to learn new things and there were times to play to your strengths, and when you were hungry and knew you'd be able to eat sooner rather than later if you used a fork, well, forks were the way to go.

"I see your point," he said. "But let's not forget that we're trying to identify a killer. And though maybe murder is different, it's almost always easier to do something the second time."

Half a forkful of shrimp-fried rice dropped onto my plate. "Why, Rafe Niswander. If I didn't know better, I'd say you're worried about me."

"Well, yeah." He expertly twirled rice noodles onto his chopsticks. "Just put a nonrefundable deposit down on our wedding photographer."

I frowned. "I thought that friend of yours was taking the pictures." Whose name escaped me at the moment. Fred? No, that wasn't right. But similar. Frank? What other name started with an F?

"Six-pack of bottled craft brew," he said, sounding aggrieved. "Not the cheap stuff I get."

Since he always bought whatever beer he wanted,

I didn't use up any of my sympathy allotment for the day on him. "We were talking about setting some sort of trap." Or at least I had been. "Outside of the acknowledged safety issues, do you think it's a good idea? More to the point, do you think it could work?"

He slurped in a huge bite of noodles while I strong-mindedly averted my ears from the noise, chewed, and finally, after a thousand years, swallowed and said, "Sure. A trap could work."

"Did you hear that?" I asked Eddie, who was sitting on the floor, equidistant from Rafe and me. I wasn't sure if he was criticizing my non-use of chopsticks or hoping for something worthwhile to fall on the floor. Or both. "He said it could work."

"Has to be a good plan, though." Rafe looked at Eddie. "If you have any ideas on that, now would be a good time to speak up."

Eddie stared into space, unblinking.

"Right." I stood to collect the empty plates. "What are you up to the rest of the night?"

"Mrr."

"Not you. I know what you're doing."

Rafe gathered the napkins and utensils. "Toss-up between watching hockey or watching baseball."

Since I knew perfectly well he was going to work on the basement, I said, "Go with hockey. The season is almost over. There will be baseball for months."

Rafe grinned. "Look at you, knowing so much about sports."

I stopped short, plates in hand. Was it true? Had spending so much time with Rafe oozed sports knowledge into my brain? Not that I had anything against sports; it was just that my interests lay in different directions. Opposite directions. Yet . . . it was true. Spending this much time with Rafe had expanded my horizons, exposed me to new things and new ideas. And I'd probably done the same for him.

The thought gave me a warm, fuzzy feeling, one that lasted through my own chore of raking out the flower beds and bagging crumbling leaves.

"What about you?" I asked Eddie, who was sitting statue-like about ten feet away. He'd sat in the kitchen window, howling at me, until I couldn't stand it any longer and let him out, thus rewarding bad behavior. "I've learned a lot from you. Especially the part about making sure to use a lint roller before going to work. Are you learning anything from me?"

He stared at me, his yellow eyes unblinking.

"How does that work? If I looked at you like that, my eyeballs would dry up and fall out of my head." I gave him a long look, trying to match his stare, and couldn't do it.

"You win," I muttered. "I know, I know. The cat always wins, I get it."

"Mrr."

"Well, you don't have to sound so smug."

As I raked, I thought about the theoretical trap. "By the way, like Rafe said, we'd be happy to hear your trapping suggestions. Oh, you'd like a summary of the final suspects?" I asked, even though he hadn't so much as twitched. "No problem. We have two—Ian Breece, farmer with a Conti, and John Pinnock, the cranky neighbor. I'm leaning toward the cranky neighbor. He keeps trying different ways to scare off Sylvia, so it just makes sense that. . . . What are you doing?"

Eddie ignored my question. He was intent on fishing something out from between two of the many fieldstones that created the raised flower beds. He was also making an odd snorking sound, the kind of sound that meant one of two things: he was about to hack up a hair ball, or he was about to hack up a piece of the grass he'd just eaten. On the plus side, he was outside, which meant the effort to clean up his mess would be minimal to nonexistent.

"Mrr!"

He batted a scrap of something in my direction, bounded up the back stairs, and sat with his back to me.

"Right," I said, picking up his prize. "Thanks so much for finding this fine piece of"—I eyed the scrap of thin plastic—"former candy bar wrapper." From the bit of writing I could make out, it was sour apple something or other. Laffy Taffy, maybe. Cats are so weird.

I shoved the scrap into my pants pocket and went back to rake wielding. "Anyway, like I was saying, John Pinnock is at the top of my suspect list and—"

"Mrr!"

"Well, sure, I'm trying not to be biased just because I don't like the guy. That's the whole reason for a trap. What we need is proof."

"Mrr!"

Even my cat thought the idea was dumb. To some extent, I was inclined to agree, but the alternative was doing nothing, and Ryan was depending on us.

As I raked, something tickled the back of my

brain. Someone had said . . . something. A something that hadn't seemed important at the time. Who had it been? What had it been?

I closed my eyes and let my mind wander back and forth across the last few days, skipping about . . .

My eyes flew open. "Rake Man," I said out loud, staring at the rake in my hands. Skyler's neighbor. What exactly had he said about Skyler? That he'd never seen him go anywhere overnight. That didn't mean that Skyler never ever went anywhere; Rake Man couldn't see everything that Skyler did. But it did mean that Skyler might have lied to me about being in Chicago for that art gallery opening. And it did mean he might not have an alibi for the night of Pug's murder.

We were back to three suspects.

Chapter 19

The next day dawned clear and bright. I'd gone to bed hoping that my subconscious would come up with a trapping idea, but I woke with nothing in my head but a fuzzy dream of John Pinnock in a rowboat with Pug, Sylvia, Graydon, and Kristen. It was a crowded boat and I surfaced into wakefulness hoping that no one fell in.

So much for my subconscious mind doing anything useful. Still, it was a glorious spring day, so I jumped out of bed singing a happy tune and Eddie jumped with me, singing his own song. Post-shower, I toweled off my way-too-curly hair, listening to the refrain to which he kept returning.

"Mrr. Mrr. Mrr." Pause. "Mrr. Mrr. Mrr." Pause. "Mrr. Mrr. Mrr."

"Has a good beat," I said, "though I'm not sure I can dance to it." I tried a few steps that might have resembled a grapevine twist but probably didn't. "Yeah, not so much. How about a tango?"

Eddie gave me a dirty look and stalked off.

"Don't go far," I called after him. "It's a book-mobile day."

He thumped down the stairs without saying a thing, which probably meant he was annoyed with me. Luckily for both of us, he'd recovered from his sour mood by the time we needed to leave, and even luckier for me, he stayed quiet on the drive up to the library.

"How's Mr. Ed this morning?" Hunter put the carrier on the floor in front of the passenger's seat and strapped it down, as I was going to drive in the morning and he was taking the afternoon. Thursday was normally a Julia day, but she and her husband were headed to Chicago for a long weekend of theatergoing. I'd asked her to bring me back a small present and she'd put on such a thoughtful look that I was a bit concerned.

"Mr. Ed was vocal earlier," I said, "but he's quieted down."

Hunter leaned down to look into the carrier. "Anything wrong?"

"Mrr."

"Now you've done it," I said.

Hunter laughed and buckled his seat belt. "Poked the Eddie bear, didn't I? Sorry about that. What's today's question? Do we have one yet?"

Julia and Hunter and I had recently started a habit of choosing a discussion topic for each trip. This had come about because I'd been trying hard to get Julia to share insider New York theater stories, which she wasn't always inclined to do. She'd successfully diverted me by announcing that the question of the day was going to be "If animals could talk, which one would be funniest?" and voilà! we had a new tradition.

I considered making "What's the best way to trap a killer with a fake Conti?" the question, but instead went for "If we could ask a question of any author, living or dead, who would it be, and what should we ask?"

"Good one," Hunter said, and we launched directly into discussion. My first suggestion was asking James Joyce about his punctuation choices in *Ulysses*, but Hunter brought up the excellent question of finding out, once and for all, why Agatha Christie had vanished for eleven days. Then, as we arrived at the first stop and started opening preparations, we agreed that the ultimate authorial question was for Dr. Seuss, asking how he got the cat to put on a hat in the first place.

"We tried putting a Santa hat on Eddie last Christmas," I said, unlocking the back door.

"Did it work?"

"Only if you consider half a second a success."

"Ms. Minnie. Hunter M." Lawrence Zonne climbed the steps and nodded at us, his thick white hair combed neatly back. "Success is in the eye of the beholder, don't you think? And a good thing, because waiting for someone else to declare me successful might cause my ulcer to start bleeding again." He made a face. "Once was enough, thank you very much."

"Are you all right?" I asked, concerned. It was hard to believe the agile and sprightly Mr. Zonne would ever be anything but hale and hearty, despite the fact that he was in his mid-eighties. He was too alive for anything else.

"Fit as a fiddlehead fern." He patted his midsection. "All I needed was an adjustment to my medication. Annoying it took a night in the hospital to determine the correct dosages, but that's the medical establishment for you."

Hunter and I made noises of commiseration.

"Thank you," Mr. Zonne said. "And at least I didn't have it as bad as the gentleman in the bed next to me. He was there for an adjustment to his pacemaker and was going to be there at least two nights. Johnny P., I told him, you have my sympathies. Said I'd send flowers, but he wasn't interested."

Could it be? No . . . could it? "Are you," I asked slowly, "talking about John Pinnock? From Chilson?" Because, that first time we'd met, hadn't he said something about the hospital? About doctors? Heart doctors, that was it.

Mr. Zonne's gaze sharpened. "Why, yes. Is he a friend of yours?"

"When was this?" I asked. "When were you in the hospital?"

"Oh, not long ago." He pursed his lips. "It was a Monday night, I remember that, so not quite a month ago."

"You're sure?" I held my breath, waiting.

"Dear child. My memory isn't what it was, but I can remember that much."

I sat down heavily on the carpeted step. John Pinnock had been in the hospital on the night Pug was murdered. There was no way he could be the killer.

That evening, Rafe and I drove out to meet Ryan. It was Thursday night, and though we were far closer to finding out who'd killed Pug, we still didn't for sure know the killer's identity, and we didn't have proof of anything. We'd come up with the bare bones of a plan to discuss with Ryan, but we still had two suspects.

"John Pinnock couldn't have done it," I said. "So it's either Ian Breece or Skyler Ellison."

Rafe looked grim, an expression so rare on him it took me a minute to recognize it. "What you said about Ian. All those financial setbacks. He's a good guy. I like him. But if you have enough money troubles that you might lose your home, your livelihood, the life you've been building for yourself and your family?" He shook his head. "I can see how that would drive you to desperation. To do things you'd never consider otherwise."

I'd been thinking the same thing. Briefly, I tried to put myself in Ian's place but gave up quickly. Until you were in the middle of a situation, could you know what you'd do? Know for sure? "And there's Skyler."

"Yeah, I know he's the other one on the list," Rafe said. "But I don't get the why. What's the motive?"

I was having the same problem. Money didn't seem to make sense, as Skyler had already walked away from a huge inheritance and, if we could believe what the neighbor had said, he could walk back to it anytime he chose. "Doesn't mean there isn't one," I said weakly.

Rafe nodded. "Everyone has secrets."

"Not—" I stopped, because there were indeed a handful of things Rafe didn't know about me. Embarrassing things that weren't important in the grand scheme of things, but was there any real reason for him to know that I'd once mistakenly sent a text to my graduate school adviser that had been meant for my then boyfriend? No, there was not. I faked a cough and said, ungrammatically, "Not hardly anyone has a secret worth killing over."

After a quick glance at me, Rafe said, "And there's always the chance that the killer is someone we haven't considered."

I didn't want to think about that, but since I was trying to be a better person, I sat up straight to face the truth of his statement and said, "Well, if Ian and Skyler don't show up tomorrow night, the trap will let us know that, too."

"What if one of them is the killer but has something else going on?" Rafe asked. "How will we know?"

"Got that figured out," I said. "The Breeces have a farm blog, and yesterday Felicia posted that Ian is giving two half-hour presentations on growing plants from seeds, one Friday evening, one on Saturday morning."

"How about Skyler?"

"Called the gallery this afternoon. He wasn't there, so I said I was working with him about maybe buying a piece and asked when he'd be there. Turns out he's working Friday from noon to seven, and Saturday from ten to four. He might have social plans, but if the Conti sculpture is the underlying motive for Pug's death, dangling one for sale at a rock-bottom price of next to nothing will lure him out from the best party ever."

Rafe made a noise that sounded like agreement, and we worked on fine-tuning the plan as we parked and walked to Ryan's cabin, or rather, what we hoped soon *wouldn't* be Ryan's cabin, but would be an old log home back in its former role as a quiet spot in the woods.

"Hey," a soft voice said.

Both of us jumped, Rafe going significantly higher than I did. "Ryan Anderson," I said after a moment, putting a hand to my panting chest. "You have got to stop doing that."

"Good trick, though," Rafe said, still gasping a bit. "Deer hunting will be a breeze for you come fall."

Ryan sidled out from behind the trunk of a massive maple tree. "If I get out of this mess okay," he said, "I never want to set foot in the woods the rest of my life."

It was the closest thing to a vow I'd ever heard outside a wedding ceremony. "We have a plan," I said confidently. At least we had the beginnings of a plan. Okay, technically, we had the skeleton of a plan, but that was why we were here, to figure out the rest of it.

"Yeah?" Ryan's gaze was restless, darting left, right, and all around. The look of the hunted. "What are you thinking?"

"Have you heard about that new website? *The Chilson Diversion*? Blog, I guess, technically." I explained how it had started as a kind of bulletin board for informal events around the community, then organically morphed into something bigger. "It started a few months back," I said. "A high school Advanced Placement project, but it's taken on a life of its own. It's not just events that are posted, but local jobs that are open, and"—I paused dramatically—"items for sale."

Ryan's reaction was not what I'd expected. He looked blank. "Um . . ."

"This morning," I said, "we posted a short paragraph about selling this old sculpture that had been in the family cottage for decades. That we were from downstate and would be Up North this weekend only to open the cottage and would be happy to sell the sculpture, first come, first served."

Rafe saw the puzzled look on Ryan's face. "We wrote just enough to make it clear it was a Conti," he explained. "And made it sound horrible enough that the only people who'd be interested would be people looking for a Conti."

"But . . . there isn't a Conti. Is there?" Ryan was still puzzled.

"No," I said cheerfully. "That's the beauty of this plan. All we want to know is who shows up. If one of our suspects is there, that's the killer. We don't even have to talk to him. We just identify who it is, tell the sheriff's detectives what we've learned, and let them take care of the rest."

"Okay," Ryan said slowly. "I get it. This could work. Where are we meeting him?"

We? I blinked. "Um, we'll take care of this. You don't need to—"

"I'm going," Ryan said.

His voice was so firm that I knew there'd be no budging him. I glanced at Rafe, who shrugged. "Okay," I said. "I get it. There's only one problem."

"What's that?" Ryan asked.

"We haven't decided where to have the meeting."

Ryan stared at us. "What? That doesn't make any sense. How can you get someone to show up if you don't have a place to show up to?"

He was right, but the problem was that Rafe and I hadn't been able to agree on a location. With the weekend's weather looking to be perfect for morel hunting, we needed to arrange the meeting the next night, ahead of the hunting hordes. The problem was that Rafe had already promised to attend the middle school's track meet, an away meet in a town two hours away. He wouldn't be back until late.

"It has to be somewhere public," he'd said then, and said again now. "This guy has killed already and I don't want you out there by yourself in some lonely spot."

"But I'm going," Ryan said. "If you pick me up, I mean. My car's in the barn at my house."

"Perfect." I nodded. "This will work out. Ryan will be with me, and there won't be any danger, anyway, because we're just going to wait there and see who shows up. Take pictures is all we'll do."

"Wait where?" Rafe asked, folding his arms.

"It has to be out of the way," I said. "Whoever it is won't want anyone else to see him show up, so it has to be quiet and secluded."

"Sounds like something out of a horror movie," Rafe muttered.

I turned to Ryan. "Do you have any ideas? I was thinking maybe the parking lot of that restaurant just past Dooley. You know, the one that's been closed for years?"

Ryan stroked his chin, which was sporting a thick brown beard. "Or there's that canoe livery on the Mitchell River. They don't open until May."

"Not just a horror movie," Rafe said, "but a bad horror movie."

This time he was ignored by two people.

"I know." Ryan snapped his fingers. "How about that county park, the one on . . . What's the name of that little lake? Moss. It's not far from the highway, so whoever meets the sellers will assume we've just driven up from downstate. And there are three parking lots. We can leave your car in the lowest one and put a note on the blog to meet in the upper one."

Now Rafe was the one stroking his chin. "Well . . ."

"Excellent idea." I smiled with satisfaction. "This will work out great."

I really should have known better.

Chapter 20

The next day started out rainy and windy. I tried to see out the kitchen window but couldn't see anything except rivulets of rain running down the glass.

"What happened to that perfect mushrooming weather?" I asked.

Rafe laughed. "This is perfect weather for mushrooms. I thought you knew."

Maybe it was good for mushrooms, but not for the hunters. Or for anyone at a track meet. "You're taking your rain gear, right?"

He kissed me and hefted his backpack. "Already packed. Text me, okay? Before, during, and after."

His voice held a tone that was extremely unusual for him: that of worry. And so, instead of making a joke, I nodded. "Promise," I said, kissed him again, and waved as he drove off.

It was now decision time. The bookmobile was headed out for an all-day run, and, once again, Hunter and I were doing the morning route and

Hunter and Julia were taking the afternoon shift. "To Eddie or not to Eddie," I murmured.

Last night, Rafe and I had posted a time of eight o'clock to meet anyone who was interested in our Conti-like sculpture. There'd been no response, but we hadn't expected one, either. And there should be plenty of time to get Eddie back home and me out to the park well before eight. Before seven, even. Still, I hesitated.

I was standing there, dithering, when I felt a furry *thump* on my leg. "Mrr?" the thump asked.

It sure sounded like he'd said please, but with Eddie it was hard to be sure. "Did you really say please?"

"Mrr!"

Which was the same thing he said to Hunter when we got on the bookmobile and the same thing he said to Julia when she climbed aboard in the afternoon. I assumed he'd say it again at six o'clock when they came rolling back, but when I went out to the parking lot at the end of the day, there wasn't a sign or sound of any of them.

I rubbed my upper arms against the brisk wind in a vain attempt to stay warm. Where were they? I walked around in a small circle to keep my blood flowing and pulled out my cell phone.

No calls. No texts.

Which could mean something, or it could mean nothing. There were many areas of Tonedagana County that didn't have cell phone coverage. Maybe the bookmobile had broken down in one of those areas. Or maybe they'd hit a deer. Or maybe . . .

"Don't worry," I said out loud, and immediately ignored my own advice. At a quarter past, I started texting Julia and Hunter.

Nothing.

At half past, I started calling them.

Still nothing.

At an hour late I called the central dispatch line at the sheriff's office. Both fortunately and unfortunately, the dispatchers hadn't heard a thing. They kindly said they'd keep an ear out and would let me know if a call about the bookmobile came in.

"Thanks," I said, "much appreciated."

I called Graydon, and just as we were planning the route of our search and rescue, I heard the unmistakable noise of the vehicle I'd been driving for years. "They're back," I said, trying to see through its windshield. "And it looks like . . . yes, I see both Julia and Hunter. They're smiling and waving, so everything must be okay."

"All's well that ends well," Graydon said. "Let me know what happened."

"Will do." Then, before I lost my courage, I added, "Say, I know you can't talk about a closed board meeting, but is there anything you can tell me?"

"Uh, sorry? What was that?" he asked. "You're cutting out on me. I'll talk to you later, okay?"

Huh. So my boss was a worse liar than I was. Good to know.

I slid my phone back into my coat pocket after glancing at the time, which was ticking away.

"Minnie, I am so sorry!" Julia piled out of the bookmobile. "We should have let you know how late we were going to be, but you know there's no cell reception in the valley. This family who's up at their summer cabin because their power is out downstate hiked to the bookmobile stop, and it started raining buckets just as they were leaving."

"It's my fault," Hunter said. "I told them we'd be happy to drive them to their house."

Julia nodded. "But it didn't have a landline. And they were so thankful they made us stay and eat cookies, and fed Eddie special treats, and then the kids wanted to put on a thank-you puppet show and both our phones were out of power and I couldn't find the cable to charge them and—"

I threw up my hands in the classic referee's T position. "Stop," I said, laughing. "If even half of that is true, you're forgiven. You can tell me the whole story later, but right now I have to get going."

"Sorry again," Hunter said, handing over the cat carrier.

I told him I'd come up with a suitable punishment and wished them both a happy weekend.

"You have to come with me," I said to Eddie as I clicked my car's seat belt around his carrier. "There isn't time to take you back to the house." As it was, I barely had time to pick up Ryan and get settled into the far parking lot. I drove to the road where we'd decided to meet. I gave the prearranged signal—a quick double honk—and waited.

No Ryan.

That was odd. I was late. He should have been waiting.

I tapped the steering wheel, thinking, then turned and drove down the narrow road until the track petered out to nothing. I jumped out of the car and ran all the way to the clearing, legs pumping, lungs burning.

"Ryan?" I called out as I crossed to the cabin. "Ryan!" The door was shut and I banged it open.

Inside, the dim light showed a dirt floor empty

except for a slight Ryan-shaped hollow that marked the spot where he'd slept. But there was no sleeping bag, no tidy stack of food, no small set of dishes, no lantern. And no bicycle.

He was gone.

I pelted back to the car and flung myself behind the wheel. Heaving out great panting breaths, I started the car, dropped it into reverse, and made a three-point turn. In days gone past, I would have taken a turn like that in fits and starts, but time spent driving a bookmobile was useful in a myriad of ways.

"Hang on," I told Eddie, and roared down the two-track, back the way we'd come, only twice as fast, which was hard on the car, hard on me, and hard on my poor cat.

"Mrr!" he protested at each bump. "Mrr!"

"Sorry, buddy. I really am, but—ow!—we're almost there, okay? Almost—"

And then the car's front tires reached asphalt. With a *screech* of rubber, we pulled all the way onto the road. I slammed the gas pedal to the floor, pushing my little car's acceleration to the limit.

"Hope that seat belt is tight," I said as calmly as I could, which wasn't very calm, but at least I was trying. "We have to hurry. I don't know where Ryan is, and I have a horrible feeling that he's riding his bike out to the park." All by himself, which was really, really not a good idea.

I posed a question to myself. "Maybe he left just a few minutes ago?" But if so, I'd be able to catch up to him, and the closer we got to the park, the less likely that was, because there was no sign of him. Not on the county highway with its wide paved shoulders and not on the side road with its potholes and dirt shoulders. Hills, trees, curving roads, and small lakes. No sign of another human as far as the eye could see.

My concern for Ryan grew. Ballooned. And there was the added element of guilt. "Did he leave because I was late?" I asked Eddie. "Or had he planned to do this from the beginning, and left hours ago?"

"Mrr!"

I sent my furry friend a quick glance. "That sounded like you knew what you were talking about." Once again, I wished I could talk cat. Talk Eddie, anyway, because he was so unlike all other cats I'd met, I was half convinced he was his own species.

"Mrr," he said, pushing his nose through the gaps in the wire door.

"Sorry, but no matter what, you have to stay in the car." I flicked the turn signal and made a right onto the gravel road that led to the park's entrance. "Sorry about these bumps, too," I said, my molars rattling against each other. "Guess the road commission hasn't made it over here yet."

When I saw the park's sign, I slowed to a more sedate speed, mostly because I didn't want the noise of the car to reach anyone who might already be here. My car's dashboard clock said it was three minutes past eight, three minutes past the time our blog post had said for anyone interested in the sculpture to show up.

I mentally chewed on the limited possibilities.

What if no one came? Or . . . what if someone was already here, waiting, and Ryan was down there meeting him alone?

The car's tires bounced on a series of washboard bumps. I winced at the noise and came to a sudden decision. "Time to stop," I told Eddie. "The upper lot isn't far. I bet that trail over there goes down to the lake. I'll take that and see what I can see."

"Mrr!"

"Thank you for your vote of confidence," I said as I parked on the road's shoulder. "See you soon. I need to make sure Ryan's okay." And to see if we could identify a killer.

"Mrr!"

I put my finger to my lips and, concerned about noises reaching anyone with ears to hear, shut the door as softly as I could, while also shutting my own ears to Eddie's protests. He must have resigned himself to his fate, because as I walked away, I didn't hear any further cat noises.

"It'll be okay," I sort of said to him and sort of said to myself as I hopped into a slow jog. Because what could go wrong? All we wanted to do was see who showed up. If it was one of the two people we suspected of killing Pug, we'd tell the police. We weren't going to confront anyone, weren't going to capture anyone. Pure identification, that's all.

That was my internal monologue as I trotted down the forested path. Only the closer I got to the lake, my inner tone grew more and more anxious.

"It'll be okay," I murmured. But what if it wasn't? What if no one showed up? What would we do about finding Ryan a new place to stay? Because he certainly couldn't stay at the cabin any longer.

My thoughts grew even more dire as I started seeing bits of lake through the tree branches. What if Ryan wasn't here? What if he'd gone on the run, dooming himself to a lifetime of hiding? How would we ever find him again?

"Please let him be here," I whispered. "Please let him be safe. Please let this work. Please . . ."

I rounded a final curve in the trail and came to an abrupt halt, blinking at the scene taking place not twenty yards from me.

The trap had worked.

But too well. There were two cars in the parking lot, not one. And there, facing each other across the parking lot, were two men. One with long dark hair in a ponytail. The other with bright ginger hair.

Ian Breece.

And Skyler Ellison.

Chapter 21

My mind didn't—couldn't—absorb what was in front of me. Two people. There were two killers? How could that be? It didn't make sense. There was no reason for—

"Hey," said a quiet voice.

I jumped. It was Ryan, but he wasn't talking to me. He was walking out from behind a row of picnic tables, set for the winter vertically with two legs on the ground and two up high leaning snug against its neighbor. All his attention was focused on Ian and Skyler. I made a move toward him, but instinct kept me back. *Wait*, something told me. *Wait and see what happens.*

Slowly, I dropped to a crouch. Birds twittered all around, treetops swayed slightly in the mild breeze, and Moss Lake was a blue so deep it was nearly black. Peace and calm pervaded the scene. Unfortunately, none of it was being absorbed by the librarian in the shadows.

I stayed still as a stone, barely breathing, watching

and waiting. For what, I didn't know, but surely I'd know it when I saw it.

Ian and Skyler had their backs toward me, Ryan was facing me, but since I had no idea if he'd seen me or not, I had to act as if he hadn't. Had to assume that Ryan thought he was alone. And Ryan was nearing desperation. Was maybe there already, and desperate people did . . .

My mouth went dry.

No. Nothing bad would happen to Ryan. He'd be fine. This would work out. Everything would—

"Both of you here for the sculpture?" Ryan asked.

Ian had been standing with his hands in his pockets, his shoulders slouched. At Ryan's question, every muscle seemed to freeze in place. Even the bright red hair on his head appeared frozen.

I felt my own body stiffen. Was Ian about to attack Ryan? Was he about to steal the Conti, the one that didn't exist? I pulled my phone out of my coat pocket and thumbed it on, getting ready to call 911, until I looked down. No bars. Absolutely zero reception.

Grimly, I put the useless communication device back in my pocket.

Skyler Ellison, still wearing the lime green shoes, turned to look at Ian. "Thought you said you were here to fish."

Ian shrugged. "I fish here sometimes. Just not today."

There was a long pause during which no one said anything. It felt possible that the four of us, that group of three and me off to the side, might have stayed stuck in that formation forever, waiting for someone to speak, waiting for . . . something. And we might have done so, except something happened.

Crack!

A tree branch plummeted down and hit the ground close to the men. All of us jumped.

"Whoa, that was close." Skyler laughed nervously.

Ian, his hands still in his pockets, glanced at the branch. The very big branch. "Widow-maker," he said. "It could have killed us. Easy."

Three sets of male eyes took stock of one another. A fourth set of eyes, my female ones, watched them.

"Anyway," Skyler said, and his tone had an impatient edge to it. "If you have a Conti, I want to see it. If you have provenance, great. If not"—he shrugged—"my price drops. Either way, I want to see it."

Ryan looked at Ian. "You want to see it, too?"

"Well . . ." Ian scuffed the ground with the heel of one of his well-worn work boots. "What I was mainly hoping for was a deal. But sounds like you"—he gave Skyler a lopsided smile—"want this a lot more than I do."

Skyler didn't say anything, almost seeming like he was waiting for something. Finally, he said, "If it's a Conti, I'll give a lot for it."

This time the impatient edge was gone, but something else had taken its place. Something harder. Something darker.

"Okay, then." Ian edged backward, increasing the space between them. "Have at it, pal. All yours." He nodded, walked over to his truck, and in moments was gone, leaving behind a trail of dust that swirled in the air before drifting back down to earth.

I crab-walked a bit closer.

Now that Ian was gone, what was Ryan going to do? None of this had been part of the plan we'd gone over ad infinitum the night before. What happened to the Watch Only part, which as far as I was concerned had been pretty much the most important part if we wanted to get out of this alive and unhurt?

And then I realized. It was different for Ryan. His stakes were much higher. Though I truly and deeply wanted to find the murderer and prove Ryan innocent, if we didn't, if we couldn't, I'd go home to my own house, to my own bed.

I was so stupid.

How could I not have thought about it from Ryan's point of view? Why hadn't I anticipated that Ryan would be willing to take huge risks to find Pug's killer? And now, with him facing Skyler, had my mistakes set up a situation where—

No.

It would be fine. Nothing would happen to Ryan. It couldn't. I wouldn't let it.

Still crouching, I very slowly and carefully inched forward. There were trees enough that I was mostly hidden from view, so unless Skyler turned completely around, I'd stay hidden. Unless, of course, my movements happened to catch Ryan's eye and his change in attention made Skyler turn and—

"Stop it," I told myself. "Stop it. You can do this."

And, just like the magazine articles said, saying it out loud gave me a confidence boost. After all, nothing horrible had happened yet. Not even a hint of anything horrible. It really would be fine.

Skyler, who'd been watching Ian's dust settle, turned back to Ryan. "Don't think he's coming back, do you?"

"Doesn't look like it."

Ryan had said the words. I'd seen his lips move. But his voice hadn't sounded like anything I'd ever heard him say before. This was a Ryan I'd never met. This was a man who had nothing to lose.

This was seriously not good.

"Where's the Conti?" Skyler looked around. "One of the small ones, is it? From his bronze period?" When Ryan didn't say anything, Skyler snorted. "Don't worry, dude. I don't care if it's legit or if it's stolen. Won't pay as much for stolen, though, so don't even try going there."

Ryan still didn't say a word.

"Don't tell me you didn't bring it." Skyler laughed. "Let me guess. All you brought is a picture on your phone." He gusted out a huge sigh and gave Ryan a hard look. "Well, hand it over. Let me see what you have. I know Conti's work backward and forward, and if it's genuine, I'll pay you what it's worth."

If I'd had a thousand years to guess, I would never have come up with what Ryan said next.

"Did you kill Pug Mattock?"

Skyler's head jerked back. "Did I what?"

"Point a gun at Pug Mattock's chest and pull the trigger."

"Look, man, all I want is to buy a Conti. That's the only thing that matters here, right?"

He hadn't asked who Pug Mattock was, hadn't

blinked at the accusation, hadn't denied it. It wouldn't be proof enough for the sheriff's office, but it was proof enough for me. Skyler Ellison had killed Pug.

Now we could go talk to Ash and Detective Inwood. We could give them what we'd just learned and they'd do the official law enforcement thing. This would, without a doubt, be the biggest step in the plan to rehabilitate Ryan's image. A statement from the police, a bit of timely social media posting, and Ryan could get back to his life.

Time to go, I tried telling Ryan via mental telepathy. *We have what we need, let's leave.*

But either my powers of mental telepathy were on par with my cooking abilities, or Ryan just plain had other ideas.

"You killed him, didn't you?"

Skyler looked left and right—though happily not behind him—and shrugged. "What do you care? He had a Conti. I needed it and he wouldn't let me have it. What was I supposed to do, just leave?"

Yes, I thought.

"Contis are the only things that matter," Skyler said. "I get another Conti and no one will have as many as I do. No one in the world. That will show my parents that I'm successful. They won't be able to deny it any longer."

The primal part of my brain started shrieking a layered warning. Down at the bottom layer was the certainty that Skyler's obsession with Vittorio Conti and his sculptures was beyond unhealthy. The middle layer of concern was that someone with an unhealthy obsession was likely to behave unpredictably. But the top layer was the biggest and it was yelling the loudest.

Skyler had killed Pug for the sake of a hunk of metal. If he thought Ryan had a Conti in his possession, there was no guessing what he'd do.

Run! I silently yelled. *Get out of there!*

"Because of you," Ryan said, "I've been on the run for weeks. Everyone thinks I'm the one who killed Pug Mattock."

Skyler laughed. "You must be that Anderson guy the cops have been looking for. Robber and murderer downstate, and now you're trying to sell me a Conti? Where'd you steal it from? Can't be the Valeras; I picked that one up last fall."

Mr. Valera's sister had cried over that sculpture. And this guy was *laughing* about it? My hands curled into fists.

"There is no sculpture," Ryan said. "The post was a fake. Made it up to get you out here."

"What?" Skyler asked, his voice quiet and still. Deadly quiet.

Ryan smiled, and it wasn't a nice smile at all. "I have a cell phone in my pocket. It's been recording our entire conversation. Pretty sure I stand a good chance of clearing my name."

"I didn't admit to anything," Skyler said.

Ryan shrugged. "Maybe not directly. But I bet it's enough to get the cops looking at you. And we both know that's not going to go well, don't we?"

My mouth dropped open. What was he doing? Skyler was taller and bigger than Ryan; if he attacked it wouldn't be anything close to a fair fight. I started looking around for a weapon. A stick. A rock. Anything.

"You'll be better off if you turn yourself in, you know," Ryan was saying. "Tell them it was an accident. If it's a first offense, you probably won't get much jail time."

Skyler's right hand started moving, behind his back, out of Ryan's view, and mostly out of mine. "You think so?"

"And who knows? Maybe you can get reduced time because of mental issues. What is it they call this, diminished capacity? Because no offense, but killing someone over a sculpture is way out there."

Skyler's face twisted into a mask of rage. Or maybe it wasn't a mask. Maybe this was his real face, the frightening one no one was ever allowed to see. "Conti sculptures," he said, his voice rising, "are the only thing worth killing for!"

His hand went around his back and came out, pausing . . . And then I knew what he was doing, and knew I had to act.

"Ryan!" I yelled. "He has a gun! Safety is off!"

Quick as a snake, Skyler punched Ryan in the stomach with his left fist. He bent over, gasping. Skyler lashed out with his foot and kicked him forward to his hands and knees. He sank his fingers into Ryan's hair, pulling his head back, and put the gun to the back of Ryan's head.

"Whoever you are, come on out," Skyler growled.

Though my body moved slowly, my mind was racing. Rafe knew we were here. Maybe the track meet had wrapped up early and he was on his way. Maybe he was driving down the park entrance right now.

"I know you," Skyler said, staring at me. "You were looking for a Conti for your boyfriend."

Fiancé, but whatever. If he thought Ryan was my

boyfriend, maybe that would play to our advantage.
Wasn't sure how, but there was always that possibility.

"You," Skyler said, nodding at me. "Get his cell
phone out of his pocket."

"Sorry," Ryan muttered.

I wasn't sure why he was apologizing. He was the
one who had a gun to his head. "What pocket?" I
asked him, pleased that my voice didn't sound like
I was terrified. "For the cell phone?"

"Left front."

I pulled out the solid rectangle and showed it to
Skyler. "Burner phone," he said. "Smart. But not
smart enough." He grabbed the phone from me and
threw hard. It landed in the lake with a quiet *plop*.

"The recording is gone," Ryan said in a whispery
voice. "No reason to keep Minnie here. Just let
her go."

I glared at him. As if I'd run away and let Skyler
do . . . whatever.

"Don't think that's going to happen," Skyler said
thoughtfully. "Seems to me the best thing is to get
rid of you both. Cleans up all sorts of loose ends."

No way was he going to get away with a double
murder. Triple, counting Pug, which I did. The man
had serious mental problems. Which was obvious,
really, given the sculpture obsession thing. I tried to
take a calming breath, but it didn't help much. My
heart was pounding, my hands were sweating, and
my knees were starting to quiver. There had to be a
way out of this.

"Okay," Ryan said. "But what are you going to
do with our bodies? One body you could bury in
the woods deep enough so the coyotes and bears

wouldn't make a mess in hours. But two? That's a lot of digging. Not sure how you're going to do that."

I stared at him in disbelief. He was trying to deter a killer from killing by using disposal concerns? Seriously?

Skyler made a noise that, under other circumstances, would have been called a laugh. "Like I'm going to worry about hiding anything. All I have to do is make sure I'm not caught. No one has come down this road for the last hour, so I think I'm good. It's not like anyone has security cameras out here."

Reflexively, the three of us looked around. And, sure enough, there wasn't a camera in sight. Not on a post, not on the corner of the restroom building, not in the branches of any tree.

I pulled in a breath. Because there, in a maple tree just overhead, was something I was pretty sure was the lashing tail of a black-and-white tabby cat.

Eddie. Oh, no. The car door must have not shut all the way. And the cat carrier door must have unlatched itself with all the bumps. How had I not checked? How—

I jerked my attention away, not wanting Skyler to see. *Keep away*, I said, once again trying mental telepathy. *Stay up there!*

"Maybe you're right," Ryan said. "But that still leaves you with a big problem."

"Only one?" Skyler sounded amused. "Tell me."

Ryan spoke quietly, and I marveled at his calm. "There are two of us and only one of you."

"That's not a problem," Skyler said. "All I have to do is make sure you're far enough apart and—"

"Mrr!!!"

Three things happened at the same time.

Ryan hit Skyler's wrist, pushing the gun down and away. It clattered to the ground.

I hurled myself at Skyler, jumping onto his back and looping my arms around his neck, clasping my hands around my wrists, hauling back as hard as I could.

Eddie dropped out of the tree, panther-like. He landed on Skyler's head and dug his claws deep into his long, thick hair, all the while howling at the top of his lungs.

"Hang on, Minnie!" Ryan shouted.

That was my intention, but it was hard, as Skyler was turning in circles and grabbing at my arms, at my wrists, at my hands. I put my knees against his back and pulled harder. This man was not going to kill Ryan, not going to kill me, and certainly wasn't going to harm a hair on Eddie's furry head.

"Mrr!!"

"What I said," I panted out, holding on for all I was worth.

Ryan put his head down and rammed Skyler's solar plexus. Skyler's breath went out in a *whoosh!* and he staggered. I shifted my weight, trying to tip him off balance, and he staggered a second time.

"MRR!"

Ryan cannoned into Skyler again.

He went down to one knee. I gave him a hip check and sent him to both knees. As he fell, I spotted the fallen branch, grabbed it, and whirled around, whacking Skyler with it just as he was starting to stand, sending him back to the ground.

Ryan, scrabbling around in the gravel, jumped to

his feet, holding the gun at the ready. "Don't move," he said. "Move and I'll—"

"Get that mangy ball of fur off me!" Skyler roared.

Eddie, of course, ignored him, and I was sure I saw him flex his claws. Skyler moaned with pain, which in any other circumstance would have concerned me, but this time absolutely didn't.

I released my grip on Skyler, got to my feet, and was starting to take my jacket off to tie his wrists together, when a car roared into the parking lot. Then another. It was Rafe. And Ash.

"Mrr," Eddie said, very casually. Using Skyler's head for leverage, he leapt to the ground and trotted over to the newcomers.

I smiled at Ryan. "It's just like I've been saying all along."

"It's going to be okay," he said.

And then he smiled.

Chapter 22

Minnie! Are you all right?"

Rafe crushed me against his chest. I said something into his jacket that he couldn't hear, so he uncrushed me, gave me a long kiss while a purring Eddie twined around our ankles, then looked into my face. "Sorry. What was that?"

"Why is Ash here?" Not that I wasn't grateful, because I was indeed very pleased to see a law enforcement officer put handcuffs on Skyler, but I was puzzled.

"Oh. Him. Well . . ."

The slightly sheepish story came out. Ash had attended the same track meet and, longtime friends that they were, they sat next to each other, and somewhere between the running of the three-hundred-meter hurdles and the four-by-four-hundred relay, Ash asked what I was doing tonight.

"Telling the whole truth and nothing but the truth was the only option?" I asked.

The love of my life shrugged. "Why wouldn't I? Good thing, too, don't you think?"

"We would have been fine," I said, but there was a slight quaver in my voice that wasn't so sure. I bent to pick up Eddie, and, minor miracle, he let himself be scooped up and cuddled.

A sheriff's vehicle drove down the road, its headlights sweeping across the parking lot, and came to a stop next to Ash's vehicle. The uniformed deputy got out, conferred with Ash, and soon Skyler was tucked in the back of the deputy's vehicle.

Ash and the deputy and Ryan went into a huddle slightly apart from Rafe and myself.

By now it was completely dark. The only light was from the various cars, and the sparkling of the stars up in the clear sky. I looked up, studying the cloudy dust of the Milky Way spreading from northeast to southwest, and tried to grasp that those clouds were actually the light from zillions of stars in one spiral arm of one galaxy.

"You're cold." Rafe put his arm around me.

"I'm fi-fine," I said through chattering teeth. It wasn't that cold, not really, so I wasn't sure why I was shivering.

"Yo, Wolverson!" Rafe called. "Minnie's turning into an ice cube. What's the timeline here?"

After a short consultation between Ash and the deputy, it turned out that if the park entrance was taped off, none of us needed to be there at all, so Ash did that and we drove to the sheriff's office in a small caravan, Ryan's bicycle in the back of Rafe's truck and Ryan himself riding with Ash. I selected my Happy Songs playlist and by the time we reached Chilson, I'd stopped shivering.

Detective Hal Inwood met us at the front door. "Ms. Hamilton. How nice of you to drop by."

"Thought you might be missing me," I said, thinking of all the hours I'd spent in this building, but the grin I tried to send him must have been a sad failure, because instead of tossing out an edgy reply, he gave me a long look and said, "Would you like some water? Or maybe coffee? Half caf, but it's fresh. Made it myself not ten minutes ago."

I smiled. A real one, possibly the first true smile I'd ever given him. "Thank you. Coffee sounds fantastic."

We were dispersed into two tiny interview rooms, Rafe and me in one, Ryan in another, with Skyler in another part of the building, as he'd been arrested and was in the holding area, being processed into jail.

It took hours to explain everything. I fell asleep more than once, and it was long after midnight that Rafe and Eddie and I went home.

The next morning we were back. Only now I was wide awake, breakfasted, and had a nice hot travel mug of the Round Table's coffee in my tight grip. Ryan was there, too, along with Hal and Ash. It made a tight fit in the small room, but we were all friends, so it was okay.

Hal, the elder statesman in the room, spoke first. "You look well this morning, Mr. Anderson."

Ryan grinned. "It was hard to decide what to do first when I got home. Take a shower or shave off the beard."

Last night we'd learned that two days ago, the downstate police who'd been looking for Ryan had called the sheriff's office and basically said, oh, yeah, forgot to tell you. We found the guy who robbed the bank. He'd run off to Montana. Got him hauled back to Michigan last week.

I'd wanted to rant and rave about the inefficiency, about the waste of Ash's time and energy, and especially about the unnecessary trauma Ryan had suffered, but I'd been too tired. And now Ryan looked so happy and content that there seemed little point in bringing it up all over again.

"Then I remembered. My shaver works in the shower. I could do both." Ryan laughed, and I smiled. The old Ryan, the cheerful Ryan, was still with us. I only hoped the old plumbing in his farmhouse was up to the task of washing away four weeks' worth of beard.

Hal flipped through a stack of papers and extracted one. "Here's what we've learned since last night," he said, skimming its contents. "Skyler Ellison's parents were appalled by his early interest in the art world and did everything in their power to divert him from a career in that direction."

Though he was still looking at the paper, I could tell by the lack of eye movement that he wasn't reading any longer.

"Skyler Ellison's father," Hal went on, "had a dislike, even a hatred, for that profession. His father's sister married an artist who abandoned her less than a year after he'd moved them to New York. She was too ashamed to go back home and died a few months later of a cancer that could have been treated—and likely cured—if caught earlier."

It was a sad story, tragic on many levels. I wondered what it said about Skyler's relationship with his parents, that he would embrace something that must have been abhorrent to his father.

"Art has a pretty broad scope of professions," I said. "It doesn't seem fair to assume everyone in it is a manipulative gold-digging schemer."

Hal nodded. "True. But the former brother-in-law was a sculptor."

Ah. Well, there you go. It seemed beyond the realm of possibility that Skyler's obsession with Conti sculptures could be anything but a reaction to his childhood. And that brought up another question. "Are Skyler's parents still alive?" I asked.

"His father died ten years ago," Hal said. "His mother passed two years last Christmas. Congestive heart failure and a stroke, respectively. There were no other children."

So Skyler was trying to prove himself worthy to parents who had been dead for years? What a messy tragedy for so many people, but mostly for Pug. And Sylvia.

Hal seemed to be waiting for another question, but it wasn't going to come from me because I was preoccupied with wondering how it would feel to have both parents gone from the world. It was the natural order of things, I understood that. Still, knowing that someday my mom wouldn't be asking if I ate my vegetables and that my dad wouldn't always be around to remind me to check my car's windshield wiper fluid made me want to call my brother. An odd reaction, but there it was.

So it was Ryan who asked the question. "If Ellison didn't have any brothers or sisters, did he inherit his parents' estate? Or because he went to art school, did they cut him out of the will like they threatened?"

Hal nodded. Apparently Ryan had asked the right question. "Skyler Ellison did, in fact, inherit the full estate, excepting a few donations to non-profits."

"Because his dad died before his mom did." Rafe put his arm around me. "If it had been the other way around, I bet he wouldn't have seen a dime."

"Perhaps," Hal said. "But I doubt we'll ever know for certain. What we do know is that, in spite of having liquid assets in the seven-figure range and less-liquid assets of even more value, Skyler Ellison worked for little more than minimum wage in a Chilson art gallery, lived in a marginal upstairs apartment, and drove a vehicle with bald tires and no muffler. Yet . . ."

He paused and tilted his head slightly. "Yet in Mr. Ellison's apartment, we found the sculpture Mr. Breece had sold to Mr. Mattock, along with seven other Conti sculptures, ranging in market value from the mid–five figures to mid–six."

Doing math so early on a Saturday morning was making my head hurt. "Up in that ratty apartment, Skyler had sculptures worth more than a million dollars?"

"Yes," Hal said. "And who they'll end up with is beyond my pay grade." He flipped through his stack of papers again. "Now, about Mr. Ian Breece, who was also at the park last night."

"Yeah, that messed up." Ryan shook his head. "For a while I thought maybe they killed Pug together."

Hal tapped the paper that was now on top. "While

Mr. Breece was, and is, in serious financial difficulties, his motives regarding the Conti were straightforward. He and his wife, Felicia, had been given a Conti sculpture as a wedding gift. It was from her parents, but neither Felicia nor Ian cared for it. They decided to sell it, but they also didn't want to hurt her parents' feelings, so Ian sold it quietly, to Pug Mattock, after getting an approximate cost from Mr. Ellison at the art gallery."

So simple, once you knew.

"You said you don't know what's happening to the Contis. What about the Valera sculpture? And the Conti that Skyler stole from Pug?" I asked. "He bought it from Ian. By rights it belongs to Sylvia."

Hal looked at his notes. "Let me clarify. I was speaking about the Contis outside of those two. They are being processed as we speak and will be returned to their owners today."

I peered at the detective. He'd sounded content. Pleased, even. But maybe I was projecting my feelings onto him. I sent Sylvia a wish that she'd find comfort, if not in the lakeside cottage, then wherever she could. And if Mr. Valera didn't take their sculpture so his sister could see it, I'd do it myself.

"One question," Rafe said. "Why was Ian at the park last night?"

Ash grinned. "You should know. You're the one who posted the ad on that blog."

"Mr. Breece," Hal said, "was there for the reason he stated at the time. To get a deal on a Conti. He'd hoped to offer a low price to someone who didn't know any better, then turn around and sell it at a large enough profit to shore up his farm's finances."

Parents and children. Wills and weddings. Two men from two families, and vastly different roads the men had taken, both leading them to Conti's works. One via what seemed like a thumbed nose to his parents, the other concerned with hurting the feelings of his in-laws. One obsessed with artwork ownership, the other only wanting to save his farm, but their roads had crossed long enough to result in the murder of Pug Mattock.

My thoughts wandered away. I'd spent a lot of time in this room, talking about death. About murder. About the gray aftermath of crime that went on and on for the people left behind. I sighed. Maybe this would be the last time. Maybe after today I'd never have to walk into this room again.

Rafe's arm tightened around me. He leaned over and whispered, "When Inwood leaves, I have a plan."

That sounded intriguing. "A good plan?" I whispered back.

He scoffed. "Like I have any other kind."

Since I had a vivid memory of what had happened last winter after his plan to surprise me with a drive to Mackinaw City to see the blue ice during a near blizzard ("We'll have the whole beach to ourselves with this kind of weather"), that didn't rate a reply.

But he did sometimes have good ideas, so I waited patiently while Hal told us the probable months-long timeline for Skyler's arraignment, trial, and sentencing.

"Any questions?" he asked. When we all shook our heads, he shot me a suspicious look. I looked back with wide, innocent eyes, and he left, shaking his head and muttering about the youth of today.

Personally, I thought that today's youth couldn't possibly compete with today's older folks. Aunt Frances was one of the sneakiest people around— on top of her boardinghouse matchmaking past, she'd been quietly working for years on a Minnie Needs to Marry Rafe campaign. And Sylvia Mattock had texted me her plan to squelch John Pinnock. Every time he did something to make her life miserable, she was going to play the lonely-widow card. If he played loud music, she'd bring him a casserole. If he ran the lawnmower under her bedroom window at five a.m., she'd ask him to fix a leaky faucet. Sylvia was confident that Pinnock would, eventually, make the connection and give it up. I was betting two months; Rafe's bet was four months, because he said men really weren't all that bright.

Ryan looked at Ash. "So, I can go, too?" When he got the nod, he jumped to his feet. "Minnie, Rafe, thanks for everything. I can never make it up to you, but I'll try. Talk to you later, okay? I'm meeting Keegan for breakfast." And he practically flew out of the room.

I smiled after him and got a bump in the ribs from Rafe's elbow.

"Ready?" he murmured and, without waiting for a response, pointed his index finger at Ash. "You're an idiot."

Wincing, I said, "That's a little harsh, isn't it?"

"You think?" Rafe asked. "What would you call someone who walks away from someone he loves and who, bizarre as it seems, actually loves him back, just as much?"

This was his plan? He thought berating Ash

would change something? Really? "It's not that easy," I protested.

"You ask me, he's taking the easy way out, not figuring out how to fix things."

"That's just not true. They tried to make it work. He tried."

"Yeah?" Rafe's eyebrows went up. "Seems to me that Chelsea was the one doing all the trying."

Ash was watching us, his head going back and forth. But he hadn't said anything. Until now. "What do you mean, Chelsea was trying?"

I was curious what Rafe meant, too, so was glad when he said, "Minnie figures part of the deal with Chelsea is seasonal affective disorder. Anxiety, fatigue, all that. One of those lights can help, so she borrowed one from Minnie."

That wasn't exactly how I remembered it, but whatever. "She texted me the other day," I said. "It seems to be helping."

Rafe nodded, as if that proved his point. "And what are you doing?" he demanded.

"Well, I . . ." Ash stared at the table. "I'm glad the light is helping her, but that's not the only thing. She doesn't put down roots. And deep roots is who I am. Nothing is going to change the fact that we want different things."

"What if you're both looking at it wrong?" Rafe asked. "What if it isn't about roots, but about not being stuck in one spot forever?"

Suddenly, I saw where Rafe was going and jumped in. "What if," I said, "you make plans to travel?"

"You get a ton of paid time off," Rafe pointed out, "and you hardly ever take any. You lose vacation time every year because you're a moron. And you never spend a dime you don't have to, so I know you have cash stashed away. Use it."

"But—"

I talked over whatever his objection was going to be because whatever it was, it didn't matter. "This is what's called a compromise. You go places a few times a year, and she doesn't have to stay in one place forever."

Rafe started to say something, but I elbowed him into quiet. We'd done what we could; anything else and we'd start repeating ourselves.

Sighing, Ash reached into his shirt pocket. "Got this at Thorington Jewelry weeks ago," he said, sliding the small object across the table.

I stared at the ring. The engagement ring. The gorgeous engagement ring, with a round-cut diamond in a rose-gold filigree setting that had tiny diamonds dotted all around. Though it looked vintage, since he'd bought it at the local jewelry store, it had to be new.

"Ash Wolverson," I said, pushing the ring back to him. "You go propose to Chelsea or I'll do it for you."

It's possible that I was shouting at the end. Likely, in fact, because Rafe said, "You know she will."

Ash was grinning. He picked up the ring and slid it into his pocket. "All right, you two. You've convinced me. But I know who to blame if this heads south."

And he was out the door before Rafe or I could say that it wouldn't go wrong.

"Cool." Rafe stood and stretched. "That was a

job well done. What's next on the agenda? Finding Cleopatra's tomb, or figuring out how to keep socks from sliding off inside shoes."

I frowned. "We don't know where Cleopatra is buried?"

"Look it up," he said. "What's next?"

Since I figured we'd more than earned a treat, next was walking down to Tom's to get cookies. We were standing in front of the glass display case, trying to decide between oatmeal raisin, chocolate chip, peanut butter, and chocolate no-bake, when the bells on the front door jingled and my boss walked in.

"Morning, Minnie, Rafe," Graydon said. "How are you two doing?"

Since he was going to hear the story eventually, I decided it was better if he heard it direct from me. "Well," I said, and gave him a very abbreviated version of last night's adventures.

By the time I was done, Rafe had chosen and paid for the cookies, and the three of us were sitting at a small, round marble-topped table, choosing from the wide selection of baked goods.

"So," I finished, reaching for a no-bake, "Pug's killer is in jail, the bank robber is in jail, and Ryan is free to do whatever he wants."

"Quite the night." Graydon took a chocolate chip. "All I did was sign a new employment contract." He smiled and lifted the cookie in a toast. "For three years."

I made a noise that could have been called a squeal. "That's great," I said, grinning. "Really, really great."

"Thanks," he said, eyeing me, then looking at Rafe. "Do you know what she did?"

"Probably not."

"She wrote a letter to the library board support-ing me. Every single staff member signed it, and so did a number of patrons."

Rafe reached for an oatmeal raisin. "Sounds like something she'd do."

I felt my cheeks grow hot and studied my cookie crumbs until the heat subsided. All I'd done was write how I felt. It wasn't a big deal. I hadn't thought to have anyone else sign it, but once Donna heard I was writing a letter, she told everyone and my office had been stampeded with people wielding pens.

Graydon tapped the table. "It was a risk for her to write that—you know what boards can be like—and I'm grateful. I appreciate the board's support, but knowing that the staff thinks I'm doing a good job means more than I can say without getting all gooey."

The three of us sat and chatted until the cookies were gone, and on the walk home, I kept telling Rafe how happy I was that Graydon's contract was renewed. And how happy I was that Pug's killer was in jail. And that the good Ryan was free to go back to his regular life.

"You're just happy inside and out, aren't you?" Rafe said, amused, as he opened the front door.

Buzz!!

Both our phones started vibrating at the same time. I pulled mine from my coat pocket. "Kristen," I said, as Rafe pulled his from his pants pocket and said, "Scruffy."

The air around us stopped moving. Part of me was excitedly shouting *Baby!*, but my mouth wasn't working at all, because fear suddenly grabbed hold of my insides. What if something horrible had happened? What if they'd had an accident on the way to the hospital? What if something had gone wrong with the delivery?

But the small and brave part of me took control of my thumb and hit Accept, and as I put the phone to my ear, I saw Rafe doing the same thing.

Two seconds later, we were jumping into the car and on our way to the hospital.

Aunt Frances stared at us across the restaurant's table. "Kristen had what?"

"A girl," I said, grinning from ear to ear.

"And a boy. Names soon to be announced." Rafe lifted his beer glass in toast position. My aunt, Otto, and I followed his lead. "To twins," he said, "twice the diapers, half the sleep."

"To twins," Otto said, winking at me. "Because that's when you find out who's a good friend and who's a great friend."

"To twins," Aunt Frances said. "Two miracles instead of one."

It was my turn, but I couldn't think of anything funny, or profound, or clever. All I could come up with was how I felt. "To the twins," I said, "who will have the best parents in the world."

"Hear, hear," Otto murmured, and we drank deep of our adult beverages.

The four of us had gathered at Angelique's for lunch, a restaurant where I rarely went because librarian's wages. But celebrating the birth of Twin One and Twin Two required more than sandwiches.

"I can't believe they didn't tell anyone they were having twins," Aunt Frances said.

"They didn't want anyone to fuss." I thought back to the gleeful expression on Kristen's face when we walked in the door of the hospital room and saw her with a baby in each arm. "Plus, the shock value was probably fun for her."

But Kristen was right; people would have fussed. It had been bad enough when we'd thought she was having one baby.

"Speaking of shocks." Aunt Frances glanced at Otto, then looked at me.

I put my hand over my heart. "Please, no. I can't take much more today."

She laughed. "More a surprise than a shock, then. I've decided on a post-retirement job. One that will keep me busy, but only as busy as I want."

"You're going to teach sky diving."

"Close, but no," she said. "Wedding planning."

"Excuse me?" I thumped my head with my palm. "I could have sworn you said 'wedding planning.'"

"Stop that. You'll give yourself a headache. Yes, wedding planning, but with a twist. I want to specialize in working with couples who want low-key Up North weddings. Women and men who want to get married up here and don't want all the bells and whistles. People like you two."

Rafe elbowed me. "Hear that? There are other people like us."

"Hopefully not too much like us." I elbowed him back. "Sounds like a great idea, Aunt Frances. Really. And with all the kids you've taught over the years, I bet you get a nice client base in a heartbeat."

"The thought had crossed my mind." She tipped her wineglass in our direction. "But here's another surprising part. I'd love it if the you two became my first clients. No charge, because I don't have a clue what I'd doing."

"Sold," I said immediately, holding out my hand to shake. "You'll be fantastic at this." And she would be. Not only was she super organized at anything she did, but she knew every business owner and venue for miles around and was one of the calmest people on the planet. Who better to soothe the worries of pending grooms and brides?

We talked about our wedding until Rafe and I got bored with the topic—almost ten minutes, a new record—and when lunch was over, the two of us drove home and went for a walk on the waterfront.

Though the day had started cloudy, a light breeze had pushed the clouds to the east, revealing a baby blue sky and bringing air that you could think was actually warm. It was nearly May. Maple syrup season was over. The trees were greening up so fast you could almost see the leaves growing. Daffodils were in full bloom, tulips were coming up, and the woods would be filled with, in addition to the morel mushrooms, trout lilies and marsh marigolds and, my favorite, trilliums.

"Have you decided?" Rafe asked.

I blinked.

My mind was a million miles away, but we hadn't gone far from the house. A hundred yards, maybe, almost to the marina where I'd formerly moored my adorable little houseboat. I was pretty sure, although not completely sure, that he hadn't said anything else, so I took our location as a clue. "About the houseboat, you mean?"

"If you want to sell, I know a guy who might be interested."

"Of course you do." I took his hand. If there was ever a situation in which Rafe didn't know a guy, I'd start looking around for zombies, because the apocalypse was surely on the horizon.

"If you don't want to sell," he said, "I'm okay with that, too."

I squeezed his hand. "So if I hang on to it, and rent it for the season to someone, you won't think I'm hedging my bets, just in case this marriage thing doesn't work out?"

"Nope. I'll think you're smart. Making the most of your original investment."

My heart sang. He really was an excellent human being. And he understood me. "Then that's what we'll do."

"Um." He gave me a sidelong glance. "You already have it rented, don't you?"

"Let's just say everything seems to be working out," I said smugly. But then my smugness evaporated. Because there was one thing that wasn't working out at all.

I stopped in the middle of the sidewalk and turned to him. "We need to talk about the house."

"What about it?"

His puzzled look raised my annoyance level from flat zero to a solid seven. I did my best to push it down. "The fact that I'm not paying for any of it except for utilities. That I don't know how much you paid for it, how much you spent on the renovations, and how much you're paying for the mortgage. That we're getting married in"—I did some quick mental math—"less than five months, and I don't know what kind of debt I'm getting myself into."

"Five months? Really?"

The annoyance level did not drop an iota. "Do not divert," I said, and he must have finally grasped how serious I was.

"Minnie. Sweetheart." He lifted my hand and kissed it. "The former owners were friends of friends of my parents. They'd bought it to renovate but soon lost interest because grandkids started arriving. I picked it up for a very low price. And renovation costs, because of the barter work I've been doing, have been next to nothing. The student loan payments you were making? Change the name on the payments to the bank that holds the mortgage, and we'll be splitting costs almost exactly. Although I'm thinking we should combine accounts and not worry about who pays for what."

"But . . ." So many thoughts were in my brain that they got jammed up and nothing came out. I shook my head to loosen them up and said, "Why did it take you so long to tell me this?"

He shrugged. "Thought I did."

My annoyance soared into the red range. Seriously? *Seriously?* Then, because honestly, there wasn't any point in being angry, I started laughing.

"What's so funny?" Rafe asked.

"Life with you," I said, "is never going to be boring."

With the sun on our faces, we walked hand in hand, down the waterfront. The sparkling water of Janay Lake was on one side, the town of Chilson on the other. Our town, the town where I'd summered as a child and later been lucky enough to find a permanent place, the town where my fiancé and I would be married, and where we'd grow old together.

Back home, Rafe headed to the basement to start painting drywall and I sat at the dining table with my laptop to update the financial spreadsheet.

Eddie immediately decided that his needs were more important than anything I was doing, so he jumped from the floor to my lap to the computer keyboard. In a few seemingly random paw steps, he managed to close the banking website, shut down the spreadsheet, and launch the photos of the infant twins I'd taken a few hours ago.

I snuggled my cat. "You know what? I have to go back to Pam's. One child-sized wicker rocker won't work when there are two children. Looks like I'm going to buy that rocking horse after all."

"Mrr," he said and, since he'd had five full seconds of snuggledom, struggled to get free.

Since the cat always wins in the end, I put up only a token resistance before letting him go. He oozed to the floor and pranced over to the closest bookshelf.

"Eddie, don't you dare—"

My words, of course, had no effect on his actions. He jumped three shelves high, clambered over the top of our collection of natural history books, and disappeared behind a copy of the *Field Manual of Michigan Flora*.

And then I remembered. Last night. The tree branch that had fallen. The branch that turned out so very handy for me to pick up and use.

Had Eddie been up in that tree? Had he made that branch fall?

"Did you?" I asked.

His furry head popped up from behind the row of books.

And he winked.

Ready to find
your next great read?

Let us help.

Visit prh.com/nextread

Penguin
Random
House

Photograph by Jon Koch

LAURIE CASS is the national bestselling author of the Bookmobile Cat Mysteries, including *Checking Out Crime*, *Gone with the Whisker*, *Booking the Crook*, *Wrong Side of the Paw*, and *Cat with a Clue*. She lives on a lake in northern Michigan with her husband and two cats.

CONNECT ONLINE

 BookMobileCat

*Librarian Minnie Hamilton and her rescue cat, Eddie,
are ready to pin down a bank robber in the newest
installment of the charming Bookmobile Cat Mysteries*

Late March is prime reading weather in the small northe
Michigan town of Chilson. Though snowfall and cloudy sk
deter outdoor activities, life inside the bookmobile is wa
and cheerful. But as Minnie and Eddie are making the roun
to deliver comforting reads, they see something strange: lo
bookmobile patron Ryan Anderson speeding away. When s
discovers the police want to question Ryan about a bank robb
and the death of a security guard, Minnie realizes she's one of
only people who doesn't think Ryan is morally bankrupt.

After an additional murder victim is found, the police i
mediately suspect her patron, but Minnie isn't convinced. A
when she encounters Ryan hiding from the police, she decid
to help him by investigating the crimes. Minnie and Eddie v
have to fight tooth and claw to prove the young man's innocen

Praise for the National Bestselling Series

"With humor and panache, Cass delivers an intriguing myster
and interesting characters."—*Bristol Herald Courier* (VA)

"Library lovers, cat aficionados, and cozy-mystery fans
will adore the latest in this always entertaining series."
—Kings River Life Magazine

$8.99 USA $11.99 CAN   Mystery

ISBN 978-0-593-19773-8

5 0 8 9 9

Cover art by Mary Ann La

A BERKLEY
penguin

9 780593 197738